More Praise for
The Redtape Letters

"C.S. Lewis fans should take devilish delight as *The Redtape Letters* turns the table on the Devil. Lee Whipple's book is both fun to read and highly instructive."

—Robert Holland,
The Richmond Times Dispatch,
author of *Not With My Child You Don't*

"Whipple deploys good arguments and accurate observations...."

—Thomas G. West,
Professor of Politics, University of Dallas and
Senior Fellow, The Claremont Institute,
author of *Vindicating the Founders*

"*The Redtape Letters* offers a unique and interesting way of presenting the reasoning behind modern-day liberalism....It is entertaining as well as thought provoking and would make excellent supplemental reading for courses in political science or political theory."

—Gary Wolfram,
George Munson Professor of
Political Economy, Hillsdale College

"*The Redtape Letters* is a marvelous exposé of the inner workings of modern-day liberalism."

—Burt Folsom,
Senior Fellow, Mackinac Center for Public Policy,
author of *The Myth of the Robber Barons*

"*The Redtape Letters* is a modern classic....Wit and lightness of tone, even while presenting serious subject matter, is a skill that Mr. Whipple exercises with great ability."

—W. J. Rayment,
The Conservative Bookstore Newsletter
CONSERVATIVEBOOKSTORE.COM

A NOVEL

the REDTAPE LETTERS

A NOVEL

the REDTAPE LETTERS

Unmasking the DEVIL
in latter-day liberalism

LEE WHIPPLE

Rhodes & Easton
Traverse City, Michigan

Published by RHODES & EASTON
121 East Front Street, 4th Floor, Traverse City, Michigan 49684
To order additional copies, please call: (800) 706-4636.

Publisher's Cataloging-in-Publication Data
Whipple, Lee.
   The redtape letters: unmasking the devil in latter-day liberalism/
   Lee Whipple. – Traverse City, Mich. : Rhodes & Easton, 1999.

        p.   cm.

   ISBN: 1-890394-34-3
   1. Religion and politics – United States.
   I. Title.   II. Redtape letters.
BL2525 .W45 1999   98-89607
322/.1/0973 – dc21   CIP

PROJECT COORDINATION BY JENKINS GROUP, INC.

03 02 01 00 * 5 4 3 2 1

For Jim Schaberg,
without whom this book would not exist

Contents

Author's Note

This book really owes everything to others. First, my debt is to C.S. Lewis for the book concept borrowed from *The Screwtape Letters*, and occasionally for the content where our subjects overlap. Second, I owe a debt to Edmund Burke, the patron saint of conservatism, particularly for his *Reflections on the Revolution in France*. Next comes Russell Kirk, without whose scholarship—from *The Conservative Mind* to *Redeeming the Time*—I would have been lost. Thomas Sowell's *Vision of the Anointed* and Robert Bork's *Slouching Towards Gomorrah* were highly influential. I am deeply indebted to the Founding Fathers for works and public words too numerous to mention, and of course for the country in which this book might be written.

In addition to many other writers and their books, worthy but too numerous to mention, I owe a debt to all those who have influenced me in columns, articles, and speeches over the years. William F. Buckley Jr. stands at the forefront.

Allow me to also mention in appreciation the great body of Judeo-Christian writings, and the Judeo-Christian tradition itself. Abraham, Moses, Jesus, Matthew, Mark, Luke, John, and Paul, Aquinas and Augustine, C.S. Lewis, again, T. S. Eliot, Malcolm Muggeridge, G.K. Chesterton, John Henry Newman, Fulton Sheen, Aleksandr Solzhenitsyn, the list could go on, all embody the conservative spirit that I have attempted to place at the heart of this book: the present and future firmly grounded in the traditions and wisdom of the past, a belief in one God, and an absolute morality.

Redtape, the villain who serves as main character

i

in this work, is all that the above saints, prophets, and writers, religious and political, would in the world have *not*, and by implication what they would have. At least, that is my intention.

A special thanks goes to Jim Schaberg, a longtime friend and reviewer on previous books, who suggested the idea of a politically oriented takeoff on *The Screwtape Letters*. His suggestion was in the spirit that Lewis himself played off Bunyan's *Pilgrim's Progress* to create *Pilgrim's Regress*. The idea grew quickly beyond politics to the moral questions that are at the root of all political thought. Jim was a part of the book's growth and story development. He stayed on as a valuable reviewer throughout the project.

With so much debt, and because this is in reality a hybrid work of essay and novel—for which, by the way, I owe yet another debt to C.S. Lewis and to George Orwell––I felt the need for footnotes throughout, both to give credit to sources and to expand upon certain points. At times, I felt the need of a note to explain to readers that even though what they had read was outrageous beyond belief, it was true. Fact in this book is far stranger than the fiction. Footnotes, however, would have spoiled the flow of the book and intruded upon the illusion a novel must maintain to function. Accordingly, I have included an "underbook," letter-by-letter notes, placed at the end. Mark Kundmueller, who helped me with research, is its primary author. Thanks to Mark for perseverance and care.

I work in full knowledge that no writer creates a new approach but builds, more or less consciously, on the past. As T.S. Eliot said, "To aim at originality would be impertinence." At most this book is an original arrangement of ideas which do not belong to me, become fiction for enjoyment and ease of understanding, I hope.

Thanks to Jerrold Jenkins and his fine staff at Rhodes and Easton for believing in this work, and for invaluable assistance and advice. Also thanks to Michelle Kundmueller for her assistance in editing the final draft. And, of course, thanks to family and friends who have been supportive and patient during the writing.

LEE WHIPPLE

St. Augustine, Florida
    3 January 1999

A NOVEL

the REDTAPE LETTERS

"Seldom have so few cost so much to so many."

The Vision of the Anointed
—Thomas Sowell

PART ONE: PREPARING THE GROUND

"Readers are advised to remember that the devil is a liar."

—C. S. Lewis
Preface to *The Screwtape Letters*

Letter the First

~

Dear Ticker,

Glad you're settled in—and in old Portland Hall, where I stayed when I was at school. Are the Ivy League girls still lookers? Say hello to Dean Flap and President Slough for me. They have long been friends of the family. How else would someone with your scores have gotten in? Ha ha. Just teasing.

Seriously, though, you must study hard. When it comes time to run for Congress, a gentleman's *C* could haunt you. The niggling press. Grades aside, Ticker, books can be useful. They hone the political edge. The Caesars are buried in *tomes,* my boy. Ho ho. Food for the enterprising bookworm.

About your roommate—I think it's a wonderful idea. Is he really a conservative? The admissions people must be slipping. Happily, the error allows the enterprise you suggest. By all means, convert him! It will be a good exercise, and should prove amusing.

In fact, this may be just the thing for you—one must know his liberal catechism well to teach it. Count me in. I will happily advise.

You must be careful at first with terms, my boy. "Liberal" has become a bad word, the *L* word. Don't insist on it right away. In my day it was the *P* word, "progressive." What shall we call ourselves next?

"Social democrat" has a nice ring. No matter what, stay away from the *S* word, "socialism." Act like you don't understand, if anyone mentions it in the same breath with liberalism. Shake your head and look vexed. New words, son, but it's the same ol' game.

Write to me of your progress with Dan, our soon to be liberal young friend. Tell me a little about him. How in the world did he end up in the Ivy League?

Your affectionate uncle,

RED

Letter the Second

~

Dear Ticker,

It sounds like your boy is going to be a tough one. When the working class produces a conservative, he's invariably the worst sort. Hard to make the son of a steel worker feel guilty about the plight of the working class. Mother *and* father, you say. Mother stays home with the kids. Dad works two jobs to help with college. Partial academic scholarship. The full catastrophe. Our work is cut out for us.

You acknowledge in your letter that Dan "maybe" got the better of you in a little dorm-room debate— your boy wants everyone to take castor oil twice a day, of course, and be personally responsible and so forth. And "he seems to make a lot of sense."

Sense? Great Caesar's Ghost! Physician, heal thyself. He *maybe got the better of you*? It sounds more like he kicked your behind, boy, and it's rattled your brains—and in the presence of your suite mates. Don't mince words with me, son. If you got a public spanking in the opening round, say so. You and I must be totally honest with each other, always. Within the family, you must never sugarcoat anything.

About the Lovelies, by the way, Mses "Jewelry" and "Plain Jane," as you call the. Tiffany and PJ. Don't underestimate their importance. A sympathetic audience is almost as good as a stuffed ballotbox. You must all become pals. *Sweet* mates, as it were. Ho ho. The liberal ladies next door could become your secret weapon.... But I digress. We must deal with Dan's little victory.

Stop debating immediately! Don't debate *anything*, boy. That's leading with your chin. Simply focus on the fact that Dan's conservatism fails to make things *Perfect*. If his tax cuts, and so on, seem to result in the employment of all but ten people on earth, focus on the ten. Dig in your heels. Look sad, shake your head, and point relentlessly at the ten. Learn their names, tell their stories. Wrench hearts, not minds. You're a liberal, son!

That should get you started. It's defense, but your opening stumble leaves us no choice. We will take the offensive shortly.

Your stern but affectionate uncle,

RED

Letter the Third

~

Dear Ticker,

Of course it worked—you must learn to have faith in your old Uncle Red. A "slick trick," indeed. *Perfect*, I'd say, and more important than you might think.

Friend Dan is playing our game, my boy. He has accepted a basic rule: for every problem, there is a Big Idea out there, somewhere, that will result in a Perfect Solution. Anything less will *not* do. *"Le mieux est l'ennemi du bien,"* said Voltaire. The best is the enemy of the good.

Think of *Problems* as the latter-day liberal racecourse, son. *Big Idea*s are the horses, *Perfect Solutions* the finish line. You're off and running in the Latterday Liberal Derby, Ticker.

The Answers to all of society's ills are out there, my boy, somewhere in the indefinite future, just waiting to be grasped by keen liberal minds. Anything concrete, present or past, must be weighed against this phantom future. Life is a grand experiment, son, and Man is the scientist who *will* find all the Answers: that is the liberal leap of faith. Our boy is airborne and doesn't know it. Ho ho. Your lessons begin.

I am encouraged by how easily you tumbled Dan— and by the way Ms Jewelry and Plain Jane weighed in on your side. But let's not get cocky. Only a few days ago, our boy was holding his own.

Let Dan spin his wheels awhile, before we show him the Perfect light. A little frustration will do him good. Fundamentals son—we will have Perfection or nothing at all. *Le mieux est l'ennemi du bien.*

You are taking French, I hope. It is the natural language of liberalism. You must read Voltaire's attacks on the Church and Rousseau's on private property, in their native tongue. Nothing like it, my boy. Stirs the blood, no pun intended.

I'm proud of you, son. Keep up the good work and tell me more about the ladies. They will be important before this is through. I must get to know them better.

Your guiding uncle,

RED

Letter the Fourth

~

Dear Ticker,

Tiffany sounds like a throwback to the 1960s, in ways. Indian beads traded in for gold chains. "Ms Jewelry" wants to do away with all those cumbersome courses and tests, does she? Have students find solutions to *real* social problems. "Vitalize" the learning process. Now! Makes me homesick for the old ivy covered walls.

Let her rail, Ticker. She has grand ideas. She wants instant change. She'll do, my boy. She'll do. What fun!

Now comes Dan, in old-fogey opposition, revering the Great College, respecting the professors, honoring tradition, wanting to *learn*. Ms Jewelry meet Mr. Passé. Let her at him, Ticker. Incite, my boy, incite— and sit back and watch and wait.

Give Dan time to get to know the Great College firsthand. Let him find out what he is really defending. Don Quixote meets the Ivy League. Life can be cruel. Ho ho. What will our boy do when he finds out the Old Ivy Girl has become a whore? Will he join up with Tiffy, or continue to play the fool? We win either way.

Little PJ sounds bland, as you say, but politically correct enough. We'll have to find her some whales to save.... Dan will probably place a higher priority on people. See what you can do with that one, son. Ask if

all living things aren't of *ultimate* value? No special status for man. See what Plain Jane thinks about what Dan
thinks about that. It should make a nice little brouhaha.

It sounds like things are shaping up well, everything on the right—that is the *Left*—track. A little free-
for-all between Dan and the girls should get things
rolling. You, however, my boy, must remain above the
fray. Take no impulsive stands. Make no headlong
rushes. "Be cool," as we said in my day. You want to
manage this mud wrestling, not join in. Public positions must be taken with care, Ticker.

Ideology is one thing, son, family fortune and
power quite another. Keep rhetoric and reality in their
places—don't step on your own feet. It's like *Monopoly,*
boy. You don't want to go lowering the rent on prop-
erties you own, or building hotels on someone else's.
Talk the *need* for Change, but be mindful of what must
remain *unchanged*. In politics, son, "the more things
change, the more they stay the same."

Mark that phrase. It's the family motto, our politics
in a nutshell. Family *realpolitic*. Our liberalism is, shall
we say, "enlightened."

Your crafty old uncle,

RED

Letter the Fifth

~

Dear Ticker,

"The more things change, the more they stay the same?" You don't get it. "Family *realpolitic*"—what do I mean? Oh my. Oh my. This is distressing. We have much to do. How can you imagine converting Dan, when you understand so little yourself?

For the Love of Money, boy, have your parents neglected your real education entirely? Didn't anyone tell you the Life and Times of Old Ned, the *real* story? So much catching up to do. We must bring you up to speed, Ticker, before seriously engaging your Dan—let him bout with the Lovelies, for now. Where to begin?

Old Ned—

It was the early 1900s when Old Ned came to this country. This was in the days before government, in the modern sense. Before the Smoot-Hawley Tariff, the National Recovery Act, the Wagner Act.... The country was wide open, low taxes. Anyone could take a crack at getting rich as Croesus.

Old Ned, as everyone knows, made the family fortune. After that, he started the family business: maintaining our wealth and power. No sugarcoating. I must speak frankly. It's time for you to grow up.

Once Ned was rich, he saw a problem. Other people were getting rich too. There would be endless competition. On top of that, back then, rich people were scared to death of the masses—uprisings in Russia and China. Sooner or later, we, the family, might lose out to competition or be swept away by revolution.

So Ned switched the family to politics, in order to keep things the way they were. Freeze our position, while we were ahead.

Ned envisioned a society of three classes: common folk, the well-off, and an elite. The elite, to maintain their position, would have to keep the well-off from becoming strong enough to compete, and the common folk from becoming desperate enough to revolt: the one from rising too high, the other from sinking too low.

It occurred to Ned—and others with his problem—that this could be done by pitting the two classes against each other, lower versus middle. The elite would champion the lower class in the name of social justice and *redistribute* wealth, that is the rich would give the middle class's money to the "poor." The elite would remain high above the fray, ensconced in privilege, unscathed. Ned and his pals had discovered social democracy.

In one stroke, Ticker, the well-off would be stymied and the common folk made compliant, and both groups kept busy loathing each other, and it wouldn't cost the elite a nickel. Add Machiavelli to your reading list: "*You can be very free with wealth not belonging to yourself ... it is only spending your own wealth that is dangerous.*" Ho ho. Voltaire, of course, understood this too: "*In general, the art of government consists in taking as much money as possible from one class of citizens to give to the other.*" An important lesson, my boy. Mark it well.

Of course, rich guys like Ned were only riding a wave—leaders in Europe, and intellectuals everywhere, were also discovering social democracy. Ned and his pals weren't the only ones looking for a ride. Politicians and bureaucrats, even some ministers, were figuring out similar angles about the same time. It was a defining moment: socialist sparks of pure intellect igniting ambitions, history pulling the strings. Everyone dancing in the same general direction.

Ned's particular angle fit like a jimmy into what was happening all around. You see his genius, boy, and the demon, history, coming together? Ned could protect his money by giving away someone else's.

But why would the well-off pay the bill, you ask? Politics, Ticker, big government. *Progressive* government: one part federal family-feeling, one part box on the ear. An iron fist in a jersey glove. Big Nanna, the nation's keeper was born.

Genius, history, and luck came together, son, and we, and some others, ended up in the catbird seat, off the radar screen, turned into congressmen, governors, and heads of foundations, living off tax-sheltered fortunes and government protected businesses. Some long-time politicians locked themselves in with sinecures (look that one up, boy) and fat pensions. Big bureaucrats did the same. A few ministers became perpetual preachers of the new order.... The liberal elite was born.

The common folk and the working well-off found themselves on a merry-go-round, down below, perpetually switching horses, chasing each other to the sound of *progressive* music. Of course an occasional titan rises up, but no problem. There is always a little room at the top, if some one elbows-in hard enough.

Ours is a dynamic new order, Ticker, and not a bad one as history goes. Not a bad deal at all in the long view: a benevolent stewardship by the best and the brightest. World without end, Amen. *"Plus ça change, plus c'est la même chose."*

"The more things change [everyone switching horses on the Equality merry-go-round, down below], *the more they stay the same* [no one gets off the wheel and into the elite's lunch]."

It's history, young man—an elite *always* calls the tune to their own advantage, one way or another. It's the way things are and have always been, and, not-withstanding the naiveté of this nation's Founding Fathers, it will always be.

You were blind, but now you see?

Your Dutch uncle,

RED

Letter the Sixth

~

Dear Ticker,

This naive talk of right and wrong must cease. Your ignorance of *family-realpolitic* can be tolerated—ignorance is a problem, something we can correct. But squeamishness is a sin.

You should never have been allowed to get this old without learning the facts of life. Someone did tell you about the birds and the bees, I hope.

Naiveté, creeping moralism, incredulity, confusion.... It is fortunate I am such a patient man. Ticker, Ticker.

Uncle Red will set you straight—

Yes! It's all true—and you'd better start learning to like it. But no, it is not a *conspiracy*. Get that out of your head. It is not a conspiracy. It's history! I explained all that. You're not listening, boy. The time was ripe, and Old Ned and a lot of others rode the wave. They seized the new day.

We're not in this alone, son—and no *one* is at the top. The game is played by many in many ways. You'd be surprised who dines at the liberal table, or preens in the *L* mirror. It's not just politicians and bureaucrats and families with fortunes to protect. Movie stars, journalists, college professors.... There are even genuine zealots, blind followers not making a penny or turning a trick. But more on all that, later.

As for us, Old Ned positioned the family and I've carried on, as you must do, leveling the ground down below to protect our money and power above. Tax shelters, subsidies, tariffs, progressive taxes, minimum wages, work rules, product and production restrictions.... All this you must learn to manage, Ticker, and much more. Senator Ticker, I hope. You're in line for my seat, boy.

It's all true, son, but not simple. Your lessons in liberalism have only begun. Don't jump to conclusions. Listen and learn—and stop this childish moralizing. It's time for you to grow up.

But, then, on the other hand, maybe we should see things differently, throw open the floodgates of American myth. Transcendent order, natural law, true competition, social mobility.... Founding Father stuff. A world, perhaps, more to your liking? Of course, you might, in this world, not have an allowance (upon which most families could live) or a Ferrari or a Ralph Lauren wardrobe, and might not be going to the islands on spring break or "studying" in Europe next year.... Think it over.

Warmest avuncular regards,

RED

Letter the Seventh

~

Dear Ticker,

Whoa. Let's slow down and talk this over. We are nephew and uncle, after all. Forgive me if I seemed abrupt.

No intimidation was intended, perhaps a little sarcasm, well-deserved—and a hard look at reality, by which I stand. But no intimidation. No, no. I was just being honest.

You will find, son, that I *am* an honest man. I look the facts in the eye. I see what I see, and pretend nothing. I am an honest man, Ticker, though not an honest *politician*—the private and public Reds. There, you see? Brutal honesty. You are my nephew. With you I will share myself, and the family jewels as it were. But, enough about Uncle Red for now.

I have a suggestion. Let's get on with converting Friend Dan, but with a new understanding: I recognize your independence, you recognize you have much to learn. You keep an open mind. I live, for the moment, with your prickliness about Old Ned and the liberal elite—we have yet to even introduce you to the liberal rank and file. So much to learn, my boy.

Make the attempt to turn Dan around, as you originally set out to do, and you will learn all you need to know to make up your mind about liberalism.

What exactly is liberalism? Already you begin to grasp the larger question, the real issue—you begin to see that it is not merely a political but a moral question. Or is it? What is morality? Does it exist?

Let us answer the questions by trial. I advise, you advocate, Dan tests our case. Liberalism stands or falls.

I will wager that, with *full understanding,* you will stand with me. Ho ho. Our little game takes on new meaning.

Uncle Red will hold nothing back, not with you. I will show you the inner workings of not only liberalism but the world. I will strip *everything* bare.

In the end, it is up to you—but no jumping to conclusions. Wait until my case has been made to decide. I will trust in the strength of my argument, if you will only listen and test my case through the fire of advocacy, as in a courtroom. Yes. What could be more fair?

Let's get on with the business at hand: Friend Dan. What do you say?

Trust me, Ticker. There may be duplicity in liberalism, as you have already begun to see, but under it all are facts of life that will set you free. The *facts* will set you free. I will show you a mountaintop above the ruck—beyond morality.

It is a brave new world I offer, my boy.

Stay with me, son. I will crack liberalism open for you like an oyster, and show you the pearl. All to you will be revealed.

Your loyal uncle,

RED

Letter the Eighth

~

Dear Ticker,

You accept the challenge! Glad to hear it, boy—I had confidence in you all along.

Your question is salubrious—a healthy self-interest. You need not worry, however, about people "finding us out." The things I have told you are between us, all in the family. Officially, we are the Champions of the Common Man, saving the world.

Nothing is illegal, my boy. Don't worry about that. We write the tax code, and the fine print in rules and regulations.... Ho ho.

Now, listen closely. Before we call your little group to order—let Dan and the Lovelies spar a while longer—we must expand your liberal universe to include another constellation, the liberal rank and file. Old Ned and the elite are only half the story.

The great body of liberals, Ticker, the ragtag and bobtail, think liberalism really is a crusade to save the world, to Perfect it. Heaven on Earth, et cetera. This is useful but nonsense, of course.

In the real world, once you outgrow the supernatural—at least you don't believe in fairies or a Grand Old Man in the sky, my boy, thank the stars for that—there is only better or worse from someone's point of view. I prefer mine. Better is my way—I told you I would speak plainly.

Keep the players straight, son, two levels of liberals, us and them, the initiated and the starry eyed—

Foremost are the liberal elite, the few, *us*—assorted inner circles and individuals—who have the big picture: naked self-interest. Hardball liberals, boy, realists, those not afraid to stand tall. A thousand variations on three themes: power, fortune, fame. Liberalism, to this select few, is a convenient ideology, albeit containing a central truth, the pearl—I will show it to you in due course.

The liberal remainder are the minions, the many, *them*—the True Believers—those who think there really is a Santa Claus and a Perfect world for all someday. Amen.

This outer ring is to be the orbit of Friend Dan—as well as, already in orbit it seems, Mses Jewelry and Plain Jane. Think of Dan as a novice True Believer, a "Troob" in training. We will bring him to the Holy Order of Saint Ned. Ho ho.

Enough for now, more on the Troobs as we go. It's time to focus on Dan. Let's not lose our advantage, shall we? It would be a shame to give back the ground we have already gained. Dan's head is still spinning, I hope. Seeking Perfection—getting that last ten people on earth employed—and battling the Lovelies. Ha ha. Let me know how things proceed.

Your rarin' to go uncle,

RED

Letter the Ninth

~

Dear Ticker,

Professor Feather agrees with Ms Jewelry. That puts Dan in a fix. Our young Don Quixote must now, by his own code, take seriously this *Mea culpa Manifesto* of professordumb, first written on the unisex-john wall, probably by Ms Tiffany herself, or commit a breach of conduct. Disrespect for a professor! Ho ho.

> "STUDENTS, CUT TO THE CHASE
> —BYPASS PROFESSORS—
> TEACH YOURSELVES!"

Let Dan figure a way out of this. He sails between Scylla and Charybdis, my boy, Ms Jewelry and Professor Feather on one side, the Great College, his Lady Dulcinea Del Toboso, in harlot's dress—that is to say stark-naked—on the other. *Pons Asinorum*. Dan finds himself on the "ass's bridge" of modern higher education: if the student's opinion is as good as his professor's, why is he there? You see the dilemma?

How does the conservative cross, or not cross, the bridge? He must oppose truth or the crown, striking his colors, either way. It tortures his conservative soul, one way or the other. Don Q., the elder, escaped into madness in a similar fix. Not our steel-town boy,

I'll wager. He'll cross—and the Great College, after all, will have been instructive.

I told you Ms Tiffy would soften Dan up for you, Ticker. Professor Feather, of course, gets an assist. *"In politics, the professor always plays the comic role,"* said Nietzsche. Ha ha. But seriously, boy, this is a good stroke of mischief. You will see.

Let the drama unfold, my boy. The interests of you and your allies—the professors—coincide. Your cause is advanced, and you lift not a finger. Watch closely and learn. Keep me informed.

Your Machiavellian uncle,

RED

Letter the Tenth

~

Dear Ticker,

Friend Dan has made a small bow to liberalism, my boy: he rejects authority, laughing privately at professors, but accepts the collegiate imprimatur and boon. The Great College is a "sham," but he still seeks her blessing. Sneering, he kneels to be knighted by the Infidel. His salute becomes a Bronx cheer. Hierarchy is stood on its head, or knocked flat. Utility reigns. Ho ho, Uncle Red waxes poetic.

"Welcome to the modern world, Friend Dan."

Our boy has made the *smart* choice. We progress—don't underestimate the importance. Yesterday, the Great College was the Colosseum in Dan's mind, today it is a cubist habitat. Where one *lives*, Ticker, shapes one's mind. A thousand small steps will bring our boy into the liberal fold.

Your instinct not to twit him on this is sound—you might only stir up the fire we would see burn itself out. I question your motives, though, son. This is one time you don't need to feel other's pain. Let the boy suffer, it will do him good. You haven't switched your major to social work, I hope.

Now, in a similar vein, we must have a word about socializing with the Troobs. It's fine that you're playing a little handball with Dan—did he really whip you, and he has never played before? Embarrassing. This family prides itself in manly athleticism, and winning! Perhaps you should practice, or find a game with a better chance of cheating. But I digress. It's fine to play a little ball with your boy, but don't get carried away. There is a thin line between customary social contact and fraternization.

I must speak plainly, son. Always know what you are *using* someone for—never forget it, not for a second. I detect admiration when you speak of Dan. Resist that. Remember what this is about. Dan is a learning tool, a disposable pal.

We are champions of the Common People, Ticker, but that doesn't mean we bring them home for lunch. Keep them in their place. Remember when Patsy had puppies. They were cuddly and cute—but that didn't make them your cousins.

You must be perpetually on guard with True Believers, never hinting at the real facts of life. A careless word in an unguarded moment—an aside that lifts the curtain—and Troobs will turn on you like snakes. Never doubt it—the unwashed have no sense of humor. A bit like you, sometimes. Think about that.

It's an easy mistake to make, my boy, letting down with the Troobs. You can get fond of Believers, become attached to them, especially the women. Don't make this mistake. Maintain your perspective. Remember who you are. You must make Dan and the Lovelies feel that you and they are the Brothers and Sisters Simpatico, while keeping them at arms length (three of your *three thousand* best friends).

In my next letter, we'll get down to brass tacks. It's

time we took the initiative. Smile, boy. You're inheriting a fortune, as well as the need to protect it.

Your older and wiser uncle,

RED

Letter the Eleventh

~

Dear Ticker,

Down to brass tacks—

It's time to focus your pals' attention, get this little free-for-all organized: you need a cause to come together behind or a downtrodden group to champion. You mention "the homeless" coming up all the time in your classes. College math: two homeless, plus one—what is the appropriate public policy? Ho ho.

The homeless is not an imaginative topic, I know—but a good place to start. Perfectly politically correct: I can see Dan now, under the hard glare of the Lovelies.

Turn your pals attention to shepherding this nation's growing flock of homeless sheep. Millions of them! That should do nicely. The homeless, of course, are only the sheep of the week. Many others work as well or better.

Stress the *feelings* that your group shares for these Unfortunates. Keep the focus on that. If Dan suggests practical solutions, trip him by holding up a single homeless gentleman left out on the street: the gentleman remains down and out—perhaps forced to choose between work and the city limits—if Dan has his way. I feel I know our boy already. A "tough love" advocate, I'll bet. Art of the possible, and all that.

Perfection, Perfection, Perfection.... Don't give an inch, Ticker. *All* must be saved, completely, every wretched one, rehabilitated in every way, or no deal!

Make the bums *real*. Names and places. Fill out your characters. Put faces on them. Use your imagination. Sketch in the details, bad childhoods, bad luck, and never, never a hint of personal irresponsibility. These are *victims*. This was done to them by society. Never let up on that for a minute.

Work on fundamentals, son, blocking and tackling. Pathos and Perfection!

Discourage discussion of Dan's real steel-town homeless. These fellows you say he has mentioned, haunting the fringe of his hometown neighborhood, are not—as you might think—an asset. Keep them out of your discussions! You will understand why in due course—all cannot be learned in a single lesson.

Work on what I've given you for now, son. It prepares the canvas.

Your artistic uncle,

RED

Letter the Twelfth

~

Dear Ticker,

You sound much improved, my boy—and in the face of adversity. You warm to the game, I think.

I am sorry that my warning did not come in time. I can imagine the sudden chill you describe when Dan told his tales of flesh-and-blood steel-town bums. At least no one fainted. The picture of Mses Plain Jane and Jewelry trying to take it all in would be comical, if this were not such serious business.

Allowing Dan to introduce the *real* homeless was a tactical error. Not one, however, for which I hold you responsible. You are, after all, only a boy, and my warning came late. We will deal later with the nature of your error. Right now, you need damage control. Listen closely.

The feeble defense you have improvised is doomed. Cease this effort at once. How can these bums who refuse offers of showers and jobs be *the exception*—never mind if they are—if we demand the solution to the problem be Perfect and therefore universal? 100%! You see the trap you lay for yourself by allowing exceptions?

The bubble containing the universal homeless problem is pricked. The door flies open for differentiated, local, incremental, even partial, solutions. Where would Big Nanna fit in? "Big Nurse," in this case. Nanna has many guises. The national issue would be gone, taken over by states, communities, families, even individuals behaving responsibly. A disaster. No, Ticker, the homeless must be the homeless, period.

Furthermore, there are larger interests at play— interests you must be mindful of as you proceed. The homeless are not a throwaway group. A long-term management perspective is required, not merely a fix.

You see, we created the homeless a few decades back—here I get ahead of myself in your education, but this you must know in your current predicament. Yes, Ticker, we *created* the homeless. Big Nurse was totally eliminating mental illness through scientific expertise and government largess—but psychothera- pies failed more often than not, and mental health in- stitutions all over the nation were on the verge of col- lapse. Do not think of this as a contradiction. It's all part of the normal government-business cycle.

Before this mental health debacle could come to full light, the denizens of mental hospitals, coast to coast, were dumped on the streets, that is into *real-life thera- peutic milieus*. This, of course, was the very latest theory of rehabilitation from the best and the brightest, bands playing, bows taken. A smoke screen. When the smoke cleared, the mentally ill had disappeared and there were the *homeless*. Voilà. A trade: prob- lematic mutton for fresh lamb. Ho ho.

Take note, boy. If you manage your sheep properly, you can drive them back and forth between two cliffs forever, simply switching names as they turn—the Public Memory is short—Shropshires to Suffolks,

Suffolks back into Shropshires. "The more things change, the more they stay the same."

Now, it's nowhere near time to recycle the homeless. They are years away from the cliff, maybe decades. Keep these sheep *homeless*, as we would currently have them, in one saintly, homogeneous flock— no unholy exceptions—and they will serve us well, not just today but in the future, when we round them all up and turn them back into the mentally ill.

Big Nurse will need to step in once more and house them and feed them and provide expertise to make them Perfectly well—more on such maneuvers later. We must turn to specifics, to smoothing the little bump Dan has put in our road with his steel-town bums.

Do not, as I said, make exceptions of Dan's misanthropes. *Differentiate* them. Rename them. Disappear them. These fellows aren't homeless at all: they are transients, drifters, vagrants.... Cut them out of the flock of suffering homeless saints. We can spare the few to protect the pristine (piteous and pathetic) image of the many.

Life has its little sacrifices, son. Drive these goats and donkeys away from your sheep. Transients, drifters, vagrants are another issue, for another time.

"Let's stay on the subject, Friend Dan, the 'homeless.'"

Rename Dan's bad boys, make them disappear. Ban them from discussion. Protect your flock. Do this now—we will give your boy something else to think about soon. It's clear he has too much cerebral free time.

Your elastic uncle,

RED

Letter the Thirteenth

~

Dear Ticker,

Good, good. That's my boy. Now that the "drifters" and "vagrants" have been driven off, we can breathe easier. But let's play it safe, broaden our base. We need to complicate things, give Dan something more to think about. Liberalism is to him a foreign language—let's give him the course. Total immersion.

Expand your discussion of the homeless to include the plight of the poor in general. Do this at once. And let's get a little gender into the mix, say "abused wives." That should be a good one: some very personal bruised and battered new faces. It will get the girls fired up and into the fray. But be careful here. Though individual instances are dramatic, they are rare.

Test the water—make this a habit—to see if anyone knows anything about the subject before you start in. Do you see how your "homeless" error in this manner might have been avoided?

The statistics on *spousal abuse*—less actual assaults on married women than any other group in society—are in reality dismal. Volume can only be generated through definitions that include such things as husbands stomping out of the room. You must be on guard. But all this seldom comes up—the topic is large in the Public Mind, where it counts. I doubt you will have trouble. Switch to some other "abused," one your pals know nothing about, if you should meet intelligent resistance.

Add the plight of the poor and abused wives to the homeless. And throw in something "endangered"—there is always a beached whale somewhere. That should get you rolling, and give you room to maneuver. Switch around when things become troublesome in any one spot. Rule of thumb: if you encounter reality, change the subject, redefine terms. You must learn to juggle Misfortune, my boy. Ho ho.

Ticker, in the end you must have many sheep: separate little flocks of lambkins within one big flock of poor, pitiful, much-maligned ruminants. All in dire need of Big Nanna in her many guises—all in need of caring liberals to give them a political will and a voice. When the liberal speaks, it is always for millions!

Do as I have advised, and you will soon have some running room, lines of retreat—and mental exercise for Dan to keep him out of mischief in the first place.

Put this little "homeless" blip safely behind us, so we can get on with your education, and Friend Dan's conversion. Follow my advice and all will be well.

Your prudential uncle,

RED

Letter the Fourteenth

~

Dear Ticker,

My compliments on damage control. It sounds like you're back on track. The girls, of course, were Believers in the first place—they have merely responded to the smelling salts. Their heads are now clear and they can no longer remember why Dan's true-life tales of the homeless were so disturbing. Abused wives are "taking off like a rocket," good. And PJ has a pet kangaroo rat. Endangered, she thinks—outstanding.

The bums are behind us, the homeless restored. Our sheep multiply. Bravo. Consider the liberal starter kit sold: lost lambs, sentimentality, and Heaven on Earth someday. What's next?

It's time, my boy, to fill out the product line. Time for you to start preaching the latter-day liberal Beatitudes and dispensing some liberal Grace—

Blessed are those who feel other's pain, those who *really* care about people.

Blessed are those who worship the planet Earth, those who venerate animals and flowers and trees, rain forests and whales....

Blessed are those who realize that all imperfection in this world stems from greed and bad management—from others not being as good and wise.

Blessed are those who can see in the future
a manmade Perfect world, inhabited by Perfect women and men living in Perfect liberty,
equality, and fraternity.

And blessed are those who have a thousand
theories about how to change things to bring
about this Heaven on Earth, *rapidly, through the
power of Science and central government.* Amen.

Look carefully at the final Beatitude, Ticker. That is
where you make the sale, where the novice surren-
ders. The *way* is added to the *light*. Heart and mind
fuse. Pity is transformed into piety, self-righteousness into missionary zeal.

Scales fall from the initiate's eyes. The way to salvation ignites like a beacon, the latter-day liberal
Mission:

"GO FORTH IN THE NAME OF BIG NANNA
AND PERFECT THE WORLD!"

In a luminous instant, liberal Grace is received, an
excellence and power granted by the ghosts of
Franklin Delano Roosevelt and Lyndon Baines
Johnson. Ho ho. The True Believer, the *Troob,* is born!

The anointed goes forth, singing of Himself, to bring
about Heaven on Earth, through social democracy,
liberal policy, Democratic action, *liberalism* (work
the *L* word in slowly, slip the big *D* past them when
they're not looking). All will be Perfect, in time. The
Greatest Good for the Many is by the faithful to be
achieved: everything anyone could want in quanti-

ties unlimited, passed out free!

Now, who could be against that, Ticker? I'll tell you who! Listen closely—the deal is only half made. The darkness must be cursed, if ever there is to be Perfect light. Who could stand in the way of earthly beatitude, everlasting Grace, and a horn of plenty? "The Adversary," that's who, the greedy, mindless, uncaring *conservative*! The "Right"—

> Cursed are those who do not worship Man and the planet Earth, those who shrink from the quest for worldly Perfection.
> Cursed are those who oppose rapid change, those who reject the grand theories of liberals who would lead mankind into the future.
> Cursed are those who accept human differences, those who accept social complexity and seek only a measure of liberty and equality.
> Cursed are those who wish to limit government, trusting in family, local institutions, and human tradition instead.
> And cursed, most cursed, are those who put God above all, traffickers in religious superstition.

Meet the *Adversary*, Ticker, our mortal enemy. Selfish, superstitious monsters! Liberal and conservative: light and dark, two sides of the coin of our realm, and equally important. Opposing conservatism is a *necessary* part of receiving liberal Grace.

A Troob must be equally dedicated to defeating the Adversary—the "Right," the "far Right," or the "radical Right," depending on just how annoying—and to leading the remainder of the human race into the Promised Land!

Liberalism, boy: a mission, an Adversary, and a badge of honor. Your boy, Dan, and all the Tiffanys and Plain Janes and Dean Flaps and Professor Feathers of the world get to walk in the liberal light, if they will only bow down to Big Nanna, oppose the Adversary, and seek Heaven on Earth, Amen. Sell the *Blesseds* first. Save the *Curseds* for later, especially the last one about God.

Anoint your boy, bless him, and keep him in the faith. Tempt him. Share the grandeur. The Greatest Good for the Many! Take the high ground, Ticker. Whip Dan into shape—and bring the others along for the ride.

Leftward ho!

Your impassioned uncle,

RED

ps. Don't go buying this wholesale yourself, boy. Us and them, remember? Elite and Troob....

Letter the Fifteenth

~

Dear Ticker,

The Beatitudes are selling well. Keep up the good work, son. Tend your sheep. Anoint, bless, and keep the shepherds....

The question you pose is keen—you tug at an interesting string. Let's see how it unravels, shall we, boy?

The girls and the new boy hanging out with your group—Jake, is it?—are not really upper crust. They are merely well-off. As you observe, Ticker, they, unlike Dan—his family paying little if any taxes—are reaching into their own pockets to line ours, and they seem to love it. They subsidize us, the super rich, as well as the common folk. "Grossly unfair, a double whammy," as you say. Tsk tsk.

Why such willingness and good nature? One can understand a certain sloppiness in thought, when giving away someone else's money. But not when giving away one's own! This is, indeed, a mystery. Uncle Red will explain—

First of all the well-off, in general, never seem to comprehend that they—the upper-middle income group, about twenty percent of the population—pay over fifty percent of the taxes. It doesn't seem to register that people like us don't pay any, or token amounts for show. My Senate salary, for instance, is duly taxed. Ho ho. Spare change, my boy. But I can say I pay my taxes too.

The well-off understand progressive taxes only in theory, son. Take from the rich, give to the poor. Robin Hood and his merry men come to mind. They think of the super rich who pay no taxes, if they think of us at all, as few (in numbers, yes, but in dollars, no). Ha ha.

Maybe they miss the trick because they're so busy working. Maybe they don't stay well-off long enough to learn the game. Maybe they're scared to death of the IRS. Maybe they're just creatures of habit, and don't think about anything much....

Choose all of the above—and be thankful, boy. Bless the merely well-off, Ticker, and keep them in this beatific state of habit, ignorance, and fear.

That's half the story, my boy, why the well-off pay up. But, the more interesting question remains. Why do some liberals, like your new pals, *love* to pay? What's behind this self-flagellation? I've given you a hint there, Ticker. Can't you guess?

Think about it. You said yourself, the girls feel badly about *everything*: because they are in the Ivy League and the homeless aren't, because everyone else doesn't have a sports car.... Yet, you say, they seem "above it all." "Arrogant and haughty...." Why the split personality? What do they care if some bum in Duluth never went to Harvard?

Son, they don't love their fellow man any more than I do—but they love the *idea* of loving him. They want to be their brother's keeper, so long as they don't have to have him around. This produces a very special disease, upper middle-class guilt: a hyperactive conscience, with telescopic sights. Troobs feel guilty about everything that's far away. They accept the blame for things that happened in other states before they were born, for earthquakes and floods in other countries, for babies born deformed to people they don't even know....

Progressive taxes are an antiseptic way of assuaging this guilt, the perfect penance for hubristic transgressions, abstract and impersonal. A way of loving your neighbor without having to have him around— helping out without getting your hands dirty. The Good Samaritan who never crossed the road.

A special disease, upper middle-class guilt, and a special cure, progressive taxes—a marriage made in heaven, as it were. Ho ho.

This is an understandable blind spot for you, boy, growing up as you did. Your father and mother may not be politicos—someone has to run the family foundation—but they are hardly Troobs. You'll come to understand all this better as you spend more time with your pals—that's part of what college is for, getting to know the voter.

Why, then, the next question—let's run this string out—don't these liberal penitents simply give to the poor around the corner or even next door? Why the long-distance line? They wouldn't have to have tea with the common folk, just send money. Why send money all the way to Washington, to have it sent back?

You know the answer, Ticker. They are Troobs— elevated above simply helping one's neighbor. Merely helping those in need won't do. Would it solve everything for everyone? Would a *Perfect* world ensue?

No Troob is about to settle for just helping out the guy next door. A drop in the bucket. Only Big Nanna can save the world. You see the beauty? Better to send your money to Washington, play for the really Big Score. Save *everyone*, control the weather, cure cancer and the common cold....

Your pals have recited the liberal Beatitudes since the first grade, Ticker, probably in public school. And their parents, before them. They didn't go to prep school in Switzerland, like you. They know their catechism, boy. What the world needs now is not charity but Change. Heaven on Earth, coming soon.

They buy the notion of Perfecting the world, and we have the market cornered—the Adversary won't touch it, blasphemy to him, against his religion. Money is sent to Washington to *fix things once and for all*. What a relief, the burden lifted.

So the liberal penitent pays his taxes, and loves it. Sometimes he even sends a little extra to Ethiopia or other far-off places to subsidize the poor (and rich) there. Old Ned never dreamed the lambs would learn to love being slaughtered. Almost makes you believe in God—and on our side.

Be thankful, boy. Count your liberal blessings. Drink them in, like the bouquet of a decades-old Chateau Mouton Rothschild from our cellar.

N'est pas?

Your rhapsodic uncle,

RED

Letter the Sixteenth

~

Dear Ticker,

Sounds like things are going fine. Good boy, but don't coast.

The new boy, a "yellow-dog" Democrat you say— so no problem. No! Not good enough. Stretch, boy. Set yourself a goal. Before we are through, this yellow-dog Jake should vote for the Devil himself before he would vote Republican. Yellow-dog Democrats are only lukewarm. Preferring a yellow dog over any Republican simply won't do. It's not enough. And don't let up on the girls, either. Stay at them until they *ooze* sincerity. If they don't make you sick, you're not doing your job.

Go the extra mile. Get into it, boy. Preach the Beatitudes. Bring Tiffany and PJ and Yellow-dog Jake to new levels of liberalism, secure their souls for Nanna (and Ned). Get your pals to compete as to who's the most outraged about abused wives. See who feels worse about the homeless and who cares the most about the poor. Get everyone to oh and ah over Plain Jane's rat, and bemoan the plight of its poor endangered cousins put out of their homes by people building houses and farming their fields. The Fiends!

Dan, you say, seems in a daze, "stunned." I've seen this before, the bright lights of liberalism working strange wonders. The Great College, taking its toll. Your efforts, and mine, lighting the way. For some converts, it's like watching a sunrise, an instant epiphany. Then, for others, as with Dan, it's like catching the flu, a slow process of brooding and discontent, wondering what's going on down in the bowels. Ho ho.

Don't let him brood too long, Ticker. Now is the time to bring him into the fold. Wrap him tightly into your little group. Get him to join in the fun. Explain to him that the strange way he feels is because he is growing so fast and cares so much. All quite natural, for one who has never before seen the liberal light.

Your proud uncle,

RED

Letter the Seventeenth

~

Dear Ticker,

Hmmm. I thought we'd have Dan alongside the boat by now, ready to net. A little thrashing about would not have surprised me, but this is perplexing. He sounds like a fish that's played out but won't come in, just lying on the bottom.

Let's play him carefully. We'd better slow down. Do exactly as I say. This is a delicate time. I underestimated the boy, I admit. But no harm done, so long as we don't hurry him. Steady now, Ticker.

Your immediate task is to turn up the heat about poverty and the homeless and the abused wives and rats.... Bring up the heat slowly. Take your pals from feeling bad about social injustice, and eliminating it someday, somehow, to going to war about it with the Adversary. This is the natural progression, the next stage of development—though I'd hoped to have Dan fully on board first.

You must create the feeling of impending action, a *brewing* war. Everything must be in the indefinite future. Not today, not tomorrow, not even the day after. No pressure to sign on the dotted line. A good salesman is a good fisherman.

Keep the focus on *whom* the war is with. Keep away from *how* the war will be fought—later for that. Notice that in reality nothing changes. You are simply intensifying the sentiment. Play the game of names and faces, *personalize*, but this time the Adversary, the enemy.

See how many images of rich Republicans taking the food out of the mouths of poor babes you can muster: the heartless Right-wing! Picture the homeless being put out on the street and whales being beached, by conservatives. They do this for fun! Get your hands dirty. Sling a little mud, throw some stones, and watch the sparks fly. Yellow-dog will growl and the girls will howl.... They'll be screaming for the political scalps of those Republican pigs in a heartbeat. Who could help but hate the brutes?

All you do, my boy, is instigate. Get things going, then lie back and wait. Let the emotion build. Play the loyal comrade, support your Troobs.

Focus the images, heat up the sentiment, frame the Adversary. That's all for now. Let's see if we can't coax your boy up off the bottom, get a few more hooks in him. This is turning out to be more interesting than I had guessed it would be.

Your angling uncle,

RED

Letter the Eighteenth

~

Dear Ticker, Ticker, Ticker,

I might have expected this question, but not from *you*: "Who isn't against poverty, I mean, who would be for it or anything?" I've read this deplorable, mealy-mouthed run-on sentence of yours three times, and it only gets worse. My own nephew. Great Caesar's Ghost!

Don't think about it, boy. *Feel* it. You haven't been listening. Now get this. The Adversary likes poverty. The Right wing! Greedy, uncaring exploiters of the poor. Picture them. See their pointed teeth, watch them drool. They only pretend to care about people, making themselves grotesque. We, on the other hand, *really* care. With us, it's true compassion.

The sincerity of True Believers is here a great strength (a wonderful front). The Troobs really do care, in their way, and the Adversary will seldom accuse them of not. But, never fear, we *will* accuse the Adversary: THEY DON'T CARE! It's our mantra, boy. Repeat it loudly and often, until it soaks in.

Keep in mind, you're selling a package deal. Those who would receive liberal Grace may not pick and choose. THEY DON'T CARE is a part of the package. No package, no deal! No anointing, no Grace.

Get this through your head, and drive it home with the others. This is central to your current task, preparing for war. Cement it within the minion minds you manage (and learn to at least half believe it yourself). THEY DON'T CARE! Get verbal assent from your charges, and reward it.

Let's get down to cases, the how-to—

"You are against poverty, aren't you, Friend Dan, and against the greedy, heartless exploiters of the poor?"

"Why sure, yes," says Dan. Of course he is!

"Ah, good," you say. "Please wear this ribbon in recognition of your stand, to differentiate you from all others who do not care as much as you."

If the situation is too informal for ribbons, simply look pleased with your boy, a somber, *sincere* pleased. Touch him. Squeeze a shoulder or firmly grasp an upper arm. Blood brothers, amigos (partners in crime).

In the end, Troobs must value pathos in and of itself, and must be able to believe things divorced from all reason and reality.

THEY DON'T CARE. It's only a step now to the Adversary exploiting the poor, and only one more to the Adversary actually being *for* poverty, liking it, glad to have others in squalor, children starving. Remember Alice and the Queen of Hearts: the Queen could "believe as many as six impossible things before breakfast." So can your boy, and the others, all but Dan, probably already do. What about you?

Who isn't against poverty, indeed.

Your incredulous uncle,

RED

Letter the Nineteenth

~

Dear Ticker,

You're starting to worry me boy, one fainthearted slip after another. Get a grip. This is good news. No time to go soft.

You must get used to the sound of war drums. Let Jake and the girls dance around, go native as it were. Don't take it so seriously. No need to go to the window—the trees are still there. You've done your job, my boy. Be proud. Join in. Coax Dan out onto the dance floor. Get with it. It's all in fun. Your pals are just letting off steam.

If you start to reel, if the victims and oppressors you've conjured up start to seem a little too corporeal, remember this: it's only a puberty ritual. There are liberals who have made a lifetime sport of this. Lighten up.

The liberal Beatitudes have been poured on the open wounds of social injustice, on *feelings* about it that is. It seems there is the smell of burning flesh, the hiss, the yelps and moans. Pshaw. Smoke and mirrors, none of it's real.

There are poor people out there, and oppressors too, to be sure. But that has no more to do with the little party you're having than real cops and robbers have to do with Hollywood thrillers. This is only high sentiment and finger-painted images, and only half true. Enjoy the colors. Smear a little paint, yourself. Experiment. Build on the half true. Half-truths are our liberal bread and butter—but more on this later.

Now, get hold of yourself. Get back in the game. Don't get real, boy, get ahead and stay there. That's what Old Ned would say.

It sounds like things are really going swell—and I'm right here, standing behind you all the way. Remember our deal.

Your stalwart uncle,

RED

Letter the Twentieth

~

Dear Ticker,

That-a-boy! You sound much improved, and the progress you report is significant. Dan's little dance steps may not seem like much, but remember it wasn't that long ago we couldn't get him out on the floor. Now, this little do-si-do with PJ. He's coming your way. A little indignation here, some crocodile tears there (bow to your partner) and away he slides down the *sliberal* slope. Ho ho. Don't hurry him, Ticker. Our boy must be a volunteer, when the real action comes. Give him room. Let PJ teach him to dance. We can cover some fine points, and do a little review, meantime.

Let's go a little deeper into the psychology of the True Believer, the inner workings of the minion mind (you won't find this in your course catalog). You must study the inner Troob, Ticker. They are the front line of liberalism, and must be managed. Not always an easy chore. There is nothing nastier than a disillusioned Troob—or more dangerous to the cause.

You must understand the Troob mind, son—but never slip into this quicksand yourself. We have things in common with the Troobs, *and much that is not.*

The Troob psyche has three layers—like a parfait. Yes, that's apt, a rich and colorful dessert in a delicate glass. A sweet goo. At bottom is the Believer's self-image, a pudding of sincerity, caring, and out-rage—a psychological landfill of alleged injustice and other people's pain—divorced from reality, yet half true. It is *based* on reality.

Half-truths maintain the phantasm in an other-wise normal mind: injustice and injury do indeed exist (but not everywhere, all of the time, and some-one did not always do it to someone else, and when someone did the perpetrator was not always Right-wing). You and I know all this, Ticker, but, of course, let sleepy dogs lie. Ha ha.

Half a glass of half-truths and sentimentality—color this bottom layer of psychic pudding, purple. All the Troob's passion and power is drawn from here.

The middle layer of this parfait is the liberal Mission: "Go forth in the name of Big Nanna and Perfect the world!" The images of injury and injustice, deeper in the glass, blend upward into reverence for central government and the crusade to bring about Heaven on Earth, liberal zeal. Color this layer sky-blue: *Man, the Perfecter of the universe.* Hubris, my boy.

A dangerous game, Ticker. Never take hubris too far. We are accidental gods, you and I, in an acciden-tal world—the lizards may reign, one day, in our place. Remember that. It is the absence of illusions, not grand ones, that keeps you in the saddle. Illusions are for Troobs.

The topping would be, let's see ... whipped cream and nuts. Ah yes, just so. Tactics, my boy, *au liberel*. A swirl of political maneuvers and rhetorical tricks, the Troob intellect: Perfection or nothing, THEY DON'T CARE, white ribbons of sincerity....

You've learned a few tactics already, son. You must add to the list. You must know every Troob trick, and many more. Tactics will soon become all important.

Enough for today, I find myself fatigued. At my age, after all I've seen and done and been through, outrage and indignity are difficult constructs to fathom. I find probing the deeper levels of Troob psychology exhausting. But you are young and strong. Carry on. Wade in—but always wear rubber boots. Understand the Troob mind, but don't indulge yourself. Don't start believing all that you preach.

Your old-warhorse uncle,

RED

ps. Keep the war dance going with your pals.

Letter the Twenty-first

~

Dear Ticker,

I understand your concern, but this a false alarm. Ms Jewelry working one night a week serving mashed potatoes and green beans to bums is a world away from Dan's living with them nearby. This seems to violate the rule of keeping the Adversary's victims, our sheep, at arm's length, lest reality intrude—I understand. We have here a special situation. I'll explain.

It's much like a child studying zebras, who takes a trip to the zoo. This, of the child, does not Tarzan make—nor will a little volunteer work make Tiffany into Mother Teresa. No danger that any preconceived notions will be seriously challenged, about zebras or bums. A false sense of intimacy and knowledge is the more likely outcome. Useful, from our point of view.

The danger you mistakenly foresee—understandable after your experience with Dan—is that injustice and injury, the root causes of homelessness, will be diluted with instances of misfortune, irresponsibility, human perversity, and addled brains. It's good to be on guard, but the abstraction is safe back there behind the mashed potatoes and the green beans. If Tiffany had to actually eat while she was there, she might reconsider being a liberal. Ha ha.

The general rule holds: malice may be tolerated

toward someone nearby, but generosity and love should be directed toward those far away. However, there is no harm in *visiting* the zoo. A fine point. Glad you asked, that's how you learn.

I look forward to your next letter, to hear more of your progress with Dan. The first stage of Dan's conversion appears nearly complete, blast off of the second stage soon. He sounds almost ready.

I almost forgot. Did you really come in on Dan praying, actually contemplating an image of Calvary? This seems to have disturbed you. Forget it. It is odd, but probably not dangerous. Religion has a way of getting absorbed into nascent Troob psyches—more student crucifixes than you could count have disappeared into this quicksand—the process seldom even noticed. Jesus gets transformed into a social reformer or philosopher king....

Let's keep an eye on the religious tendency in our boy, but leave it alone for now. It will probably take care of itself, a little wrinkle that will iron itself out.

Your undaunted uncle,

RED

Letter the Twenty-second

~

Dear Ticker,

Sounds like our boy is becoming a regular Fred Astaire, thanks to PJ. She and Dan are becoming "special friends." But no romance. That's perfect—romance and conversion can be a problematic pair. By all means, let PJ keep leading her pal on the war-dance floor. Men are always least wary with female friends. Stay out of the little Troob's way.

Note that it is *spousal abuse* that has captured Dan's imagination—for him the most abstract of all your sheep. PJ, and the others, have probably never seen an abused wife either. Yet the issue inspires them. This is quite normal, Ticker, and highly instructive.

The True-Believing tone can rarely be struck with clarity in the presence of firsthand knowledge. Recall Dan's acquaintance with the homeless, how it muddied the waters. Firsthand knowledge complicates things and begs an individual response, and, too often, a resolution—one either acts or leaves things alone.

PJ, Dan, and the others have, no doubt, seen a child who has had his eye blackened by another. Uninspiring, mundane. Children, even grown men, beat each other senseless, every day. Large dominating small.... But there are laws. Enforce them. What's the big deal? You see?

Spousal abuse, for your little group, is not an *instance*, however regrettable, to be dealt with in usual ways. It is an *idea* that grows ever larger in their minds, and therein lies its political power. The rally-round factor, Ticker: a *cause*.

Causes, not instances, are what we're after, boy, the bigger the better. Causes can go on forever. Instances can be resolved. Mark the phenomenon well. It has gotten me elected more than once.

Let your pals beat the drum about "battered wives" for awhile. Soon enough, someone will call for a vote, one way or another, and we will have turned the corner with our boy. Some one of your pals will demand a loyalty oath. Stand up and testify, or lose one's standing in the group. "Are we agreed then...?" "Ain't it awful...?" Stand up, stand up, and be counted.

"Friend Dan, you are with us on this point, at least. There may be differences among us, but surely we are all together on this...."

Dan is human. He doesn't want to be alone. How many friends would you guess he's made in the Ivy League? He won't disappoint us. You just wait and see if I've not read the politics of your little dance-floor correctly. I've watched this shuffle a thousand times, and it always goes the same way.

Your prescient uncle,

RED

Letter the Twenty-third

~

Dear Ticker,

Keep them dancing, boy. We're nearing *escapist* velocity. Ho ho. The second stage of our rocket blasts off soon. Meantime, let's build on what's selling, the *idea* of "battered wives." Here's what you do—

Establish inequality, men versus women, as the common soil from which spousal abuse *(and all other social ill)* springs. The downtrodden wife, the homeless, the poor, even poor put-upon kangaroo rats and whales—all have been deprived of something by the Adversary. You see? At the root of all social ills are the Adversary's insatiable *greed* and his need for *hierarchal power*. What else could it be?

From here, Ticker, one little turn of the screw, and a Grand Cause emerges. "Liberals unite, we must LEVEL THE PLAYING FIELD!" I love that phrase, liberalism in a word, as it were. The Perfect headline, boy. *Equality*!

Sex, income, education, there must be equal everything for all! See Big Nanna, arms akimbo, looking sternly down. She will redistribute power, money, intelligence, strength, sex.... Why not? Today's impossibilities are the whims of tomorrow in this modern world—all lies just ahead. Are you with me, boy?

Wrap all the indignation and gnawing grief you've

been fomenting under one heading: *Equality*! Load everything onto the Equality bandwagon, and hook the whole thing to Big Nanna. Who but a super hero like Big Nan could even attempt to pull such a load? Who else could even dream of bringing Perfect social justice to this foggy world of woe? Who but She could stanch the bleeding heart? Who but She could make things *equal*, for all?

Catch the drift, Ticker? Do you see where we're headed? So far, we've just been building up steam, getting angry and feeling sorry. Liberal piety and missionary zeal. Victims and oppressors, alarms ringing. Big Nanna positioned to answer the bell.

Our heroine, Big Nan, is about to engage the Adversary in combat. She will fight the war you've been brewing.

Victims, an Adversary—and our hero, Big Nan. It's a thriller, my boy, and the plot thickens. What will Nan do? *Level the playing field*, of course, the first step in building the Perfect world.

There will be no more homeless or battered wives. Kangaroo rats will stand tall. All will be the same size. All will ride prancing steeds (on the Equality merry-go-round). Ah ha! Ha ha.

Hi-ho.

Your schemeful uncle,

RED

Letter the Twenty-fourth

~

Dear Ticker,

Yes and no. Yes, the "liberal phantasms," as you call them, will now become more substantial. The moral questions that cling like leeches to political thought will become clear. But no, no ventures into the real world, not yet. It's all in the dorm room for awhile.

It is not yet time for our Dan to try his liberal wings, to test liberal theory against reality. We must first inoculate him against the "heartache and the thousand natural shocks that flesh is heir to." We will not make Shakespeare's mistake, carelessly turning our character loose to be infected by the world. No, no.

Hamlet, you see, was never immunized. He was never given to understand that heartache and shock are not natural at all, but completely manmade, *100%* inflicted, committed, p-e-r-p-e-t-r-a-t-e-d. Only with this knowledge firmly planted will it be safe for our boy to suffer the world and remain free of conservatism, or despair.

There must be no outrageous fortune to suffer and bow before, only human error and inequality—the giant liberalism will slay. Outrageous fortune is the stuff of comic books, like *Hamlet*. Only when this is fully understood, can the illusion of omnipotence be maintained outside the dorm room. Only then, can the task of rearranging the stars and recreating life begin. Then, and only then, from this elevated hubristic plane can it be seen that it is only a matter of time and money and expertise before man Perfects Himself and brings about Heaven on Earth, Amen. Ho ho.

Behold, Ticker, I describe the mature Troob, no longer needing to fear being mugged by reality. Our Dan has a long way to go—he is yet a babe. Our boy must be immunized before we turn him loose to suffer slings and arrows. He must know, *and take to heart*, the third Beatitude before he leaves the nursery: "Blessed *are those who realize that all imperfection in this world stems from greed and bad management—from others not being as good and wise*."

Soon, Ticker, Friend Dan's inoculation begins. We will graduate him from causes to *issues*: the liberal arithmetic of social problems. He, and you, my boy, must learn the new math of public policy, in which two plus two equals whatever we choose.

Step by step—and all in the dorm room for awhile. Soon enough, our Dan will grow impervious to Hamlet's human frailty and doubt, ready to try his liberal wings. When it is time, we will let him fly. Not even liberals can live forever in a college dorm room. Ha ha.

Wallow in self-righteousness and pity with your pals a little more. Play at going to war. Praise Big Nanna. Set the stage. Let PJ do her thing. Soon Dan's immunization shots begin—and therein, a Ph.D. in liberalism, for you. You lucky boy!

Your calculating uncle,

RED

Letter the Twenty-fifth

~

Dear Ticker,

Our boy is nearly ready for stage two. Let's make sure you're ready too. Here's a little learning exercise, just for you—

I want you to create an issue—go beyond the grief fests and indignity sing-alongs you've been holding. Make a problem on paper for your fellow man. Not another cause, my boy. Create an *issue*.

Provoke action as well as emotion. Don't take this as a criticism of what you've been doing, son. You've got to knead the dough before you bake the bread, form attitudes before molding opinions and beliefs. We progress, step by step—your education proceeding *pari passu*. "Side by side," Ticker. You've much to learn, my boy. Do they still teach Latin at the old school, or have they dropped that too?

Of course, issues in real-world politics are usually ready-made—it's only a matter of mastering the detail and figuring the spin. Lots of practice, straight ahead. But first, I want you to build an issue of your own, from scratch. It's the only way to really learn.

Look to your courses ("The Impoverished American," "What's Wrong With the U.S.," "The Dark Side of the Land of the Free," all long-standing freshman offerings of which I'm sure you are taking one) and pick out a problem. Add some statistics and a little imagination, and produce a Crisis. Think of it as creating a recipe for disaster. Cooking up a catastrophe, as it were. For example—

Step One: Take the total number of Americans currently in poverty ...

(Never mind if a large percentage of the *defined* poor have two cars, television sets, and microwaves, or that most have a standard of living that is the envy of the world—poverty is in the eye of the beholder, which means whatever definition gets you the numbers that will make a stir. Shop around.)

Step Two: Mix in a National rate of population growth, and deduce the mushrooming number of poverty stricken that there will be in the United States in just five years ...

(Use China as a base line for population growth, and assume Mexico and Central America become U.S. states.)

Step Three: Marinate the above numbers in some projection or other for the Nation's future food supply and extrapolate the numbers of "poor" who will actually be starving ...

(Define "starving" as anyone getting below the government minimum standard of *any* nutrient, vitamin, or trace mineral—you can't be too careful about such things—and see that the U.S. gets only its fair share of the world's food supply.)

Step Four: Put all this in a pot, stir vigorously, and bring to a rolling boil: "MASSIVE POVERTY AND STARVATION STRAIGHT AHEAD ..."

(Get several prominent, liberal scientists to endorse this conclusion—far easier than you might guess.)

Step Five: Serve hot, explaining, in excruciating detail, the grave danger facing the Nation, if not the entire Civilized World, maybe the Planet, perhaps the Universe itself ...

(Use colorful charts and graphs that look like angry weather fronts to present a "computer model" of the disaster, preferably developed at a prestigious university—easy enough to do.)

Step Six: Ring the liberal dinner bell, and call out for all the world to hear: "The sky is falling! The sky is falling! SOMETHING must be done!"

(Explain that only central government, Big Bread Winner, is powerful enough to feed the soon-to-be-starving multitudes and forestall the Crisis—not farmers, not fishermen, not ranchers or fruit growers, not Jesus with his fishes and loaves, *Big Bread Winner!*)

Step Seven: Add, just before serving: government programs, increased regulation, more taxes....

(Boxcars of other people's money may now be given away, and the Nation's food industry put in a stranglehold of gubernation.)

Once your save-the-Nation train is in motion, you sustain it for as long as you can, redefining and recreating the Crisis—a constructed reality can be taken apart and put back together any number of ways.

When the jig is finally up, run for the sidelines and

blame everything on the Adversary. They are really good sports about this. I've never figured out why.

Understand, Ticker, the above is only an example. It could be the environment in total collapse, asteroids coming at us from outer space, a new rare and deadly disease.... Do your own thing. Be creative. This exercise will give you a solid foundation for managing the issues we will soon introduce.

Get to work, son. Let's see what you can do. Mush, boy, mush! Some day you'll be playing this game for real: spending someone else's actual dollars, strangling real industries in miles of red tape.

Your slave-driving uncle,

RED

ps. Did I ever tell you how I got my nickname? Remind me later, I'll tell you the story.

Letter the Twenty-sixth

~

Dear Ticker,

A good first draft, if a bit sloppy. Check your math on the percentage of the earth that will be destroyed—you misplaced a decimal point. The Crisis is much larger than you imagined. Two-thirds, not half, of the earth will be either destroyed by fire or submerged under water from the melting ice caps.

Also, the looting in the remaining cities will be much worse than you projected. I think we are looking at a total social meltdown here. And *personalize,* boy: I want to hear people scream.

Put more emphasis on what you propose. Spend money, take control.... A *cause* becomes an *issue* when something is proposed. We are no longer merely tending our sheep. Liberal largess and caring must take form.

Finally, tie what you propose more firmly to your experts. This is essential. Tune me in, boy. The conservative bent is always and forever to be coming up with facts that undermine the need for our save-the-world programs, or, if not that, presenting modest alternatives. *Always meet facts or practical opposition with experts.*

Your line: "The situation is too serious for 'folk medicine.' We must have a professional plan. A disinterested expert [fraternity brother] must be employed to discover the *root causes* of the problem and develop a solution [a federal, caring, 100% solution, all ways and forever]." The stage is now set to employ the *Perfect* defense, once more.

You have only to reveal the imperfections (versus your expert's *theoretically* Perfect) in whatever the conservative proposes—even if it is to do nothing at all—leaving your expert's plan standing to dominate the field. Conservative approaches are never Perfect—not even the pretense. These people never learn.

It's the same game we've been playing all along, Ticker, but now we go beyond what's wrong—wringing our hands and being indignant—to *how* we will save the world. We empower Big Nanna through our experts, and win by default. The Adversary has no Perfect solution, we do. Are you with me, my boy?

I'll give you a *B+* on your Crisis, son. We are making progress. Keep me advised on developments with Dan and your pals. Time for the next step, Dan's immunization shots, soon.

Your *progressive* uncle,

RED

Letter the Twenty-seventh

~

Dear Ticker,

We'll take silence as consent. If Dan really went along with Ms Jewelry's proposal, the boy is ready. "Mandatory life imprisonment for any instance of spousal abuse"—and Dan said nothing? We've come a long way. That's our loyalty oath, Ticker. Dan has thrown in his lot. He's one of you, now.

Before we go forward, I want to do one last rehearsal. I know you're impatient, Ticker, but let's prepare a little more. Preparation, my boy, is next best to owning the judge. Let's put a few more rhetorical arrows in your quiver, before the shouting starts—we can't expect our Dan to take his immunization shots without a little fuss and holler, now can we?

You must be ready for Dan's conservative instincts to revive, as reality seeps in. Small doses and little flareups, that's how inoculation works. Old sensitivities put to rest (liberal sensibilities left in their place).

Dan has taken the big step, Ticker. He has bought the idea of saving the world. But, confronted with matters of public policy—real issues, even in the dorm room—his instinct will be to backpedal. You must be ready.

More tactics for holding sway—

Your boy, if he is deep down the conservative steel-town fellow I believe him to be, will want to save the world one step at a time.

Your answer: "Never, Dan. We must save the world now! Justice delayed is justice denied, and injustice not instantly cured is infamy infinitely compounded [let him sort that package out, if he can]."

He may counter that his step-at-a-time approach, while not addressing everything *now,* at least makes things better, and does not preclude additional steps later, as required.

Your answer: "No, no, not good enough [dig in here]. We must fix the whole thing, once and for all. For centuries mankind has been content to merely grapple with imperfection. We must prevail! Anything less is cowardice, a cop out [packaging, my boy, manliness and omnipotence—buy one, get one free]."

He will want, if he plays true to form, to incorporate in any solution the experience of things similar from the past. "The collective wisdom of past generations," or some such nonsense, he'll call it.

Your answer: "No! No! No! No! We must have new thinking, a radical change! The past had its chance and it failed. If those before us had known *anything,* we wouldn't be in this mess [another package deal, disdain for the past and radical change]."

Your Dan will probably want those involved to

participate in the solution, to take action and be responsible.

Your answer: "Foul [muster a little indignation]! These people are not educated, or equipped. They are disadvantaged. We must act on their behalf, be their Champions, do it *for* them [package number four, caring and control—are you learning the game, my boy?]."

He will want a budget, bet on it—and to know where the money is coming from.

Your answer: "Unrealistic, my friend [a sad little shake of the head]. This is a Crisis! It costs what it costs. This is a matter of caring, not money. The real question is do we care enough? If we do, the money [guess whose?] will be there [caring, largess, and highway robbery, package five]."

You see? It's really no contest. Tie up the bundles with pretty white ribbons, to show how sincere you are and how much you care. Let Dan share your ribbon, if he comes along. If he balks, explain the alternatives.

Your counter: "Friend Dan, do you really want to compound infamy? Won't you choose the manly course, instead? What will it be? Shall we improve things or leave them in their sorry state? Shall we take charge, or let injustice reign? Shall we be stingy or spend whatever it takes? You do *care*, don't you, Dan?"

Add these arrows to your quiver, Ticker, and practice the language, my boy. Without fine words to adorn them, these tactical arrows are mere sticks.

Words, the felicity of those chosen, are the feathers that make the missile fly. Feather your arrows, boy, and don the liberal mission, the pursuit of Perfection—it is your breastplate, son (and I, Uncle Redtape, am the dagger up your sleeve). Ho ho.

Your silver-tongued uncle,

RED

ps. I promise, you may try out your weapons forthwith.

PART TWO: SEEDS OF EVIL

"The great act of faith is when man decides that he is not God."

—Oliver Wendell Holmes, Jr.
from a letter to William James

Letter the Twenty-eighth

~

Dear Ticker,

Let the games begin!

Your dorm room becomes the Great Hall of public debate. Stand like Robespierre inciting terror and virtue. Dan and your pals will play the French mob.

"[T]he crowd, they need interpreters," Pindar said in the fourth century B.C. Nothing has changed, Ticker. Issues must be *interpreted*—the essential black art of politics. Causes rally the Troobs, but issues galvanize the Public Mind. Votes! He who shapes the Public Mind, holds sway. The pulpit is mightier than the sword, my boy—dead men don't pay taxes.

We begin with the Mother of all issues, Welfare—

A riddle: How is Welfare like the communications industry? Can you guess? No? All right. Uncle Red will tell you. We begin with first principles, son.

In 1844—post office in hand—the federal government gained control of the country's first telegraph wire, Washington to Baltimore. The Communications industry was in Big Nanna's pocket.

The telegraph clattered along, month after month, losing money. Slowly, in government hands, the infant telegraph would have grown up in need of perpetual subsidy. Big Mailbag could have added the telegraph to his empire and been in line to grab, one by one, the tools that have built the Information Age. Think of it: the post office become an all-purpose communications agency the size of an army, totally in charge of telephone, radio, television, satellite-transmissions, and the Internet.... The implications are staggering. What would the country look like today?

Big Nanna could have *owned,* not simply regulated, the communications industry. But the opportunity was missed. A sadder chapter is hard to find in the history of latter-day liberalism. What happened?

A few mossbacks in Congress pointed out there was no constitutional authority for the federal government to control the telegraph. Imagine, letting that get in the way. Government stepped aside, and the telegraph fell into private hands. This was in 1846—the government line still Washington to Baltimore, losing money.

By 1866 the telegraph, in private hands, had profitably spanned the entire U.S and reached under the Atlantic Ocean to Europe. The loss to Big Mailbag, then and now, is incalculable. Look at him today, no piece of telephone, radio, or television, battered by UPS, Federal Express, and e-mail.... Ticker, you let one cockroach in the door and pretty soon they are everywhere.

Well, you can't win them all. We must take our lumps and learn.

Now, what does all this have to do with Welfare? Perspective, my boy, state of mind. Welfare is not a program. It is an *industry.* If Big Mailbag had thought like that, he'd be in the catbird seat today.

Ticker, we must think like businessmen not bureaucrats: beating the competition, locking in customers, barriers to entry.... Think big, not small. Think of

Welfare as a *government program* and you'll wake up one day with the Salvation Army eating Big Nanna's lunch. Philanthropic organizations and churches could conceivably take over, just like the entrepreneurs, bankers, and brokers who pirated the telegraph and the Information Age. Beware!

Listen to the death rattle in Big Mailbag's throat. Look at him throwing tax dollars into advertising to hold customers he could have owned: tax dollars spent on advertising to get people to use a government service, and private competition still thrives. A cockroach is an ugly thing, and difficult to kill.

Your first lesson, boy: Welfare is not a program. It is an industry, with customers to keep and private competition to beat. Remember how Big Mailbag blew it, an object lesson, son. Private solution is government dilution—never forget it.

That's the big picture, Ticker, the battle lines from afar, a general's view. General Red's, your uncle. You are a lucky boy, to be so in favor with the brass. But, time for boot camp, son. I'll not spoil you. This battle, and the ones to come, will have to be won in the trenches, by you. You must learn hand-to-hand combat, as well as master strategy.

Your orders: Raise the Welfare issue, and take Dan's measure. He will have a few steel-town thoughts on the subject, I'm sure. Engage, Private Ticker, and report.

Your four-star uncle,

RED

Letter the Twenty-ninth

~

Dear Ticker,

Calm down, boy. This isn't the end of the world. Dan jumped on Welfare like old boots—OK. The boy seems well informed. Let him have this round. His conversion will be all the more solid in the end. He'll remember the time he thought his moldy conservative views were being reborn, and how wrong he was.

Relax. Dan blackened your eye, that's all. Take it as a wake-up call. This little flare up will focus your mind. You'll pay closer attention, and maybe want some revenge? Issues require answers, my boy—a lesson you won't soon forget. Your blood is up. That's good. Faint hearts finish last. Now, let's get back on offense.

First of all, you need some background. Dan doesn't have the half of it. It's worse—or better. Ho ho.

In the 1960s, the "War on Poverty" was declared by President Johnson, the liberal saint, "LBJ." The *War* on Poverty—note the imagery, boy, to fire up the Troobs. Public policy is more than drum beating, but that doesn't mean the drum beating stops.

When the *War* was declared—here's one I'll bet your boy doesn't know—poverty was actually in decline. It had reduced by almost half, in the previous two decades. Still, the issue played in the Public Mind, where it counts. A lesson there, boy.

A new government agency was formed, the OEO, Welfare Man: a new superhero in the Washington pantheon, flying to the defense of the Nation's poor, the inner-city poor, to be more precise. Don't even think about the rural poor. They were never part of the equation. The inner cities are a natural unit, Ticker, easy to cordon off and manage long term, a natural sheep pen.

Results were excellent. Welfare benefits were soon so high that employment could not compete in straight dollars, let alone ancillary benefits—locked in customers. Generations of children were raised to expect welfare and reject work: an increasing, self-perpetuating, flock. In three decades, the program budget increased by over 1000% and the number of poor *went up*. Think about that.

The hard-ball liberal elite, bureaucrats, ministers, politicians, and good-old-money foundation boys cut up the poverty pie. Dollars, jobs, influence, celebrity, votes, were heaped in the poverty war chest, liberal coin of the realm, there for the taking for those who knew how—while the Troobs earnestly preached about Heaven on Earth. The jugglers, and the clowns.

New programs popped up everywhere. Public housing, public health, preschool.... These were heady times. In a few short years, federal spending on Welfare went from 8% to 16% of GNP. That, my boy, is a booming *industry!*

The YOU DESERVE—a concept that proved useful far beyond the inner city—generation was born, devoid of natural curiosity, sapped of vitality, self-indulgent, dependent, indignant, *easy to manage*, and going nowhere. I speak here of the many, not the few.

Some folks got on their feet and got out. No one bats 1000, boy. The best of shepherds lose some sheep.

Mistakes were made, of course, from which we must learn. Goals were clearly stated, "reducing dependency" for instance—a glaring error. Reductions in urban violence and better race relations were promised—totally unnecessary. Passing out money should have been the goal. *"Preserving, protecting, preparing...."* Specific goals are a no-no, Ticker. Some Troobs, no doubt, slipped the leash. Learn from this, boy: measure process, never results.

But, all in all, round one was a thumping success. Decades of smooth sailing, more than four if you count the poverty war as an extension of the New Deal— the Social Security Act of 1935, with racing stripes. You can't ask for more than that.

That's all for now. I have an important vote coming up and have to get to the floor. Government doesn't grow on its own, you know. Let Dan hold forth, for the moment. Don't respond. Wait until you master the detail, and I give you the spin. Our innings are coming, my boy. I promise.

More on Welfare, in a liberal *heartbeat*. Ha ha.

Your hearty old uncle,

RED

Letter the Thirtieth

~

Dear Ticker,

Welfare, round two, around 1980—

The pattern Friend Dan decries becomes unmistakable, expenditures out of control, welfare-recipient isolation, dependency, and degeneration....

OK-OK. Nothing is perfect, small p.

That's right, Ticker, you can have it both ways. Big P in the ascendancy, small p in retreat. All you need is a few years between. "So we didn't exactly Perfect things *this time*. We'll come up with another big idea."

Never fear failure, boy, or acknowledge it. Look at John Galbraith, Paul Ehrilich, the Club of Rome.... Gross overstatement, reverse prognostication.... No problem, if you get the right *backspin*.

Welfare was down, but not out. Time for damage control, that's all. For openers, we claimed things would have been worse if we had not declared war on poverty. No doubt about it. If we spent 16% of GNP on poverty and it got worse, just think what would have happened if we had spent nothing. Ho ho. Besides, Welfare was the *right thing to do*, regardless of outcome. Individual recipients of Welfare were asked if *they* thought it had failed. They said, NO!

Beyond rhetoric, there were defensive maneuvers to slow the outgoing Welfare tide: Our friends on the

Court (*Goldberg vs. Kelly*) ruled that Welfare benefits were a form of property under the Fourteenth Amendment, requiring "due process" to terminate. This added an army of Welfare workers to facilitate recipients in filing cases and miles of additional red tape. The minimum wage was steadily increased, to freeze out the major competition, employers. Policies that kept fathers out of Welfare homes were quietly defended against a chorus of critics....

Deny and delay, my boy—the politics of perpetuation. In the middle of the government-business cycle, tactical maneuvers are everything. A thousand little things were done to maintain the Welfare industry.

We even let the Adversary knock down the OEO, got Welfare Man out of sight. Slipped him into a dozen federal agencies, under cover. By the way, those were my glory years. I got my nickname writing entitlements into law, sliding Welfare by other names into nooks and crannies in federal agencies, thousands of pages of rules and regulations, layer upon layer of supervision. Miles and miles of—*Redtape.*

The sobriquet came from a fellow Senate Democrat, insiders only of course. I've worn it with pride. I wrapped a decade in red tape all by myself, if you count the several pounds I added to the tax code. Did you ever wonder where *your* nickname came from, boy? It's a little family joke—you would have never understood until now. You looked so much like me when you were born, your mother, bless her, called you Ticker in fun and it stuck. *Tickertape*, after me—and I bet you thought "Ticker" was just affectionate cluck.

I've always thought you were the one to succeed

me as head of the family, son, as I succeeded Old Ned. Now don't let that go to your head. Don't make me sorry I told you—but enough of this, back to business.

Round two of Welfare was extended for more than a decade. Not a bad run for this phase. We hung in there. Persist and survive, Ticker—the first rule of debacle. Never get in a hurry (resurrection takes time).

So now the game is finally up—your boy makes the case. What do we do?

Round three—

Remember the mentally ill, turned into the homeless? Sheep marched back-and-forth between cliffs? Yes, boy, time to turn things around. We simply march Welfare down to the states, with strings of course: *purse strings*. Big Nanna sends federal tax dollars back to the states, with a few rules and regulations attached. The states get money back for Welfare *if*.... Control, son, one way or the other.

Let the states run Welfare for a while. Ha ha. Give it a decade or two—it will be your watch by then—and you can switch things around, dust off the big *P*. I doubt the states will have achieved *Perfection*, expunged poverty 100%. You can cry out for Change, pointing to failures, heart rending cases here and there. Remember Dan's ten homeless left out on the street?

Welfare Man can come out of hiding and don his cape. Maybe, who knows, he might start another "War on Poverty...."

But, for now, chalk up another round for Dan: "When you're right, you're right, Friend Dan. Let's get this problem back to the states, to the local folks close to the action...." Snicker. He'll lap this up, the rube, and you'll get points for being fair.

Keep in mind, Ticker, on top of everything else, even without Big Nanna's strings attached, state governments are governments too. Some of the best of the liberal elite start out in state government, in training for the Big Top here in Washington. The Little Nannas, all by themselves, will keep the liberal torch burning.

Call this switch "devolution," a fine word. Speak about the *"new federalism."* Announce "the end of Big Government...." Lay it on. Let your boy bask in his victory for a bit. Then we'll get down to defining just what is meant by all this. Ever play with a boomerang, boy?

Your amenable uncle,

RED

Letter the Thirty-first

~

Dear Ticker,

What a nuisance, but maybe there is an upside here.

The Republican gala Dan wants to attend is not dangerous. This is the unleaded Right, not the hightest stuff of a Heritage workshop or a *Firing Line* debate. No Sowells or Buckleys or Wills to encounter.

In fact, all Dan will find are a bunch of old guys patting each other on the back, and a few elected bureaucrats looking for votes. Mock conservatives, milling about the political center. Inspiring as flies. I know the group putting on this program—I wish there were a thousand of them.

These guys (precious few women, you'll find) are the equivalents of our Troobs. The same intellectual embarrassment, but harder to manage—at least Troobs do what they're told and don't *attempt* independent thought. Frankly, Ticker, politically speaking, I think these guys are a plus for our side.

Half of them want to take a bulldozer to the cities, make everyone live in small towns or on farms. Retreat to the past. The other half want government grants to study doing away with government, or to subsidize punctilio. Tax credits for three-piece suits, that sort of thing. Miscellaneous conservative and libertarian longings in liberal harness. Ideological as

Chairman Mao, most of them—none of the practical bite of true conservatives.

This is the *lite Right,* Ticker, no problem.

Here's what you do—

You go with Dan—show him how open-minded you are. Dan doesn't own a suit, that's good. Tell him it's OK. You and he will wear sweaters and ties, be neat and clean. A certain respect for tradition not the Brooks Brothers—that's what counts, right? You're young. They'll understand. Ha ha.

Believe me, Ticker, these old geezers will make you guys so uncomfortable Dan will wish he'd stayed home. They welcome only young people from families they know, dressed up just so. Powdered wigs and breeches traded in for *conservative* suits—little Lord Fauntleroys grown up to play House of Lords at the Holiday Inn. Ho ho. Conservatives *conserve* the past. These guys *cling* to it. It will be all pomp and circumstance, a little pageant. People introducing people to introduce people to introduce the speaker—all talking about themselves.

"Golly, Dan, is this what conservatism is all about?" Chuckle.

We can take a time-out for this. I'll write more on Welfare soon.

Your flexible uncle,

RED

Letter the Thirty-second

~

Dear Ticker,

What did I tell you? The lite-Right, prickly and pompous. Scarecrows in the conservative cornfield. Ho ho. Dan got scared away, good. You and he are now brothers scorned. "Who needs them...."

Let's get back to Welfare, keep our eye on the main event. It's time for you and your pals to discuss Welfare down at the state level. Ticker, by now should you know the drill. Propose nothing yourself. Knock down everything Dan proposes—the existing federal model wins by default. Fifty Little Nannas, federal strings attached, are almost as good as one.

What does Dan think Welfare, removed to the states, should be like? That is the question. Be prepared for a tussle—our boy's instincts will be for practical answers, results not theories. Habits die hard. By the way, it is interesting that Dan has chosen economics as a major, that he *likes* numbers and is good with them. You were right to tell me. He will be hard to snow. All the better, it will test our mettle.

Here's how it should go, if our homeboy plays true to form—

You can bet Dan will take a moral approach to Welfare—the impulse will be there, at least. The underlying argument is that social order requires a standard of virtue. If there is no right and wrong, on what basis are things prohibited or prescribed? Your boy will want rules, grounded in an absolute morality.

Your answer: "Friend Dan, everything is relative. Albert Einstein proved that. What is wrong for one person may be right for another. What is wrong in one place may be right somewhere else. Look at the high culture of the ancient Aztecs—they had human sacrifice. Abhorrent to us, but who are we to sit in judgment from another place and time? No, Dan, we should not judge others, and government *must* not judge."

(Sell this, and you're halfway home.)

We must assume Dan does some reading, and we know he likes numbers. The *father* deal is likely to come up—all the positive social outcomes correlated with fathers. Dan will want to avoid the father-disincentives in federal Welfare, perhaps even encourage the maintenance of traditional homes.

Your answer: "This is none of our business. A family is whatever those in it define it to be. Who are we to define an arbitrary structure? Are two women, or two men, of less value than a woman and man? Let's keep government out of *private* things."

(Ha ha. Bend your mind around that one, boy.)

He may now say that 10,000 years of human history must indicate something about the functionality, if nothing else, of traditional families.

Your answer: "My friend, human history has been an unmitigated disaster. Don't talk to me about history!

Open your mind to new things. This is about the future, not the past. We must look forward, not back."
(Tell him to "stop looking in the rearview mirror.")

Private charities and community-based efforts may figure large in his plan.

Your answer: "Central control is essential, and only trained experts should participate. How would we know if everything was being done *exactly* as it should be, if folks were running about willy-nilly helping others." (Would he want his appendix taken out by a mechanic?)

He may want to attack crime as endemic to the Welfare environment, his emphasis on *deterrence,* swift, certain, and severe punishment of crime.

Your answer: "The only humane emphasis is crime *prevention.* To merely apprehend and punish is to admit failure in our relationship to other human beings in the most profound way. We will never eliminate crime through punishment. Only through prevention can the ultimate goal of an ideal society be achieved."
(*Perfection,* once more, Heaven on Earth, Amen.)

Education is bound to come up, as the long-term solution. Dan will want to open up alternatives to the public school, give people choices as to where and how education is delivered. "Putting parents' hands on the rudder of their child's future," or some such nonsense.

Your answer: "The public school [and teachers' unions, our pals] staffed by highly trained and *certified* teachers [Troobs] are the backbone of this country. If we let people opt out [allow competition] the public school will be destroyed. Change, yes, but only within the hallowed walls of this great American institution [work rules intact, tenure protected] that *deserves* our support. The public schools must be part of the Welfare solution, not a scapegoat bearing society's sins."

(Ask Friend Dan, if he honestly thinks that parents are qualified, many of them with minimal education themselves, to decide what is best for their children?)

Finally, he may want to separate the deserving poor from the lazy.

Your answer: "No one can be inside another human being. What is great effort for one person may be done with ease by another. Can anyone really say another person should work for a living? It would be playing God to try to make judgments about such things."

(Our friend the half-truth, and relativity, once more.)

In the end, Ticker, the federal Welfare sheep will simply be in smaller flocks by state, and what will have changed? Sheep are sheep, in pens large or small—especially when federal inspectors stop by every week to certify the stockyards. Trust me, boy, our inspectors will carry a checklist assuring that all of the above goes our way, or no money back from Washington. Of course, this may not be easy.

A few states may get radical, producing pockets of self-reliance and productivity among the previously poor. This won't last. Time is on our side, son—we are an institution. We may lose a few rounds, but the game is long and the Public Mind short. Elected officials come and go. The spotlight on Welfare will burn itself out. Poor folks will endure, and we will prevail....

But, back to the dorm room, to your ivory-tower game of recreating Welfare in the states. You defend the federal Welfare model, moved down to the states. Fifty Little Nannas, instead of one big one. That's the goal. Let Dan take his best shots. Wear him down. Play hard, but don't expect too much too soon.

Don't be in a hurry, Ticker. We are in the second act of Dan's conversion, the toughest—the second act is where the main conflict comes. Issues demand answers, causes did not. Be happy with the appearance of a draw on Welfare, even a paper loss. In the end, ask only that our boy be fair. The devolution of Welfare to the states, after all, is the lion's share of the issue, and his. What will he give in return? Surely, an Ivy-League gentleman and scholar must concede something. I'm sure he hears much in his classes about the inherent virtues of consensus and compromise.

Your bottom line: Even though you and Dan don't agree about everything, you're on the same side. Doesn't what you've arrived at have something for both of you: a solution *local* but, with his small concessions, *controlled and humane*? Something for everyone. Give Dan a pat on the back for caring enough to compromise.

Your shrewd uncle,

RED

Letter the Thirty-third

~

Dear Ticker,

You've got the score all wrong, boy. Dan didn't win, you did.

You took the important trick: his bow to social relativity. I hadn't expected to get that one so soon. The traditional family falls your way, in time—it's all relative. Plus, an acknowledged need to "stop looking in the rearview mirror." That's 3 for you, Ticker.

Now, discount Welfare devolving to the states as tactical, no points for either side: you get the federal Welfare structure and philosophy, he gets decentralization. Both sides can argue they have bought time, or nudged things their way. The outcome won't be known for years, though bet on us, my boy.

Give Dan the remaining tricks, for now, education, privatization, personal responsibility, crime.... I make it 4 to 3, for Dan. You win! A smashing victory. I know, boy, you don't understand. Uncle Red will explain.

It is not the number of tricks won or lost, son, that carries the day, but which ones are taken and why, the total effect of ground given and gained. You've missed the main point, the dagger point: the devil's deal you cut with Dan.

You gained an unholy compromise, son. Dan's conservative impulses have led him into a snare. Our boy has confused compromising principles with practical politics, Aristotle's art of the possible. He has confused tactical concessions—choosing the lesser of two evils, taking half a loaf, playing for time—with substantive alteration. Some fancy stitching, my boy. Ha ha.

The Aztecs slipped right past him—you did well. They were, after all, just a *different* culture (merely ripping out human hearts and eating them raw). Tut tut. "It's *all* relative, you know." Indeed! What might *not* be, if this be, relative my boy? One or two mommies pales. The past, with all its teachings, becomes just another frame of reference. Absolute morality falls. A subtle trap, Redtape takes a bow.

Never crush, corrupt, taught Caesar.

In the modern spirit of *holy* compromise, Dan endorses three principles of liberalism. They fall like dominoes: 1) social relativity, 2) arbitrary family structure, 3) disregard for the past. Conservative bedrock, eroded away. You hit him where he lives, Ticker, and he doesn't even know it. I recall some talk of a cross. In spoonfuls of liberal sugar, you have smuggled in a bold alternative to not just his politics but his religion.

In the belly of liberal largess, son, lies *secularism:* "worldly not spiritual." *Man is the measure of all things.* Remove from this world the myth of a transcending order, and only the practical and the preferred remain. "Some *one's* point of view, and I prefer *mine.*" Haven't I told you? Is this starting to soak in?

The illusion of morality is for conservatives, and Troobs. *Moral* is a word the Troob applies to sentimentality. Conservatives think there is a rule book in the sky. You and I, my boy, know better. We write the rule book, and bless it ourselves (and preach selected verses to the Troobs). Morality, along with God, went up in smoke long ago, leaving those with the spit *the absolute power to choose.*

We are very near the center of latter-day liberalism, son. Do you begin to see the pearl? Aha: whatever *you* choose. The world is your oyster!

You have done well, Ticker, achieving a *liberal* compromise with Dan. You've put a tiny crack in his foundation. You've done more than you know. Mysticism, transcendent truths, absolute morality—these superstitions are the enemies of modern Man. You with a dagger, so sharp it was painless, have wounded the foe.

However, you must let Dan's superstitions die slowly. Supremacy is not our goal, not yet. We don't want to win too much too soon—all conversion is self-conversion, and that takes time. Let Dan bring himself along, and you come too. Let Uncle Red set the pace, he knows what he's doing.

Your task is to wear Dan down, not blow him away. Erosion and tiny cracks ultimately produce collapse, a permanent ruin upon which a new temple can be raised. High winds simply lead to disaster and *rebuilding*. Corrupt, don't crush. Think of yourself as a natural force wearing away an edifice, of Daniel. Ho ho.

Your prophetic uncle,

RED

Letter the Thirty-fourth

~

Dear Ticker,   A
naive moral tone infects your letter. My boy, you do
not believe in God, yet you *persist* in speaking of "right
and wrong." Do you not see the contradiction? New
levels, son! You must look things in the eye, or become, yourself, a slobbering Troob, mixing fairy tales
and hard science into a sickly stew.

It is not a matter of amorality being the "right
choice," Ticker. It is the *only* choice, for all but superstitious fools. Better a knave, my boy, than a fool.

Muse with Hamlet, son, "There is nothing either
good or bad, but thinking makes it so." Concede this,
and all else follows as night the day.

"Conscience is but a word that cowards use," said
Richard the III. That's *social relativity,* boy, without its
candy coating. Hamlet, a conservative, deep down,
proved a coward in the end. Richard did not. Troobs,
well, they take a pass.

The Troob, my boy, speaks of social relativity in one
breath and "right and wrong" in the next. Remind you
of someone, Ticker? Feeling a little foolish, I hope.

Social relativity. Your boy is nibbling at the worm.
Know what it means, if he takes the bait (even unaware). Social relativity admits no *absolute* standards,
enthroning Human judgment. Ticker, face it, that is

all there is. Practicality or preference, Human judgment, nothing more.

Think about what relativity applied to moral questions really means, and, when the light dawns, don't
tell your pals that Perfection in a morally relative universe must be relative too. Let *them* have it both ways,
but hold yourself to a higher standard.

Leave Troobs to their fuzzy pursuit of the Ideal,
while you and I pursue our own clear idea of how *we*
want things to be. Don't tell the Troobs that once cut
loose from absolute morality, *anything* goes. They
haven't the wit or the stomach for that. Do you?

What do you think *man as the measure of all things* is
all about, Ticker? Do you suppose moral relativism could
rule in a created universe on a Sunday-school planet
of Psalm-saying Christians or Jews? Do you think Moses
would have laid down his tablets if he had stumbled
upon the Aztecs on his way to the Promised Land?

"They are a different culture, brother Aaron, simply doing their own thing." Human sacrifice. Ha ha.

Cut to the chase, Ticker. Start seeing things as they
are. Troobs pursue the oxymoron of a secular Ideal.
Let them, but you must know, yourself, that there are
only different views. As Humpty Dumpty said,
"which is to be master—that's all."

This policy or that? Pink or blue? Human sacrifice?
Aha! That separates the men from the boys. If you
would condemn human sacrifice to be, all times and
places, *wrong*, what standard—be careful—do you
use? You see the trap? Once you let in the absolute,
you are on a slippery slope, upward as it were, to God.
Man is the measure, or not, and if not—feel the slide?

If sacrificing maidens is a transcending wrong, why not aborting a child? If things can be *wrong*, not merely different, what conveniences and pleasures might not fall in the winds that would blow? Absolute morality, my boy, is a straightjacket conservatives choose to wear. The Troob wears it when it is convenient, and puts it aside when not—and condemns himself to the life of a petty thief, stealing small pleasures but never large treasures. You see?

It's all or nothing, Ticker, for those who would rule. Think about that. Things are, for those who *think* (Troobs *recite*) either relative or not. It's *Man the measure of all things* or absolute standards by which you wind your way inevitably back to the cave and ritual masks and supernatural mumblings and perhaps in the end forward again to the tablets of Moses and the foot of the Cross....

Do you have the spit to live free of tradition and religious superstition—to throw off the yoke of the past and see things as they are? Think about it, boy. You too must refrain from looking in the rearview mirror. Time to grow up, young man.

Ticker, I've been blunt, but it is for your own good. Character, my boy, is not bought cheaply. You must face reality squarely, and spit in its eye. The world is what you decide and dare and cause it to be. *Yours,* if you *choose.* Starting to see what this is all about?

Your steely-eyed uncle,

RED

Letter the Thirty-fifth

~

Dear Ticker,

Thinking it over. That's good, my boy. I don't want blind conformity.

Son, it is really life, not liberalism, with which you grapple. Liberalism is only a reflection of life—a pleasant enough pond to skate on, but deep and cold underneath. All politics, my boy, plumbed deep enough, reflect some special *understanding* of the world. Most people choose impossible schemes or the fairy tales of religion. I choose the cold Facts of Life, and so, I believe, will you.

Ticker, you are, for the first time, examining the liberal beliefs you have taken for granted since you were a child. Traveling in your own soul, as it were. Not a trip for the fainthearted. Oh no. Most Troobs would come out screaming. But you are made of sterner stuff. I know you are, my boy.

Take your time, son. We are at another level—a higher altitude, a little shortness of breath for the unaccustomed to be expected—and yet we have only begun to climb. There is further to go. I have spoken plainly and must continue to do so, if you are to mature and take your place beside me. Politics is for realists, boy.

Below, I have copied one of my favorite quotations. Perhaps it will help you see the courage and iron will to which, in the fullness of self-understanding, you are being called. The great existentialist writer, Jean Paul Sartre, in *Le Être et le Néant* wrote:

> *"Man can will nothing unless he has first understood that he must count on no one but himself; that he is alone, abandoned on earth ... without help, with no other aim than the one he sets himself, with no other destiny than the one he forges for himself on this earth."*

A more eloquent and authentic statement of the latter-day liberal core—at the center of social relativity, secular humanism, "situational ethics," and a plethora of other *enlightened* doctrines—can nowhere be found. Here is the seed of latter-day liberalism, Ticker, put into words. Sartre is a true secular saint of our creed.

Look within yourself, my boy, and nowhere else, for the ultimate answers. Call yourself to glory.

Your evangelizing uncle,

RED

Letter the Thirty-sixth

~

Dear Ticker,

So glad my letter was "an inspiration." I am an eloquent old devil, aren't I?

But, once more, I must take you to task. You have leapt to an incorrect conclusion, another weed we must pluck from your garden.

"Love of learning" is not what sustains me. No. Knowledge and language are not my gods. That would be a Troob-like delusion, a trick of the mind to avoid reality. You would, my boy, by romanticizing my penchant for literature, history, and language make of me a more sympathetic character, and thereby, yourself. Ticker, you must see things as they are.

I have no "love of learning." Love is a construct that requires its object to be of value *in itself.* I do not *love* learning, I *use* it.

I do not seek meaning outside of myself, son. It is not there. Fool's gold and fairy tales or the cold facts of life, those are the choices. I choose cold facts.

Let me tell you about my *love of learning*—

Information, ideas, words: they are gunpowder, bullets, and bayonets in the rhetorical wars that decide who rules. They are Utility itself, however ornately arranged. Is the flower that catches the fly not served by its color and fragrance? Utility, boy, and perhaps some small amusement.

Spare me the "Ode on a Grecian Urn" and "The Sermon on the Mount." Give me Nietzsche and Hobbes and B.F. Skinner and his rats, and Shakespeare's villains and Ecclesiastes, for pithy prose and affect, and the black art of persuasion—a lesson we must make time for soon—to "seem a saint when most I play the devil," as Richard III put it. Richard knew the art of persuasion well but failed in others, an argument, if ever there was one, for *liberal* education. Ha ha. You'll not make a kindly old monk of me, Ticker. The spider does not love the web but the fly.

"I'm no fool, nosiree. I'm gonna live to be a hundred and three...." Jiminy Cricket was right about books, my boy, but he slipped and fell in love with them. Not me. I use them. *Utility*, Ticker. Get a grip on that, and many things will become clear.

Learning is a good servant, but a dangerous friend, and far too demanding a master. But enough idle contemplation—I've answered your question.

Ask more, if you like—your *eternal* questions are welcome, my boy. I too, once, was young and plagued by doubts. As Edward Young, the playwright, playfully put it: "By night the atheist half believes a God." Ho ho. Don't feel bad, son. It's all part of growing up. Ask anything. I am the great continent of latter-day liberalism, yours to explore.

Now, let's get back to work. That's the best tonic for this melancholy you're prone to of late. Ticker, I am pleased that you have also asked the practical question, what comes next with Dan? Shows you have spunk. Like a good racehorse, you stay the course. You like to run, boy. I can tell. Breeding shows.

I think we should wrap up Welfare now and move on, perhaps close out this round with a little *personalizing*. Feel the Welfare recipient's pain. Maybe pass out some ribbons. Get sincere and caring, and so forth. Issues, remember, though more than just drumbeating, still require the beat of the drum. A danger in discussing issues, my boy, is inadvertently focusing on outcomes and losing touch with sentimentality.

We will give our boy a new lesson soon.

Your understanding uncle,

RED

ps. I said I look for no meaning outside myself. Perhaps that's not quite true. I indulge myself in you, my protégé. Immortality, of sorts, I suppose—if you carry on.

Letter the Thirty-seventh

~

Dear Ticker,

"*Learning* to live, not *living* to learn"—exactly, and aptly phrased, my boy. You're *learning*. Ho ho.

Down to business. Yes, let's pursue Social Security as the next issue. I approve. Dan's natural interests, our budding economist, should be indulged—and we can give him a taste of the no-win scenario on this one. More than one Republican has become a Democrat out of sheer frustration, beating his head against this wall. Ha ha.

Social Security—

Dan's numbers are correct, son. SS is bust soon enough. "No argument there, Friend Dan, and no use crying over spilt milk. It's no time for 'who struck John.' We must address the future."

Refuse to discuss how we got into this mess! The responsible thing is to look forward not back—the patient lives, a postmortem would be ghoulish.

Dan is technically correct about SS withholdings going into general revenues, and, yes, in a private corporation someone would go to jail for that. True, but this is the government. Ha ha.

In the SS fine print, by the way—don't volunteer this—it says that the government cannot be held responsible for a nickel that's owed. So forget legality. The issue is power and politics. We're dealing with the Congress here, boy, not some corporation.

History and legality must be laid aside, verboten for discussion. The goal is to figure out how to put SS back on track. "Forward thinking!"

More ground rules:

A Crisis of this magnitude—a real one, this time, make no mistake—can be addressed only by Big Benefactor, another Nanna guise, the original giver of "social security." The dollars involved are impossibly large (and people are hooked to the gills on being taken care of and not taking care of themselves and each other). The solution is in Washington, nowhere else!

Now establish, rising above current difficulties, the need to be grateful for Big Benefactor, there to protect us—to look after our money and keep us from squandering it or making unwise investments. What if he weren't there? Who would get us out of this colossal mess (never mind who got us in)? Maybe Big Benefactor ought to take on health care too.

It's a shell game from here, Ticker. Move the shells around, here and there, however long Dan wants to play—by the above rules, of course. No cheating. All solutions but one, the pea in our little game, fail. Lift a shell, nothing there: "Sorry, Dan, won't work." Lift it again and show him the pea: retire older, get less, pay more.

What other choice is there? Big Benefactor is a giant, not a magician. Dan must be fair. The SS industry can only be saved in so many ways—you can't get blood from a turnip. *Industry,* boy, remember? Big Ben, unlike Big Mailbag, has never thought small.

Finally, offer a benevolent gesture, defending your flank. As a part of the final solution, suggest that Big

Ben put a little of everyone's money, a percent or two, in private investments where equity would appreciate or interest compound. People get to personally own these investments. Big Benefactor is not only a financial genius, he is generous. What a guy.

The only other option is to let the Adversary default—it doesn't get any better than this, Ticker. Lift a shell to show this one, nothing there. Lift it again, and show Dan the pea: retire older, get less, pay more....

Understand, Ticker, behind this shell game there is a deception far grander than extortion and false promises under the guise of government largess: the promise of security itself. In this accidental world, my boy, there is no "social security," or any other kind for that matter. Anything anyone owes you is only as secure as the debtor's ability to pay. Even if SS were privately invested, there are no guarantees.

Understand this, yourself, son, but, for the Love of Money, don't tell the Troobs. Never let on that Big Benefactor is a balloon, or that Big Nanna can't stare down hurricanes. You don't want to see grown people cry.

Ticker, selling "security" on this earth is like selling cheap whiskey. It's a good business as long as you don't sample the product yourself—cheap whiskey can make a man blind. Illusions are for Troobs, remember? Uncle Red tells it like it is: there is no security, only the odds— however jiggered—and the quick and the dead.

Your light-footed uncle,

RED

Letter the Thirty-eighth

~

Dear Ticker,

First, Social Security. Let Dan play as long as he likes—let him wear himself out. Just keep showing him the pea: retire older, get less, pay more.

Now, another *eternal* question—you are a pip, Ticker! "Where is the *real* difference between Redtape and the Troobs?" The line seems "fuzzy." "Shared beliefs," you charge, "shared passions." A ruthless thrust, boy, but no touché. I am far from a True-Believing twit!

Things shared, yes—things *overlapping*. Mice and men, my boy, have many things in common. Checkers and chess are played on the same board. But mice and men, chess and checkers, are not the same.

Redtape versus the Troobs—

First, let me say, I sing here only of myself, one part of the liberal body electric. I do not even speak for others in the liberal elite, who may vary from me in temperament and candor. Take me as the northern most point, the ice-cold North Pole, of latter-day liberalism, speaking with no delusions and all-in-the-family frankness. I've met no more arctic, ice-ribbed soul than myself.

In liberal geography, I am as far as can be from the steamy equatorial Troobics—a vast space between where the climate can be fickle. I speak of the extremes.

Let the Devil sort out the middle.

You ask, "What does Redtape *really* believe?"

I believe in science, Ticker—because it works. I believe in the survival of the fittest, in Myself and winning! *Our* family is important, of course, a primary means to the ends I have stated. Together we are stronger, more likely to survive and win. Big Nanna is a useful slut, nothing more. Elevating her higher is Troob stuff.

Pleasure is the bottom line. All, after survival, is pleasure: power, sex, wealth, fame.... There you have it, boy, the summed total of me. Stern stuff, and chilly.

The Troob overlaps, but he diverges more. Where? Dig back into the pudding of the True Believer's psyche, Ticker, to the Mission: Heaven on Earth, Amen. The Troob worships this idea, I *use* it. Redtape's *means* are the Troob's *ends*. You see, already, what strange bedfellows, the Troob and I?

The Troob is shot through with contradictions. Redtape is consistent, pure as arctic ice. The stuff of Troobs, my boy: *contradictions*.

The Troob casts his lot, as do I, in a secular world, ruled by science and man, but the Troob proceeds to deify Mankind. On this third rock from the sun, Ticker, we humans are divine, if at all, by default—and for how long? An indifferent meteor or climatic shift might in a moment dethrone us, perhaps leaving ants, crawling deep underground, as the new gods of earth, perhaps leaving nothing at all. The Troob does not face, as do I, that we are but flies of a summer.

The Troob is a secular beast, but he mixes in divers supernatural powers and a Grand Design. A wondrous concoction: a pagan, pantheist pastiche of mythology, Science, and magic. Titans, Test Tubes, and Sorcery....

The Troob worships a gaggle of gods, a grand pantheon of which He and Science are merely a part: add Animals, the Earth, and, for many, Big Nanna in her infinite guises. There is even room for Jehovah and Jesus, for some. Buddha and Krishna too....

It's fuzzy theology, boy, but serves the Troob well enough, particularly in its flexibility: church services on Sunday, yoga on Monday, whale sounds, magic charms, and abortion by Saturday night. An Aztec sort of thing, nothing new—I read recently that the ancient Aztecs were cannibals on top of everything else. Fascinating, don't you think?

I trust this elucidation settles the question: Redtape and the Troobs coexist in the liberal world, but we are as different as mice and men. Would you compare a crystal snifter of fine-old brandy and a paper cup of Kool Aid? Then do not compare the Troob and me.

The Troob and I both inhabit the liberal sphere, but Redtape is miles away from Troobdumb. Ho ho. I hope I have opened your eyes, my boy. Study the liberal map, Ticker, Redtape to the Troobics. What latitude are you?

Say your prayers, as it were, son. Ask Yourself who in the liberal-world you are, or, better, who do you want to be? The choice, if you follow me, is *yours.*

Your polar uncle,

RED

Letter the Thirty-ninth

~

Dear Ticker,

Glad to hear it—Troobdumb is not for you! The Sartre quotation begins to resonate: *"Man can will nothing unless he has first understood that ... he is alone, abandoned on earth...."* You seem to be "getting it."

You've come a long way, my boy.

But now, trouble with Dan. You are keeping your old uncle hopping.

Dan has broken our rules. He accepts current SS obligations, but will not concede the role of Big Benefactor. A "ninety-year" plan! He has slipped the leash, Ticker. Our shell game was based on resolving the Crisis quickly.

Let me get his plan straight. Over two working lifetimes, SS is turned into a voluntary program. Near-term surpluses, and an escalating percentage of future contributions, would be shifted from general revenues to private investment and—did I get this right—into a new forty-year Treasury bond? Compound interest and equity builds the fund to self-sufficiency, during the second half of the program. People can then opt out, take care of themselves, make their own investments, if they choose. Hmm....

The Treasury bond hedges the privatized portion

against stock market failure, while securing compound interest—paid by the government, yes, but, at the same time, reducing government's need to borrow to service the National Debt which, tit for tat, reduces government interest payments. This, Dan points out, reverses the trend of short-term federal-debt financing and forces Congress back into a pattern of living within its means. No more SS slush for pork-barrel projects. Dan is a diehard, boy.

In addition, the forty-year T-bond emerges as a familiar vehicle with which individuals can manage their own retirement savings, if they choose, and enhances the Nation's future ability to manage debt.

Further, Dan proposes a similar approach to current unemployment and government-paid health insurances. All this in a paper he has written for his economics class, and he plans to hand it in! His professor will faint.

Ticker, though I hate to admit it, Dan's approach seems sound. It's true: less than 25% of current SS withholding, subject to compound interest, bails the system out and puts it on the road to self-sufficiency. An economics major with a practical bent is a dangerous thing.

Politically, of course, one Democratically controlled Congress in the next ninety years could derail such a plan in a thousand ways—and, on the bright side, we have lured Dan into social engineering of sorts. Yet, he is socially engineering Big Benefactor out of business, and, however politically naive, he escapes the capitulation-or-default dilemma. He has upheld conservative principles in a ruthless cross fire. The boy is stubborn, and smart. Ticker, I sound as bad as you, almost admiring the brat. But be assured, that will not restrain me.

I have to call this a draw, so far. It's really my fault. I was overconfident again, allowing too much room for Dan to maneuver. But, really, who would expect anyone to do all that math?

Our new tack—

We could laugh Dan down, of course, deny his numbers and stonewall—but this is no time for derision. Our boy is halfway into the fold. We don't want to drive him back out. I think there may be another way to salvage this, if you can rise to the challenge.

Ticker, let's accept Dan's plan, in theory, if he will accept that people cannot *really* be responsible for themselves in ninety years or nine hundred. Bring in the Lovelies and Yellow-dog Jake to support you on this—they know *other* people are basically children and need oversight. People can take care of themselves *only within reason.*

You've got it, boy, time for a little *compromise.* Time to reason together, as LBJ used to say. Stroke Dan with one hand, snatch his plan for Big Ben with the other.

Give in (and take control). Accept Dan's plan *in principle*, but Big Benefactor must *administrate and monitor*—use those words.

The forty-year bond isn't really such a bad idea. Might work. But it must be compulsory, or no deal. And get Big Nanna a piece of the private investment action. Sneak her in the back door. Play this right and Big Nanna ends up owning enough stock to sit on the board, *defacto*, of half the corporations in

America, a controlling interest in time....

Think of Dan as Gulliver being roped down by the Lilliputians with thousands of threads. You and the Lovelies and Yellow-dog Jake are the Lilliputians.

Put all the hitches and fool's knots I have taught you to use, son. Rope Dan down and rescue SS from private hands. Remember the telegraph. Dan's plan is scary, even in the dorm room. Tie your knots with care, my boy, and we'll see about getting you a merit badge.

Your scout-masterful uncle,

RED

Letter the Fortieth

~

Dear Ticker,

A fine compromise. Dan's plan but federal SS stays in business as a *choice*—Big Benefactor gets to audit results for those who opt out. Payroll withholding and government control resumes, if private accounts aren't "properly set up in a timely manner" or "don't perform optimally." Well said. You get your merit badge.

Best of all, Big Nanna—this was a stroke of genius, son—controls in one giant account all the government *and* privatized SS investment dollars. A mutual fund to end all others, for efficiency's sake and to protect everyone of course. Big Nan ends up owning the brokerage business, as well as half the companies in the Nation.

Bravo, Ticker. You marched SS back to the individual and kept the purse strings—and increased Big Nanna's grasp.

All sorts of ancillary requirements, regulations, and rules might be added in exchange for the *privilege* of managing one's own money, or as *safeguards* to protect private portfolios from falling below government standards....

I can see it now—

Big Benefactor expands into other areas of "voluntary" personal saving (mandatory, of course, if not done voluntarily). Health care, transportation, vacations....

If people don't save appropriately, dollars are with-held from their paychecks. Health-care, transportation, vacation, clothing, and universal food stamps could be issued to assure people properly allocate expendi-tures. Personal spending could ultimately be totally controlled, scientifically, for everyone's benefit, by Big Homemaker....

But let's settle for your new SS, for now. You caught Dan napping, Ticker, and overwhelmed him with the impossibility of Perfect human responsibility. Your boy has come home to saving the world (and given up on individual responsibility).

You've put another crack in Dan's foundation. He is going along with taking away people's right to fail—free will. Next to God, Himself, free will is the oldest superstition of all. No choice, no road to salva-tion. Ho ho. You've stolen the path to glory, my boy, and Dan is an accomplice.

Dan has taken a big step, Ticker, gone beyond pro-tecting people from others to protecting them from them-selves. God's will has been overruled—that's secular p-o-w-e-r, son. I guess that settles *who's Who*. Ha ha.

Remember, I told you that crucifix of Dan's would disappear in the quicksand of True Believing. It's on its way down, Ticker. We are bringing our boy to Reality.

Good job, son. You and your pals need to congratu-late each other. Pass out some ribbons and hugs. You pulled this one out of the fire, my boy. Be proud.

Your relieved uncle,

RED

Letter the Forty-first

~

Dear Ticker,

Let's move quickly on Dan's new issue—I don't want to give him too much time to think about that last round. He walks straight into the liberal bastion now, our home court, Education. However, not quite as I would have him enter. I would prefer he use one of the many side doors. Do you see the problem?

Dan wants to focus on Education separately, an issue in itself. He plucks it up to study whole. I would much prefer to discuss Education relative to other things. It can be so many things to so many people, that way.

Now we will be forced into the question of what Education is for in the first place. Mark my words, sooner or later it will come to that. It cannot be avoided, with this head-on approach. Fundamental questions, political and moral, will be exposed. If Welfare is the Mother of all issues, Education is the Father. Abortion eclipses both, of course, a special case—an issue we must put off for as long as possible.

All right, we will have it his way—the hard way. Get ready, my boy, to burn some midnight oil. You have much to learn.

Feel Dan out on his views and give me a scouting report. How would he reform the public schools? Trust me, he will attack the public schools, one way or another—it is the conservative bent.

I'm starting to feel I almost know our boy, and his family. I can see his plain-faced father and mother sending him off to the Great College, fulfilling a dream. What irony! Dan's steel-town, conservative parents scrimping and saving to send their boy into the liberal lion's den to study with Professor Feather and me. Ho ho. If they only knew.

Your adjunct uncle,

RED

Letter the Forty-second

~

Dear Ticker,

Time to talk school.

"Education," the Father of all issues, shaping all others—

Education, Ticker, brooks no compromise. It plays only one way. Issues such as Defense, we can slant, be guitar-strumming, peace-loving doves or U.N. hawks policing the world. Swoop this way or that, to suit the moment. Likewise with Finance, we can spin around from deficit hawk to dove and back (spending all the way). Defense, Finance, Employment, Crime.... These are expedient issues, my boy—large or small, depending on the political winds of the day. We can assume many postures, and still have our way. Education is not like that. Education is fundamental, and we are secular-humanist hawks all the way.

With Education, there is no wiggle room. In the long run we reap what we sow, and the final product is written down and gets said out loud—not buried in bills and regulations—a million times each day. We can play with words, and, of course, we do, but the reality spills out in the classroom. Ticker, it's the toughest game of all to play, everything, at the end of the school day, in plain sight.

Education is the future, my boy, tomorrow's history

being written today. It *must* be written our way. Children must be taught what we want them to know, and become who we want them to be. Else all may be lost!

Do I have your attention, boy? Look sharp. This is the big one.

Your scouting report is excellent, Dan's position captured in a single quotation. Ironically, a nugget of conservatism from John Stuart Mill.

Mill opposes the idea of public education—didn't I tell you—as a *"mere contrivance for molding people to be exactly like one another,"* further suggesting government leave it *"to parents to obtain the education where and how they please, and content itself with helping to pay the school fees of the poorer classes of children[.]"* The boy is predictable—the Adversary in him runs deep.

Answer him, Ticker, with Rousseau, who calls for a system of public education run by the state, assuring citizens *"come to identify themselves in some degree with this greater whole, to feel themselves members of their country, and to love it with that exquisite feeling which no isolated person has save for himself...."* and that they become *"early accustomed to regard their individuality only in its relation to the body of the state, and to be aware, so to speak, of their own existence merely as a part of that of the state."* The first passage is for Dan and your pals, for Troobs, the second is just for you, elite eyes only, my boy.

Meet Mill with Rousseau, and frame the issue—a preview of things to come.

Your erudite uncle,

RED

Letter the Forty-third

~

Dear Ticker,

Study the frame for this issue: on the one side, Mill's warning against public-educated, cookie-cutter mediocrity, and his call for parental choice and control, versus, on the other far-side, Rousseau's urging of state-controlled public education, to produce the very cog, uniform, statist, that Mill foresaw and rejected.

In my letters you will find pieces of the Education puzzle to arrange within this frame. Snap each piece into place. A heroic scene will emerge: American Public Education as the faithful deputy of the state, shaping the Perfect future. Heaven on Earth, Amen. Sell each piece, my boy, as you put it in place.

The first puzzle piece—

In the Public Mind, *modern* education must be always under attack by the Right.

"The Adversary, Friend Dan, if not actively opposed, will dominate education and corrupt the minds of the young with religious *superstitions* and backward [traditional] thinking. The state's natural role is to defend against this, assuring Man's forward progress through secular public education.

Were not Thomas Jefferson, Ulysses S. Grant, and a host of other American heroes saying as much, when they called for *separation of church and state* [Ho ho]?"

Give Dan and your pals an object lesson in the perils of mixing religion and learning—

Recall for them that the leaders of the Roman Catholic Church in 1633 sentenced Galileo to life imprisonment for *observing* with his telescope that the earth was not the center of the universe. I could kiss them.

The Church fathers claimed that Galileo's observations denied earth its place at the spiritual center of things. Heresy! "Irrelevant," said Galileo—spiritual and temporal-physical centers need not be at odds. But, no, the church fathers had their feet in cement, waiting for history and science to dump them overboard and expose their folly. I can almost hear the splash.

Voilà. We have the perfect symbol of *religious superstition and backward thinking:* a faceless host of clerical bogeymen—an everlasting Ignorance that people must be forever protected against. Could the battle lines be better drawn? Enlightenment, advancement, and progress on one side, ignorance, religious superstition and tradition on the other. It's a forever war, my boy. Education is the natural front line, our children in the balance. Hi-ho.

Everyone *must* choose sides, for or against. No blurring of the battle lines.

Does it surprise you, son, that Education has so quickly become snarled with Religion? It should not. You should see by now—recall the liberal Beatitudes and the Curseds, and the cracks in Dan's foundation—that *all* political roads lead to morality and religion. Education, the Father of all issues, is a superhighway.

Paul Elmer More, of the Adversary, *Rightly* perceived the relationship:

"Politics leads to morals.
"Morals, in turn, must lead to religious faith."

More's observation, of course, is incomplete. He has spitefully *Left* out the latter-day liberal alternative. Below, Redtape corrects More:

"Politics leads to morals (or amorality),
which leads to religious faith (or secularism
or the nether world of Troobism
and other strange concoctions)."

Do you see the fork in the road, my boy? Religion or Secularism, Right or Left, black or white? My black, of course, is More's white, and vice versa—the Troobs in a world of gray, shaded my way. Politics leads to the fork in the road, not *necessarily* religious faith. This world and those in it are up for grabs.

Are you starting to get the picture? Is this piece falling in place? We begin our task of dominating modern education with an attack on religion, by putting religion and *modern* education forever at odds. With a little inflamed rhetoric, people veer Left at the fork in the road, away from our bogeymen *religious superstition and backward thinking,* and drive on to secularism and the need for the latter-day liberal public school.

Plant this axiom, for now:

Secular public education is a necessary institution, protecting people from religious superstition and backward thinking. Remember Galileo!

Go slowly with this. We must nibble our boy along. Don't trigger his defenses. Give him room to be both religious and against religious superstition, for now. Never mind the contradiction. Half the churches in America endorse it.

Your reverential uncle,

RED

Letter the Forty-fourth

~

Dear Ticker,

Today, I had planned to renew the attack on religious superstition—but, I must postpone. We need to speak immediately of Howard Bentley III, the new member of your little group.

"He's cool." Well, yes and NO! He wears a bow tie and *carries* a pipe and is a "flaming liberal." Fine. But, slow down. He is also, you say, openly, "proudly" gay.

On the issue of homosexuality, Ticker, you must be of two minds: Yes and NO! Yes to gays as a flock of liberal sheep, politically useful. But *personally*, NO! You must keep a safe distance.

Ticker, all the way back to Leviticus, the message is clear. This is bad business. Fully a third of all cultures have some sort of ban. "Gay" may seem to you quite sophisticated—you fairly gush about Mr. Bow Tie—but consider this: homosexual males live an average of less than fifty years, compared to the general population's more than seventy. Do you think maybe history and nature (forgive me for sounding conservative, but you are my nephew, boy) are trying to tell us something?

Don't believe everything you see in the movies, son.

That's the NO! A *personal* NO, for you.

Now, the other side of the coin, yes—

Gays have been given the Presidential Seal of Approval

by the 42nd President of the United States: his defense of gays in the military, a formal appearance at a gay convention, nomination of an openly gay man as ambassador to Luxembourg, a *Catholic* country. Ho ho.

Along with the 42nd President, our friends in the N.E.A. (teachers' union) have issued a formal resolution to remove "sexual orientation bias" from the public schools (in other words, gay is OK). A U.S. Congressman is openly gay. Gay is beautiful in Hollywood, where liberals reign....

"Queer Theory"—abnormal sexual behavior generalized to life in general—is being taught at numerous state universities, by more of our friends, funded in part by the National Endowment for the Arts.

What exactly is Queer Theory? A "transgressive attitude" toward *everything*. A "Queer Theory" *lecture* at New York University, for example, was a drag queen throwing food on the library floor....

Things need not make sense, son. Art is what sells, societal norms are "whatever"—social relativism, boy. Gays, for their part, hold the latter-day liberal torch high.

Let's take a concrete example, a lesson that has relevance to Education: the Boy Scouts and gay rights.

The Scouts openly operate "under God," endorsing traditional morality and social values—an Adversary organization. Extremists! The Boy Scouts are dangerous, holding on to the past and infecting the future. A hard nut to crack, until recently.

Our friends on The New Jersey Court of Appeals—perhaps heralding things to come in education—ruled that Boy Scout leaders cannot be turned out because they are gay. Think about that, my boy.

Scout leaders are *role models,* modeling what? Under the Gay-Scouts leader, traditional sexual morality becomes passé. Women and men, men and men, women and women, several of each? It's all relative, after all. The traditional family becomes simply *one* alternative of many. Gay marriage, flower girls *and boys,* of course, straight ahead....

You see how it all comes together? The politics of sexuality lead to "the fork in the road": to morals (or amorality).... Right or Left—right-and-wrong or it doesn't really matter?

Gays burn brightly, if not for long, attacking conservatism in its most private and protected bastions. Who else, in the name of Freedom, could light up the military and the Scouts?

A final point, Ticker. When discussing gays, always cast the Adversary as someone who wants to "beat up queers," punish homosexuals for their inclinations—not merely keep them from positions of influence upon children or from undermining military effectiveness or from becoming one more minority with superordinate rights. Castigate "homophobes" loudly and long. I'm sure Mr. Bow Tie will join in.

So welcome Howard Bentley III (and keep him at arms length). Yes and NO!

Your *reasonably* tolerant uncle,

RED

Letter the Forty-fifth

~

Dear Ticker,

Sounds like a great little sideshow, my boy. Is Tiffany, our bejeweled feminist, really asserting that *all* sex differences are learned, and PJ is going along? Yellow-dog, a southern boy, after all, taunting the girls to "prove it." Mr. Bow Tie, weighing in on the side of "choice." Dan, not laughing out loud, even defending his pal PJ's "right to an opinion." Oh my.

Sit back and watch, Ticker. Simply taking this seriously inches Dan along—bold new theories are a *sine qua non* of liberalism. It's one of the great things about the Ivy League, son: no theory is too outrageous for profound consideration.

But let's not get distracted. We need to get back to the Education wars, snap a few more puzzle pieces in place for Friend Dan—and for you, my boy. You'll need to spin this issue in Congress one day, in place of your old Uncle Redtape.

You'll remember, letter-before-last, the battle lines between learning and religion were drawn: Galileo versus the Church. The Church fathers, refusing to look through the telescope, set themselves up for a fall. That was 1633. Let's fast forward and see how things went down.

The 1700s was the "Age of Reason," *the Enlightenment—*

note these wonderful terms. The *scientific method* came to the fore, separating truth from falsity once and for all. Bacon, Locke, Descartes, Spinoza—throw these names around, son. Bright fellows, all, who saw the light. Add Voltaire, Rousseau, Swift, Hume, Montesquieu, Kant, Mill, and our own Franklin, Jefferson, and Paine. All were on fire, flaming advocates of science—if not Science, capital *S*—in awe of its power.

EMPIRICISM TRIUMPHS OVER SUPERSTITION!

That's the headline, boy. "The Age of Reason," the *Enlightenment*—what happy sounds.

Science versus superstition, the two faces of the modern age, the thespian masks: one smiling on the future, one frowning on the past. Below these masks is the stage upon which latter-day liberalism stands.

Watch, Ticker, as the present day, from the Enlightenment, unfolds—

Listen to the words of Erasmus Darwin, in the 1700s, the present day already being sketched in bold lines:

> "Would it be too bold to imagine, that all warm blooded animals have arisen from one living filament which the great first cause endued with animality ... thus possessing the faculty of continuing to improve by its own inherent activity, and delivering down those improvements by generation to its posterity, world without end!"

Note the inclusion of "the great first cause," a fly in the ointment. But perhaps it was wise at the time just to shoo God away—not swat him and make a commotion.

During the 1800s, Erasmus' grandson, Charles Robert, perfected his grandfather's theory of evolution, dropping the reference to any causes supernatural. It appeared one had to choose *either* natural selection or creation. Galileo would have said, "No, no, we're confusing process and cause...." But he was no longer around—and the science-mad intellectuals of this time would not have listened anyway, no more than the zealous Church fathers of two centuries before. Science was a bright comet flashing on the horizon, God already a fading star.

By the time Einstein and his "theory of relativity" came along, the 1900s, the ground was well prepared, the Public Mind ripe. Scientific relativity and absolute moral values were pitted against one another in the public square, as if they were alternatives. It was *either-or*, once more—never mind that Einstein, himself, believed in both God and the physics of relativity. He was ignored. Science is bigger than the scientist, my boy.

It was no contest, really. The theory of relativity, expanding its reach beyond physics to morality, emerged the winner, receiving the cheers of the crowd. *Scientism* was born, the new religion of modern man, soon to be taught in the public schools.

The "Scopes Monkey Trial" in 1925—Galileo's telescope, all over again—brought things to a head. It was Science *or* God, Creation *or* Evolution.... "No, no," either Galileo or Einstein might have said, "these are not *either-ors*." But who would have listened? *Scientism* was destined, over both science and religion, to reign.

Next, the "Big Bang" theory of the universe, Lemaître's "primeval atom," was applied to any lingering doubts about Creation: BANG! The world had been born, full grown, breathing fire, the great hand of Science behind it all. God, the creator, was *officially* dead. Erasmus Darwin's lingering doubts, finally put to rest.

Nietzsche had prophesied, long before: *"God is dead: but considering the state the species Man is in, there will perhaps be caves, for ages yet, in which his shadow will be shown."* A prophet, indeed. God was reduced to a pale shadow of Himself on a few Church walls, flickering before near-vacant pews of those who would evolve into the Troobs. *Scientistic* Man was stepping boldly, now, into God's shoes.

Walt Whitman put it all in a song:

> *"I celebrate myself and sing myself ..."*
> *"Walt Whitman am I, a Kosmos ..."*
> *"I have said that the soul is not more*
> *than the body,*
> *And I have said that the body is not*
> *more than the soul,*
> *And nothing, not God, is greater to one*
> *than one's self..."*

By the middle 1900s Science—radio, television, medicine, rocket ships—was at light speed bringing a Perfect future, now easy to imagine, seeming almost inevitable.

The new "Science" of psychology was growing up. It's father, Sigmund Freud, minced no words in declaring his doctrine: "Religion is an illusion," he said. Carl Rogers later took over the couch with "Client-Centered Therapy," spawning an army of secular psychologist priests, while B.F. Skinner, Freud's spiritual disciple, worked out his theories about people with rats, and took things, in his opus, to their logical conclusion, "*beyond* freedom and dignity...."

Do you hear the echoes, Ticker? Hamlet's mad musings, and Saint Richard's deft conclusion: Nothing either good or bad but thinking makes it so (conscience is but a word that cowards use).

Eternal questions, settled by Science.

Protagoras had said it all long before, of course, in 500 B.C. The Enlightenment was pregnant with a very old idea, my boy, reborn with a vengeance. Call it *materialism,* as the ancients did. Call it *progressive* thought. Call it *positivism, secularism, secular humanism....* Package it as *New Age philosophy, Scientology,* or the Playboy philosophy, *situational ethics....* Man, in each, is "the measure of all things," the maker not the breaker of rules. This is the bedrock of liberalism.

Nietzsche called it becoming the "Superman." The Adversary, in his timidity, calls it "playing God." Redtape calls it "a world up for grabs, and getting yours."

By any name, Ticker, it is what the schools must teach if latter-day liberalism is to stand: the 3 *S*'s, *Scientism, secularism,* and *situational ethics.* Forget the 4 *R*'s: *readin', 'riting, 'rithmetic,* and *religious superstition.* Put all that behind us—baggage from the past. Bury it, and drive a stake through the heart of the fourth *R.*

Start back with Galileo, ignorance and injustice perpetrated by the Church. Wrap religion, ignorance, and superstition in one dark cloak versus Evolution.

Come up to light-speed with Relativity (both moral and scientific). Then, explode: Big Bang, *beyond* freedom and dignity....

Preach the 3 S's, boy. Drop names: philosophers, great scientists, American heroes. Rehash the "Monkey Trial," Galileo all over again. Sing of yourself, Ticker, and lead the others in chorus.... That should keep you for awhile, my boy.

Put these big pieces in place, the background of our Education puzzle. Central figures and action, straight ahead.

Your learned uncle,

RED

ps. Ticker, could Walt Whitman, singing his unbridled song of Himself, or Freud, with his sexually motivated man, or B.F. Skinner, studying his rats, have ever imagined that, at the turn of the 21st century, the new-age man they envisioned, complete, would be the 42nd President of the United States? The cherry, topping 300 years of *Enlightenment* cake.

Letter the Forty-sixth

~

Dear Ticker,

Cloning upstaging Education, is it? Hot topic. Dan is opposed of course—fuzzy about why, like most people. All right. We can take this in stride. Education and Cloning are related. Education, the *Father* of all issues. Ho ho.

We can fit this into our picture—

Let's jump ahead in Education to the 1980s, to the publication of *A Nation at Risk,* the report of a national commission on public education. The commission concluded that there was in public education "a rising tide of mediocrity that threatens our very future as a Nation and a people."

International competition had thrown a spotlight on our children's lack of basic skills, reading, math, and science. The U.S. was scoring poorly, and wise-guy journalists were doing surveys that showed American high-school students didn't know who Thomas Jefferson was or where to find Mexico on a map or who fought in the Civil War....

What to do? And what does all this have to do with cloning?

Our experts studied the competition. The Japanese, scoring well, were actually way behind us in many ways. They had larger class sizes, meager facilities, fewer computers.... Other high-scoring nations were way behind too, stuck in the past, focusing on teacher competence, course content, lesson plans. Plus, most were stingy, spending far less than we do per child. With such backward competition, the answer was obvious: *bold new approaches and increased spending.*

Education was declared a National priority. National education goals were set. More commissions were formed. New federal programs were proposed, to build more schools and jam-pack them with teachers and computers.... Big Nanna even moved in on television networks, demanding more educational shows.

The number one National goal—more on the others later—was "Ready to Learn," which included nutrition, health care, and family social services. This was promptly translated into legislation to provide federally funded day-care, health-care, preschool, and psychological counseling. A comprehensive approach was envisioned, right down to prenatal care. Do you have the cloning connection yet, Ticker?

The Japanese, once again, did no formal preschool preparation. They call early childhood "the age of innocence." Children learn little things from their parents, and play. What an old-fashioned idea! The liberal theory was that expert preschool preparation would easily outperform anything parents could do.

Many lessons here, Ticker. What looked like a disaster was really an "opportunity" to push for more federal involvement in not only education but health care, social adjustment, and family life.... Big Nanna, and her little sisters in the states, if they played it right, might add the preschool years to their already solid

LEE WHIPPLE

footholds in primary, secondary, and college education. The federal Trojan Horse—swaybacked, already,
from so much work, kindergarten through Ph.D.—
might be moved inside the family's innermost walls,
conception to five years of age.

New and important ground, Ticker. Federal funding for the preschool years would give Big Nanna, in
a dozen guises, a way to enter the home. Pregnancy
Person, Big Nurse, Child Counselor, Family Helper,
Home Safety Man.... All would need to pay home
visits—be in-home helpers and monitors (certifying
families to receive federal funds, advising, and, of
course, straightening a few people out).

Consider, Ticker, the real question being addressed:
Whose children are these? The answer, of course, is
that children—remember Rousseau—belong to the
State. Parents play only a role in the National Village,
as it were, a role that might be greatly improved, now
that Big Nanna had a mandate to "fix things."

Note, by the way, blame was being quietly shifted
away from the public schools to parents. The Nannas,
federal and state, hadn't broken education—parents
had. Preschool years were the problem, the brief time
in this Nation when parents are really in charge of
their children. Government's role hadn't been big
enough! The crucial early years had been left to parents. No wonder things were such a mess.

The problem for us, you see, Ticker, at the bottom
line—the thorn in latter-day liberalism's side, nine
times out of ten—is parents and traditional, self-reliant,
families. Parents, ready to fight even Big Nanna for
their kids. Yet parents are necessary, right? Where else

do you get babies to turn into citizens to man (and woman) the state? Where else, indeed? Imagine the Perfect world of the future. Be creative, boy.

You have it now, I'm sure. With cloning, new versions of the family begin to dance like sugar plums in a true liberal's head—versions that would not talk back to Big Nanna. Families, better suited to the National Village with "parents" who understand their *role*. Even homosexuals could produce babies through cloning....

Don't slip into thinking anyone is planning all this. No, no. The liberal impulse, planted and fertilized in the public schools for many years now, needs no mastermind. Government workers and teachers protect and expand their turf. Politicians maneuver to manage and grow their flocks. Troobs simply follow their hyperactive sentiments....

Only a precious few, like your old uncle, are smart (and honest, in my way) enough to see how it all ties together, to comprehend the whole. There are precious few Rousseaus and Redtapes, who dare look a liberal universe in its cold, bloodshot eye: children as property of the state, produced efficiently, controlled completely.

Not tomorrow, Ticker, but maybe the day after. Who knows?

To the practical question, answering Dan—

Let's build on our recent lessons:

"*Enlightenment,* Friend Dan, the march of Science and the Perfection of Man, is, and should be, unstoppable. Imagine if religious superstition and tradition had been allowed to stand in the way of all that has been achieved. Where would we be now? No telescope, no television, no rocket ships, no tonsillectomies or birth control, no *clones....*"

All or nothing is your game, Ticker. If Dan rejects cloning, he loses modern medicine and *I Love Lucy* and men on the moon (and painless, safe abortions). Ask Dan if he wants to stop *progress.*

"Friend Dan, we must let Science unfold without interference. How could anyone pick and choose among the marvels and wonders Science has produced? No one has the right to say 'No' to the *advance of knowledge!*"

Now, a little flanking maneuver, some raw meat to draw the Lovelies into the fray: cloned children, Ticker, incubated in a bottle, nurtured in day-care by licensed parent surrogates, preschooled by state sanctioned child-care experts, educated by state-certified teachers— do you see the seamless web?—equals freedom for women, finally, once and for all, from the injustice of motherhood. Cloning is efficient, no wear and tear. No fuss, no mess. Women would finally be on a level playing field with men. Tiffany seems your natural ally, boy. Sick her on Dan. PJ and Mr. Bow Tie should provide support. Yellow-dog Jake may pause a moment, but he'll go with the flow. He's a good boy, deep down.

Let Dan swim, if he can, against Progress, Equality, and the Ivy League tide.

Back to *school* through the front door, next time.

Your labyrinthine uncle,

RED

Letter the Forty-seventh

~

Dear Ticker,

Dan has no answers: the March-of-Science argument is compelling, but he remains "uncomfortable." That's to be expected. Liberals aren't built in a day. Our boy becomes less extreme—that's the important thing. Be sure he understands, Ticker, that the sole reason he feels discomfort is his "old-fashioned" upbringing. Tell him this is not his fault. He will outgrow these feelings, in time.

Back to Education. Put this puzzle piece into place around 1990, right after *A Nation at Risk.*

Another little lesson in Crisis management—

Two professors from major universities looked more deeply into the question of why Japanese schools were outperforming those in the U.S. They reported: *"Teacher's salaries in Japan are 2.4 times the national per capita income, as opposed to only 1.7 times for teachers in the United States."* No wonder we have such a problem.

Our teachers are underpaid!

Here's the real story. A tribute to the Nation's professors, guardians of the educational establishment—

Consider carefully: teacher's salaries in Japan are 2.4 times the national per capita income, only 1.7 in the U.S. A National scandal. Quite obvious.

Elsewhere, however, Ticker, the professors establish

that in Asian countries teachers are at school over nine hours per day, compared with about seven in the U.S. In another place, they establish that the number of work days for Asian teachers is greater, 220 versus 180. Are you starting to get the picture?

Japanese teachers, in terms of national per capita incomes, are paid more, 41%. But they also work more, 55%. In light of pay for time worked, U.S. teachers come out ahead. The professors have stood an inconvenient reality neatly on its head. A fine trick. But withhold applause, there is more. It gets better.

Consider Japanese class size, established in yet another place in the study, at 38-50 pupils per teacher. Now adjust for cost of living, high in Japan. The American teacher lives better on less pay. And remember the high-level performance in Japan versus the U.S. At the real bottom line, American teachers earn more for time worked, work less, live better, teach fewer students, and achieve lower results than their Japanese counterparts. The professors remain undaunted.

In conclusion, they state that American teachers are not only underpaid, they "are overworked." The first of their recommendations, "decrease the teaching load[.]"

How do they dare, you ask? Will not their colleagues, in other colleges, review the research and find them out? Surely, this will be challenged. Perhaps not in the Ivy League, but out in the heartland surely.

Ticker, let's take Colorado University, far from the Ivy League, at about this same time. It resides in a conservative state, Republicans outnumbering Democrats. Both houses of the Colorado legislature have been controlled by the GOP for nearly thirty years.

What would you guess the ratio of Democrats to Republicans to be at CU?

In the social sciences and humanities departments, where education studies would be reviewed, it, not long ago, was 31 to 1 Democratic—I wonder how he or she slipped in? Ha ha.

CU has an associate vice chancellor for diversity, assuring balance in "gender, ethnicity, ability [sic], and sexual orientation." But note, my boy, no mention of politics. Not to worry, the study is safe in academia, where the Nation's future teachers are being *trained.*

Add underpaid, overworked teachers to the Education puzzle, son (with some silent applause for our acrobatic professors). Next we go into the past, to see how *modern* American education got its start.

Your far-reaching uncle,

RED

Letter the Forty-eighth

~

Dear Ticker,

Today, I want you to meet some people, liberal saints, to whom we owe much. These are the guys who laid the tracks upon which the train of latter-day liberalism in America runs: Education its mighty locomotive, boxcars full of welfare, social security the caboose. Look inside a Troob's head and you'll see a scale model, tracks and train, running around and around and around....

First, we must pay tribute to Saint Auguste Comte, a natural-born True Believer, the archetype. Saint AC was a mid-1800s French social reformer. He wrote *The Course of Positive Philosophy* and founded "positivism," standing human spiritual development on its head in his "law of three stages."

The first infant-stage of human development, according to Comte, is the *theological* (belief in the supernatural). The intermediate stage is the *metaphysical* (belief in ideas). Finally, the fully mature human being progresses to the *positive* stage (belief in observation, hypothesis, and experimentation, Science). Sound familiar?

Within *positivism*, the sciences are ranked from the lowest, mathematics, through astronomy, physics, chemistry, and biology, to the pinnacle, *sociology,* a term Comte coined himself. Here was a prophet, my boy.

In the United States, a certain Mr. and Mrs. Croly

were devout followers of Saint Comte. They, in lieu of baptism, put their son, baby Herbert, through the positivist "Ceremony of Presentation" initiating him into the "Religion of Humanity [*Scientism*]." Baby Herbert grew up to write *The Promise of American Life* (still in print) and was a founder of the *New Republic* (still published), his book and magazine a double-whammy of influence in the early 1900s and today.

The New Republic, probably Herbert Croly's own hand, editorialized boldly:

> *"[T]he community has certain positive ends to achieve, and if they are to be achieved the community must control the education of the young...."*
>
> *"We deny the right of anyone, be he Catholic, Protestant, or Jew, to remain consistently ignorant of the march of the human mind...." "No church today can hope for survival if it provokes against it the forces of modern civilization...."*
>
> *"The power to choose and control destiny is the ambition of democrats educated in an age of science."*

Comte to Croly is a fine example of the Enlightenment's march into America in the 20th century. Take note, Ticker, of the thrust in the U.S., the shape, the distinct shading and color, the flavor, the who and the how of the latter-day liberal wave as it crests on our shores. That is what this lesson is about, the American Dream—as dreamt by the Founding Fathers—being transformed, the Enlightenment of Europe taking hold of the American Public Mind.

Meet Horace Mann, another American hero, taking

his cues not from France but Germany. Mann is often said to be "the father of public education" in America. This is true in spirit, Ticker, for, though public schools existed, here and there, before him, he fathered schools as they are in this country today.

It was the 1830s. The statist Prussian system of education was the rage among American intellectuals, and the newly formed Massachusetts Board of Education—Harvard boys—were eager to try on the German boots. They appointed Horace Mann Secretary of the Massachusetts board of education and gave him license to found a *modern* public school.

Father Horace, like Comte and Croly, was the quintessential Troob, believing in Science, Man, and a pantheon of gods. Upon accepting his new position, Father Horace wrote, *"[I] devote myself to the supremest welfare of mankind on earth.... I have faith in the improvability of the race."* An echo, my boy, of Erasmus Darwin—another echo, the "master race" in Germany, yet to come.

Father Mann succeeded so well in emulating the Prussian system, imbuing his schools with the "enlightened" goal of improving the race, that he was soon recognized for his achievement and became widely revered:

The *New Englander* praised his system for producing children "with the state, of the state and for the state." William E. Channing, an influential member of the powerful Harvard intellectual elite, wrote to Mann, *"[I] shall be glad to converse with you always about your operation.... If we can but turn the wonderful energy of this people into a right channel, what a new heaven and earth must be realized among us!"*

Does it begin to fit together for you, boy? The track

was being laid on which latter-day liberalism would run, and the mighty engine, education, was being forged, breathing fire and belching great billows of smoke.

Massachusetts, with Harvard's support, became the educational model for the Nation—compulsory schooling established there in 1852 and spreading quickly. By the early 1900s prominent educational architect Benjamin Rush, à la Mann, was urging the growing educational establishment on: *"Let our pupil be taught that he does not belong to himself, but that he is public property."* The train was in motion.

As early as 1917, Big Nanna's Trojan Horse—in the form of the Smith-Huges Act, federal money for vocational education—was being dragged over the Tenth Amendment into local schools: education was no more "reserved to the States respectively, or to the people." Federal purse strings were being attached.

In 1918—about the time Old Ned was coming into his own—the U.S Bureau of Education (to become the U.S. Department of Education) in cooperation with the N.E.A. (not yet a union, a professional association of teachers) formalized the National direction that endures to this day: the "Seven Cardinal Principles." Public education was to reach beyond academics to "life preparation." Big Lunchbox, every child's surrogate parent—the schoolroom guise of Big Nanna—was born.

In the Seven Cardinal Principles, academic preparation was reduced to one of seven aims, and downgraded to "fundamentals." Study the seven principles, Ticker, and you will see the handwriting that is still on schoolroom walls today. Meet the U.S. Department of Education and the N.E.A.: 1) health, 2) fundamental processes, 3) home membership, 4) vocation, 5) civil education, 6) use of leisure time, 7) ethical character. The 4 *R*'s and foreign languages were on their way out.

Finally, Ticker, meet Saint John Dewey, author of *Democracy and Education,* who persuasively sum-totaled and sold all of the above. His influence was unparalleled from the early 1900s well into the 1950s and still echoes today. He defended the Germanic State-controlled education system, drawing heavily on Hegel's theoretical justification for the German bureaucratic state.

Saint Dewey advocated group versus individual thinking, vehemently criticizing the central role of reading in traditional education: *"The plea for predominance of learning to read in early school life ... seems to me a perversion,"* he said. Saint Dewey is philosophically the progenitor of "look-say" and the "whole-language" method of reading, the first to glimpse the social danger of phonics.

Saint Dewey was also the outspoken champion of relativity, arguing that means can not only change the end, they can *"become the end."* Process, for him, was content: *"The emphasis must be put upon whatever binds people together in cooperative human pursuits...."*

I don't mean to eulogize, Ticker, but if one man stands out among the many, it is John Dewey. He is the great-grandfather of Dick and Jane and "playing well with others," *reading circles,* and the 3 *C*'s: *cooperation, compromise,* and *consensus.*

Walk into a classroom today and watch children working cooperatively in little groups, trying to *guess* what word a collection of letters might spell, and Saint Dewey is there. Follow the children to math class and watch them—again in groups—guess at answers to equations and discuss which ones they like best, and Saint Dewey is there. Look at the number of course offerings, grown from hundreds into thousands, producing not the selfish, literate, ciphering individual of yesterday but the sensitive, cooperative, socially integrated group member of tomorrow.... Saint Dewey is there.

Saint Dewey's work gave birth to the Progressive Education Association, dedicated to educating "the whole child." The rest, Ticker, is modern history: "life-adjustment education," "school counselors," "bilingualism," "affective education," "multiculturalism," "sensitivity," "self-esteem," "relevance," "values clarification" "sex education," "new math," "revised history," "equality of outcomes," "OBE...."

We're in your own time now, Ticker. The N.E.A. and federally funded teachers' colleges control who will teach. Our friends on the Court have rethought the First Amendment, officially banning the Adversary's God from the classroom, but *not* Auguste Comte's "Religion of Humanity" come down to us in its many forms. Centralization has been achieved, a shrinkage from over 130,000 school districts in the 1940s to under 20,000 today. Teachers cross examine children, to discover parental misbehavior. There is psychotherapy in the classroom, and sexual awareness training.... Congress and federal bureaucrats are, one way or another, in every local school, through dozens of acts and bills and laws and grants and decrees.

Now *National* education goals:

1) Ready to Learn
 2) School Completion
3) Student Achievement and Citizenship
4) Teacher Education and Professional Development
5) Mathematics and Science
6) Adult Literacy and Lifelong Learning
7) Safe Schools
8) Parental Participation

Compare these to the N.E.A.'s Seven Cardinal Principles—read carefully between the lines, remembering what *literacy* and *math* and *science* have, à la John Dewey, come to mean. And what's inside "Ready to Learn."

It's back to the future, my boy, the Seven Cardinal Principles all over again, but with nearly a century of federal involvement and public-school socialization to build on. If the Nation was ever "at risk," son, we are back on the tracks now. Ho ho.

However, we must not become complacent. A new threat arises, as we speak. "Choice," an insidious suggestion put forth by the Adversary to allow parents to choose their child's school—more on this in due course.

Speaking of what's ahead, I have a little surprise for you.

Coming soon: a letter from a modern-day-education Saint, in his own words. None other than Neil Postman, of New York University, twenty books and counting, perhaps even more widely read in teachers' colleges in the latter part of this century than Dewey was in his day. I've been planning this for some time, Ticker. This guy tells it like it is. You'll like him, you'll see.

Your immediate assignment—now that you have

had a taste of the wisdom of the liberal saints—is to start preaching the gospel to Dan and your pals, the 3 S's: *Scientism, secularism,* and *situational ethics.* Plus the 3 C's: *cooperation, compromise,* and *consensus.* Revere the group, denigrate the individual. Put process and effort above results. Insist on equal outcomes for all. Drum in the essential role of Big Lunchbox as surrogate parent, integrating health and social adjustment and sensitivity and self-esteem and sex education.... Downplay the 3 *R*'s and ban the fourth—no religious superstition in the classroom!

That ought to keep you busy for awhile.

Your encyclopedic uncle,

RED

Letter the Forty-ninth

~

Dear Ticker,

Women in combat, now. Ms Jewelry, at it again. Yellow-dog in opposition—our southern boy. It's the ghosts of George Mason, John Randolph, and John Calhoun, Ticker. They haunt the south, and infect the people with a creeping conservatism, even in this modern day.

Dan is going along with the Lovelies and Mr. Bow Tie. But it seems Jake has the better argument, to you. Ticker, Ticker. You're over thinking things, my boy.

It's true, Jake's stats are correct. Women are on average five inches shorter, have half the male upper body strength, a third less muscle mass, lighter skeletal structures—and can't do 75% of combat jobs. But *theoretically* war is a push button deal and women and men can asexually coexist. No problem. Ho ho. I've heard it all in Congressional hearings, none of it to the point. Don't get caught up in the argument, son.

Feminists are a liberal constituency, equality is a liberal issue—you are for women in combat. Ticker, when in doubt count sheep and votes and align yourself with the liberal Beatitudes: "... in the future a manmade Perfect world, inhabited by *Perfect women and men living in Perfect equality.*"

This is a no brainer. Line up with PFC Tiffy—I can see her now in combat boots.

Ticker, what makes this issue difficult is that the reality, far off in one way, is very near in another. People *are* men and women—it's not like speculating about the homeless or gays. Men and women know how it works between them, and the whole idea looks preposterous. You, my boy, have fallen into that trap.

What have I taught you, son? Never fear reality! Even if G.I. Jane doesn't work out, we'll pretend it did. Anyone who says different will get pilloried for being sexist. If it's bad enough, we can always reorganize the military, fire some conservative generals, appoint commissions.... Take your natural position, regardless. Count sheep, count votes.... Never fear reality!

Paint Jake as a macho reactionary. Support the girls. This seems an excellent inoculation for Friend Dan. Give him the PC medal of honor, for playing along.

By the way, when did you learn that Dan went to Catholic school? I don't remember you mentioning this before. I must say, though, I'm not surprised. I can readily imagine his poor, Protestant parents paying the tuition to keep him out of the public schools, delivering him into one of those dens of superstition where they insist on the 3 *R*'s. A Catholic-school education fits. Makes sense of a lot of things.

Get back to the main front, boy, Education. You have much to do. I must go. I am supervising the writing of some new gun-control legislation, already at over 1,000 pages. How's that for living up to my name?

Your famed uncle,

REDTAPE

Letter the Fiftieth

~

Dear Ticker,

At last, Dan asks the right question.

"What are schools for?" Answer correctly (*politically*, that is) and the future is ours. Ho ho.

Let's focus the question. Education in America is compulsory, and all but the fringe in this country attend public schools, over 90%. That's market share, boy—we stand on giants' shoulders.

The heart of the issue, then, is defining the purpose of the public schools. "What are the *public* schools for?" It is a matter of public policy.

Present and past come together in the center of our puzzle, Ticker, revealing the future—

In 1892 a committee of ten prominent individuals was formed to address the big question, to make recommendations to the Nation's high schools regarding curriculum. School content. The committee was made up of college presidents, high school principles, and one professor. The Ten took their cue from the Founding Fathers and the past. Their recommendations, Ticker, defined the traditional path of schooling in America, from which the Great Left Turn would soon be taken.

The Committee of Ten recommended that curriculum be organized into units equivalent to a years study, later to become *Carnegie units*. Each student was to have four years, or units, of foreign languages, two years each of mathematics and English, and one year each of science (small *s*) and history. The student, according to interest, could choose six additional units from among the core subjects or from a limited selection of courses such as advanced penmanship and music. Sounds dull, huh boy? No sex education, no sensitivity training or New Age philosophy....

Of course, responsibility for socialization and avocation were left primarily to parents and community. Vocational training was the province of specialized institutions, or apprenticeship. By today's standards, the schools were guilty of criminal neglect. This was the Dark Ages of American education, son.

The Committee of Ten was not content to merely perpetuate this American tradition of academic fanaticism and social neglect, they clarified and endorsed it. Academics were enshrined in their system of units as the *purpose* of the schools, and they spoke directly to the issues of *equality* and *justice* in delivering the goods.

Below is a multiple-choice test, Ticker. Which choice is the worst? If you pass this test, you will have identified the committee's selection. It's the one of the four *not* practiced in the public schools today.

A) *democratic justice*—everyone gets equal resources and attention

B) *moralistic justice*—resources and attention in accordance with effort

C) *humane justice*—resources and attention to the weak and disadvantaged

D) *utilitarian justice*—resources and attention to the ablest

That's right, boy, they chose A, *democratic justice*—
everyone gets equal resources and attention. Said the
committee, *"[E]very subject which is taught at all in a
secondary school should be taught in the same way and to
the same extent to every pupil so long as he pursues it, no
matter what the probable destination of the pupil may be,
or at what point his education is to cease."* Imagine!

These men were leaving everything but opportunity
to parents and God! They were complete cowards,
refusing to step up to their responsibility (remember
Saints Croly and Dewey, and Father Mann) to make
the judgments required to advance society and the
human race. They would Perfect nothing, only give
people an equal chance to improve themselves. Managing society was left to individuals, churches, civic groups,
and elected bodies. Scandalous!

The Committee of Ten was openly acknowledging
that outcomes would be different for different students.
Some would garner more from the same resources and
attention, some would go further. Don't miss the implication: some Grand Creator had apparently given
different people different talents and abilities, and it
would be left to the individual and his parents to sort
these out and make the best of it. The school would
simply do its best for all. Gross negligence, Ticker.

Finally, the Committee of Ten recognized Judeo-
Christian values and natural law as a part of the
curriculum—not taught explicitly, but woven
throughout courses as a necessary part of history,
literature, and the American heritage. They made not
the slightest effort to expunge this evil. They recognized

the infection and did nothing.

Well, you see: a disastrous approach, quite unlike that being taken in Europe, especially Germany, where the Enlightenment had taken firm hold. But, remember, some of our own educational saints were already at work laying the groundwork for reform, a radical change in direction: education on behalf of Society and the improvement of the race, of which academic preparation was only the smallest part and Judeo-Christianity was no part at all, if not antithetical.

In 1918, a quarter-century later, another committee—this time made up primarily of representatives of colleges of education—was formed to take another critical look at American education: the Commission on the Reorganization of Secondary Education sponsored by the U.S. Bureau of Education and the N.E.A....

That's right, Ticker. The Seven Cardinal Principles! The Rosetta Stone of American education. This was the Great Left Turn, away from the past, setting a course boldly into the future. Health, Vocation, and Leisure, recall, became the new curricular core—with academics reduced to "fundamental processes." The Turn was on time, my boy, in tune with world history. It didn't take long to travel far.

The Committee of Ten in the 1890s had surveyed the schools and found 40 subjects being taught. By 1920, the number was nearly 300. Today, we count highschool courses in the thousands. In the 1890s approximately two-thirds of all courses were academic subjects. By the 1930s, this had been reduced to one-third.... The *purpose* of schooling was radically changed, and remains so to this day.

What is schooling for, Ticker?

Saint Croly—you remember baby Herbert, baptized into Comte's "Religion of Humanity," grown up to become a founder of the *New Republic*—answers well: The schools are *"responsible for the subordination of the individual to the demand of a dominant and constructive national purpose."* Schools, said Saint Croly, were to actualize *"the hope that men can be improved ... saved without even vicariously being nailed to a cross."* Amen.

That's half the answer, son. "What are schools for?"

In my next letter I will finish the answer, and add some modern detail. Give it some thought, Ticker. "What else are schools for?"

Meantime, start giving your pals the first half of the answer. Schooling is to improve society and the human race (as defined by the "enlightened" liberal elite).

Let's review, do a little new math—

The 3 S's: *Scientism, secularism,* and *situational ethics*
Plus the 3 C's: *cooperation, compromise,* and *consensus*
Add *vocational training*
Minus the 4 R's: *readin', 'riting, 'rithmetic,*
            and religious superstition

Equals *modern education, Perfecting society*
                and the human race.

Is it all adding up for you, boy?

Your deciphering uncle,

RED

Letter the Fifty-first

~

Dear Ticker,

"What are the public schools for?"

In my last letter I gave you half the answer: the public schools are to promulgate and indoctrinate (make omnipresent and unquestionable) the vision of the liberal saints, to shape the Public Mind and Will, to *create* Modern Man, imbued with a secular creed, dedicated to the Perfection of the human race, subservient to an all-powerful state, with Perfect equality for all (except the liberal elite, of course, who get summer homes on Martha's Vineyard). Ho ho. Sell Dan one-tenth of that and he's ours forever, boy.

Think of the public school, Ticker, as a Troob factory, not merely producing citizens who endorse the above as preeminent—whatever other miscellaneous beliefs, however contradictory, they may simultaneously hold—but who cannot conceive that any rational person could think otherwise.

Other beliefs—the limitations of Science, the Fall— must be abhorrent or laughable, the latter by far most desirable. Dan is an example of what happens when education is allowed to slip out of the grasp of the state.

Now, the other half of my answer: "What *else* are schools for?"

Let's start at the halfway mark in the 20th century,

back nearer current events, approaching *A Nation at Risk*—

In 1954, the Supreme Court in *Brown vs. the Board of Education* ruled "deliberate" racial segregation in public schools to be unconstitutional. Congress, a decade later, passed the Civil Rights Act. *Brown*—prohibiting deliberate acts of segregation—grew into the National goal of correcting "racial imbalance." A year after that the Elementary and Secondary Education Act authorized Big Nanna to spend money in local schools, lots of money for all sorts of things....

What does all this have to do with what else schools are for? Social engineers, my boy, did not need to be told that they had the makings of a grand experiment, mixing money, schools, laws, courts, and nothing less than the legacy of human slavery and the Civil War.

Engineers on the federal courts joined in, ordering school busing. Children were to be transplanted, like begonias, from one school to another. Soon, the right balance of colors, figured by Big Slide Rule in Washington, would be achieved and all would be well.

Never mind about North Dakota, where there were not enough minorities to go around. North Dakota could find some. They *needed* some—racial balance was the goal! Theoretically possible, sociologically sound.

"What else are schools for?" They are the Nation's all-purpose petri dish, son. A place to experiment—to launch grand schemes to bring about Heaven on Earth.

Note, Ticker, how we moved in a decade from prohibiting *deliberate acts of segregation* to attempting to square the eternal circle of *racial imbalance*—forcing people, black and white, regardless of inclination, to coexist in physical space in the percentages Big Slide rule ordained—a grand idea cooked up by the best and the brightest in an afternoon, historically speaking, to bring about instantaneously what had never before been achieved on earth!

If we look closely, we will find another experiment going on stage-left, while busing steals the mid-century show. As part of the Elementary and Secondary Education Act, and subsequent amendments, local schools became eligible for certain federal funds *if* they provided special programs for the disadvantaged....

Schools must be Perfect for *all*! The lame would walk and the blind would see, or Washington would know the reason why. Heady stuff. Old Redtape knows this story well. Thousands of pages of new legislation and regulation were written in Washington, burying treasure: union influence, jobs, seedling bureaucracies, program upon program developed in academia and sold to the schools.... An *industry* was born.

Money from Washington would flow, but only if schools agreed to save society's disadvantaged—equalize outcomes for all. Never before done on earth, now an overnight requirement for receiving federal funds.

The Trojan Horse, one more time, Ticker. This is the same old nag that began its work near the turn of the century—remember the Smith-Huges Act—and has worked relentlessly ever since, bringing primary and secondary schools into the federal fold, then colleges, and, now, rolling on toward preschool, daycare, and, perhaps, people's homes....

Take federal money inside the school, preschool, home, and out pops the vision of the liberal saints.

Take a close look at the "disadvantaged" slant of the Elementary and Secondary Education Act, Ticker. Mark the date, 1965. Now think back to the Committee of Ten in 1892.... What form of justice was in the 1960s being rolled—a switch—into the public schools?

humane justice—resources and attention to the weak and disadvantaged

Victims, Ticker, flocks and flocks of new sheep. Takes you back, doesn't it, boy, to when your lessons began, to crocodile tears and sincerity, to *causes* and the latter-day liberal mission: *"Go forth in the name of Big Nanna and Perfect the world!"*

Public education is the laboratory, son, where Perfection must be discovered and rediscovered every day. Change, relentless and endless, Ticker, until Perfection is achieved (the Fall exposed as wrong-headed rubbish, Salvation become the province of Man).

Wrap your mind around this, boy: the results of latter-day liberal experimentation are being taught *while the Great Experiment goes on!* The Nation's children, the white mice, whatever their color, are running a maze that is under construction. No one knows which are the blind alleys and cul-de-sacs. The answers are written, then the questions, and then the facts found that add up to the answers—and the answers change every day. Breathtaking. We do not pay educators enough.

There is a savage beauty and reckless courage in public education, son. The vision of Auguste Comte shining brightly through: his bold infant, *sociology,* become the modern social sciences and social engineering.

Endless theories, reprogramming, experimentation....

Social engineering will be your most difficult subject, boy—not a tidy process to be easily grasped. It is, like history itself, a crazy quilt of fits and starts, greed and glory: an army of Troobs—social scientists, professors, Congressmen, bureaucrats, and judges—all stepping on each other's feet, but in the end going the same general direction. All, pursuing the latter-day liberal mission.

Could anyone have planned the interaction among *Brown vs. the Board of Education*, the Civil Rights Act, and the Elementary and Secondary Education Act? No. They were all dumped into the petri dish, and "racial balance" and the crusade to equalize outcomes, save the disadvantaged, grew.

Social engineering is inefficient, Ticker, even chaotic, but an essential element of liberalism. Remember Saint Dewey: means can not only change the end, they can "become the end." Till Perfection blooms. Ha ha.

As if all this were not heady enough, *A Nation at Risk* and National education goals are breathing fresh life into *liberal* education, renewing our lease on the schools.

"What else are the schools for?" Social R & D, my boy.

Put this puzzle piece in place for your pals: schools are a living laboratory, a place of Answers discovered, not—how old-fashioned— answers taught.

Your uncle, in Progress,

RED

Letter the Fifty-second

~

Dear Ticker,

I had planned in this letter to talk more about social engineering—but, instead, we must respond to Dan. More of his economics: a National sales tax this time. What naiveté! Do away with the IRS? Ho ho. Does the boy never learn?

This is going to be simpler than you might think, Ticker. We will dispatch this nonsense quickly.

Keep in mind, you must rise above numbers. Taxes can not be plumbed with a calculator. They are more than money and math. Remember Old Ned, and what taxes are really for....

Some pertinent history: In the 1890s, about the time of the Committee of Ten, the first peacetime pass at establishing a federal income tax was made. The Founders had almost universally been suspicious of any "head tax," favoring "object" taxes like Dan's scheme. This first pass was a failure. The Supreme Court—no friend of ours at the time—ruled that federal taxes were unconstitutional. Long time ago, huh boy?

In 1913, about the time of the Seven Cardinal Principles—catch the drift?—the 16th Amendment to the Constitution authorized a federal income tax: February 3, 1913, the latter-day liberal 4th of July. About two percent of Americans were taxed on the first go-round, at a rate of 1-to-6 percent. A lesson there: start small, think big.

By 1950, typical families were still paying under five percent federal tax, *but almost everybody was paying.* In the next quarter-century, typical families paid closer to 25 percent, those that were paying that is—large numbers of people were dropped from the tax rolls. Our people, Ticker, loyal, liberal sheep.

The growth of state income and sales taxes plus local taxes—not to mention double taxation or lost wages to hidden employer head taxes—soon brought the total being paid, by those paying, to near 40 percent!

Old Ned never dreamed of anything so grand.

All right. That's basic Big-and-Little Nanna funding, to *maintain* the state. Pun intended. "The more things change..." Ha ha. But don't think that's all there is to it, pure dollars. The tax code—Redtape takes a bow—runs to thousands of pages, full of advantages for us and for those who serve us, and punishments, hurdles, and roadblocks for those who don't.

In addition, Ticker, the IRS serves as Big Nanna's secret police. Enemies that refuse to be corrupted can be crushed into dust—and there is the beauty. Dust, no blood. A person can be ruined overnight, assassinated, as it were, by a junior bureaucrat with a few dozen forms and a calculator.

Finally, the IRS is the hub of yet another industry, an industry dependent on it for survival: tax lawyers, accountants, dedicated lobbyists.... Do you think these folks are loyal at election time? Ticker, I'm not talking just votes. These guys *contribute* in more than one way.

I have told you that Education is the Father of all

Issues, Welfare the Mother. IRS is Rich Uncle.

Now, to Dan and his numbers. How many pages of them? He points to his numbers, demonstrating practicality, increased personal savings, economic growth, a rising standard of living....

Here's what you do: Sit through Dan's entire presentation again. Pretend to take notes, and punch a few numbers into your calculator now and then as you listen. Study your notes quietly for a time after Dan is through. Then shake your head sadly: "Won't work." Shake your head sadly again, as if trying to make it work. That's it.

If Dan goes back through his numbers, repeat the above. Turn to PJ and Ms Jewelry and the boys: they will shake their heads too. Why? Because they don't understand the numbers either. You've given them an easy out. Take a look at television journalists discussing plans similar to Dan's. They shake their heads sadly too: "Won't fly." They don't understand the numbers either. It's a beauty to behold, my boy.

Give in a little, to close this issue out:

"You know, Friend Dan, you're right about one thing: the code is too large and complex. But your proposal is *too radical. You've gone too far.* What we need is reform...."

Ticker, we can reform the code for a thousand years and never change anything.

Your enduring uncle,

RED

Letter the Fifty-third

~

Dear Ticker,

Worked like a charm—I've seldom seen that one fail. I can almost see your little circle, Ms Jewelry, PJ, Howard Bentley the Bow Tie, and Yellow-dog Jake, all shaking their heads sadly at Dan: "Won't work, *you've gone too far....*" Good job, Ticker.

You say Dan seemed "so bewildered." So what? Don't start feeling sorry for him, son. I've warned you about this before. Dan will be better off for the beating, trust me.

Back to education. From your comments, Dan coming along but "always holding back," I think we'd better delay social engineering once more and spend some time on tactics, get you a little more traction.

This will have to be brief. I have a meeting coming up on—would you believe it?—tax reform. Small world, huh Ticker?

Tactical advice—

Why do we need state-controlled schools? First of all, don't forget the basics: caring and sincerity.

"Why? Because children are *so important*, because we *care so much*. Only government has the resources. Only government can be trusted...."

Education must be the work of trained, certified professionals with maximum resources, the responsibility of the state! Should we let parents perform brain surgery on their children?

Work in social engineering as a positive byproduct—*Big Problems require Big Solutions*—of government's lead role in education. How else would we find the *big Answers?* Schools are the ideal place to experiment (controlled, credulous, captive audiences).

Mercilessly ridicule the Committee of Ten for their limited vision, having left all the really important stuff to family, friends, church and community. Nonexperts! Laud the U.S. Bureau of Education and the N.E.A for the Seven Cardinal Principles, courageous and visionary. The National education goals carry on the tradition....

Go for a broad commitment, whenever Dan takes a backward step:

"You are on board aren't you, Friend Dan? In the end, we all want what is best. We're just talking about fine tuning government's role. Doing the most for the children, and society. Our Nation is *at risk,* after all." Let him say no to that. Give out ribbons and hugs for progress, however small.

I suggest you continually work on the vision of the liberal saints. But gently, my boy. Get Dan to agree that *in ways* children belong to the state, that *in theory* outcomes should be equal for all, that Perfection, if a bit lofty, is the *correct* goal.... Let secularism and amorality take care of themselves—they follow naturally.

Don't bite off too much at one time. Let Dan wake up one day knowing what schools are for. Get him to give everything to Caesar that belongs to Caesar, and then just a little bit more: a conservative compromised on principles is a liberal who just doesn't know it yet.

Nibble our boy along, for now, Ticker. Soon enough, we will move to Phase Three. Yesterday, we prepared the ground with sincerity and crocodile tears. Today, we gently plow and plant seeds. Tomorrow, or the next day, be patient, it will be time for Dan to take action, harvest time. Deeds are commitments that bind.

Our Dan, all in good time, will take the silent oath, and you with him, my boy.

Your patient uncle,

RED

Letter the Fifty-fourth

~

Dear Ticker,

Back to social engineering. Where were we?

"Racial balance," if I remember: the "melting pot" of America taken to its logical conclusion, a *politically correct* ethnic mix in every pot. Plus, the vision of the liberal saints being carried into local schools through the Elementary and Secondary Education Act, the old Trojan Horse of federal funding....

What next? How do you follow that act?

The next scene may seem like a contradiction, son. Liberalism has its own internal compass. It spins around, this way and that, seeming incomprehensible, yet always settles down pointing infallibly Left. Now that the races had been pushed together, it was time to pull them back apart.

Keep thinking *experimentation*, boy (and sheep, and factions to play off against one another, and funding in exchange for federal control)—

In 1972, The American Association of Colleges for Teacher Education issued a manifesto: *"No One Model America: A Statement on Multicultural Education."* It denounced cultural assimilation—the "melting plot." Instead, schools were to pursue *"the preservation and extension of cultural alternatives."* How far we had come from the Committee of Ten's trifling academic goals.

The colleges of teacher-ed multiculturalism goals:

"1) The teaching of values which support cultural diversity ....
2) The encouragement of the qualitative expansion of existing ethnic cultures ....
3) The support of explorations in alternative and emerging life styles.
4) The encouragement of multiculturalism, multi-lingualism, and multidialectism."

More sheep!

The president of the teacher-education association, in a symposium a year later, spelled things out even more clearly, just in case anyone didn't understand the deep intent and sweeping scope of this grand experiment:

"The multicultural philosophy must permeate the entire American educational enterprise. To this end, we — the American people — must reclassify our entire societal and institutional objectives, rethink our educational philosophy.... Curriculums, learn-ing experiences, the competencies of teaching pro-fessionals, whole institutional strategies — all must adjust to reflect and encompass cultural diversity."

The Elementary and Secondary Education Act was ideally suited to provide federal support: money for multiculturalism. "What are schools for?"

The Supreme Court weighed in, declaring it uncon-stitutional to provide education in English *only*....

A federal judge in Ann Arbor, Michigan ordered a

program set up to train teachers in the appreciation of "black" English....

Six months of study by experts in Oakland, California resulted in the idea of incorporating an Afro-American dialect into teacher training, *ebonics*....

The head of the Afro-American program at City College in New York *created* a new history of ancient Egyptian civilization, an Afrocentric version promulgating the cultural and ethical superiority of blacks....

American Indians were transformed—expunging territorial wars and slavery—into an ecologically and ethically superior race....

"Dead white men" in history went the way of Moses and Jesus, out of the textbooks and into the dustbins.

George Washington and Thomas Jefferson became self-seeking villains....

Reality, Ticker, was recast in the multicultural mold. Reality, like art, is what sells.

In 1990, in the American history syllabus for New York City, total victory was declared: *"In the final analysis, all education should be multicultural education."* The goals of The American Association of Colleges for Teacher Education, in only twenty years, had become preeminent: multiculturalism, multilingualism, multidialectism....

I have a dream, Ticker: I see a Nation with three Quebecs: California, Florida, and Puerto Rico, all language-locked. I see islands of blacks in the inner cities, speaking only *ebonics*. I see American Indians, forever the children of one federal agency or another. Throwing the doors of immigration wide, *guaranteeing multicultural protections and rights,* I see islands of ethnicity emerging everywhere!

I see the United Sates as an archipelago of ethnic diversity, mandated, subsidized, each little island at odds with the others....

Ticker, the homeless and the merely poor of Welfare days are slim pickings compared to this. A liberal elite could feast forever. I have a dream, my boy: a politician's paradise (I trust you have read Machiavelli by now).

Simultaneously, another experiment gets underway: *Globalism.* Social democracy, for all. One World! Let us become *one* with the rest of the world, while becoming islands within our own stream, right after we're through becoming racially balanced. I nominate the accordion as the National Instrument. Ho ho.

The latter-day liberal game, my boy, might, one day soon, be played on the grandest scale. One World!: theoretically bringing about Heaven on Earth *entire* (never mind that we haven't quite completed the task here at home, and never let the word *totalitarian* slip in, and never, never allow discussion of China, the Soviet Union, or North Korea ... as anything but anomalous examples of central control).

The United Nations must assume a new role: Huge Nanna, Sergeant Planet, Giant Lunchbox.... United Nations resolutions pave the way. "The Convention of the Rights of the Child," apropos Education, was unanimously adopted by the world body, *"ensuring* the development of institutions, facilities and services for the care of children," *prohibiting* spanking by parents.... Social engineering, son, and the vision of the liberal saints, on the grandest scale.

Our friends in the N.E.A. passed a resolution

supporting the "Rights of the Child" and lobbied Congress to pass it into law. Globalism: one more answer to the question, "What are schools for?"

A dozen issues come along for the Global ride:

World environmentalism, pitting those who *don't care* against those who do....

World Peace, pitting those who *want war* against those who don't....

World hunger, pitting those who would *starve others* against....

Sound familiar? Any problem, do you think, getting children to pick sides?

Globalism! Taught in school today, passed into law tomorrow.... There is a world out there to conquer, Ticker: *an entire world* in need of the stewardship of a liberal elite. Imagine social engineering full grown: tinkering not with a society, but a celestial orb! Gets your blood up, doesn't it boy? Any volunteers?

"What are schools for?" Do you believe me now, when I tell you Education is the Father of all issues?

Your surveying uncle,

RED

Letter the Fifty-fifth
~

Dear Ticker,

This time, my boy, some contemporary educational philosophy from, none other than, Neil Postman, the modern-day John Dewey, bestselling author in teachers' colleges, Ph.D., Professor and Chair of the Department of Culture and Communication at New York University, writer of twenty books, mentor of pedagogues, everywhere, a former elementary and secondary school teacher—education guru extraordinaire reigning for nearly thirty years.

Neil Postman, in his *own* words.

From *Teaching as a Subversive Activity,* with Charles Weingartner, 1969:

The most strident advocates of "high, and ever yet higher, standards" insist that these be "applied" particularly to "basic fundamentals." Indulging our propensity to inquire into the language of education, we find that the essential portion of the word "fundamental" is the word "fundament." It strikes us as poetically appropriate that the word "fundament" also means the buttocks, and specifically the anus. We will resist the temptation to explore the unconscious motives of "fundamentalists." But we cannot resist saying that their "high standards" represent the lowest possible standards imaginable in any conception of a new education....

[T]he new education is new, not because it offers

more of anything, but because it enters into an entirely new "business": fundamentally, the crap-detecting and relevance business....

We now know that each man creates his own unique world, that he, and he alone, generates whatever reality he can ever know.... Reality is a perception, located somewhere behind the eyes.... "Subject matter" exists in the minds of perceivers. And what each one thinks it is, is what it is.... Relativity and the uncertainty principle are more—much more—than technical terms in physics....

In the light of all this, perhaps you will understand why we prefer the metaphor "meaning making".... The idea of man as a meaning maker puts him back at the center of the universe ....

In many varieties of Christianity, the orthodox were traditionally offered a series of relatively closed propositions... The emergence now of "situational ethics" presents a much more open set of problems....

[T]he theologically related legal concept of abortion is undergoing "selective forgetting" or unlearning.... This is one "concept" that has to turn "inside out" because change has turned the facts of the environment "inside out"....

The new education has as its purpose the development of a new kind of person, one who—as a result of internalizing a different series of concepts—is an actively inquiring, flexible, creative, innovative, tolerant, liberal personality....

And so we will now put before you a list of proposals....

1. Declare a five-year moratorium on the use of textbooks.

2. Have "English" teachers "teach" Math, Math teachers English....

5. Dissolve all "subjects," "courses," and especially "course requirements."

7. Prohibit teachers from asking questions they already know the answers to.

8. Declare a moratorium on tests and grades.

9. Require all teachers to undergo some form of psycho-therapy....

14. Require each teacher to provide some sort of evidence that he or she has had a loving relationship with at least one other human being.

15. Require that all the graffiti accumulated in the school toilets be reproduced on large paper and be hung in the halls.

From *The End of Education*, 1996—

It has not been a good century for gods .... Charles Darwin, we might say, began the great assault by revealing that we were not the children of God but of monkeys....

As Bertrand Russell once put it, if there is a God, it is a differential equation.... [T]he great strength of the science-god is, of course, that it works.... The science-god sends people to the moon, inoculates people against disease, transports images through vast spaces.... [N]owhere do you find more enthusiasm for the god of Technology than among educators....

Taking this point of view, we may conclude that science is not physics, biology, or chemistry — is not even a "subject" — but a moral imperative....

[T]he idea of public education depends absolutely on the existence of shared narratives and the exclusion of narratives that lead to alienation and divisiveness.... [I] use the word narrative as a synonym for god....

The idea of diversity is a rich narrative around which to organize the schooling of the young....

What makes public schools public is not so much that the schools have common goals but that the students have common gods. The reason for this is that public education does not serve a public. It creates a public.

[W]e use language to create the world.... We are the world makers....

These are the words of Dr. Postman, Ticker, professor and Chair of the Department of Culture and Communication at NYU, icon of American education—not a comma, not an emphasis, not a nuance added. This is exactly what he said, read by thousands of students as they become certified in our schools of higher education to teach in the public schools.

Your scribing uncle,

RED

Letter the Fifty-sixth

~

Dear Ticker,

Exactly—it's tough for Dan to assert himself against Professor Postman, Ph.D., Chair of the Department of Culture and Communication at NYU. His conservative bent, respect for authority, constrains him. Ho ho. Uncle Red knows what he's doing.

Let's follow hard on Postman, ride his coattails into the modern era of education—

Dr. Postman is a hard act to follow. I'll do my best. I've selected a little collection of overlapping laws, a sample of how Big Lunchbox, at the turn of the 21st century, is gathering up and attaching strings to implement the vision of the liberal saints.

1) THE GOALS 2000 ACT ("Ready to Learn ..."): the 1980s remake of the 1880s Seven Cardinal Principles passed into law. *A Nation at Risk* set the stage. Big Lunchbox to the rescue!

2) *REAUTHORIZATION* OF THE ELEMENTARY AND SECONDARY EDUCATION ACT: the Trojan Horse authorized and funded to continue its work.

3) THE EMPLOYMENT TRAINING AND LITERACY ENHANCEMENT ACT: the secretaries of Education, Labor, Health and Human Services—additional arms of the federal octopus reaching into education—made cochairs of a National Institute for Literacy (expenditures

authorized for such things as making "sustainable changes in a family").

4) THE SAFE SCHOOLS ACT: an all-purpose ticket for Big Lunchbox to enter the public schools, to protect the Nation's children. Only home and private schools stand in the way of making education safe for *everyone*. We must not rest until *every* child is safe (inside a public school).

5) THE SCHOOL TO WORK ACT: the issuance of a "Certificate of Initial Mastery"—based on *functional literacy*, vocational and social skills—to replace the current high-school diploma. This is our rocket ship into the future, Ticker. A government-run, Nationwide computer network is envisioned to verify each certificated student's *social and vocational mastery*. Punch in a name and up pops the student's resumé, complete with skills and sociability ratings. A government service to employers. No *official* resumé, no interview. This is nothing less than a government-controlled passport to work, an occupational ticket to ride (home- and private-school students need not apply). Now that's social engineering, my boy!

These are the fab-five new laws of the mid 1990s: intertwined tentacles reaching into a pool of billions of dollars. That's right, boy, *billions*. Federal spending on education shot up from mere millions in the 1960s to tens of billions in the 1990s.

The Tenth Amendment, reserving education "to the States respectively, or to the people," has a golden stake through its heart. Say good-bye, Ticker, with a Bronx cheer, to a most-inconvenient Constitutional Amendment.

Redtape can take some credit for all this. I've done

my part. But the great modern education Saint, Senator Edward Kennedy, must be recognized for his leadership. He truly belongs in the Education Hall of Fame. Also, credit goes to the wife of the 42nd President, an innovator and tireless worker behind the scenes.

All will take time, of course. The Adversary is fighting us each step of the way. Radical parents' groups, private foundations....

Legislation lays groundwork and provides funding, but the education battle is finally won in the schools, manipulating teachers, maneuvering principles, gaining and giving ground, sidestepping parents, circling around.... Persistence, boy, and teamwork! Our friends in the teachers' colleges, the N.E.A., federal judges, all must play their part—and you too, son. Soon enough, Redtape will step aside and pass the mantle to you. You must keep the federal dollars flowing.

How long to fully actualize the potential of these laws? How hard will you work, Ticker? The Seven Cardinal Principles were only yesterday, historically speaking. Today we have *legislated* National goals— the Cardinal Principles chiseled in stone. In less than fifty years, we have gone from zero to millions in federal education spending, then on to tens of billions! Public education is double the cost of tuition in high-performing private schools, and higher than other high-performing nations. Results: *a nation at risk* that calls for spending even more. Ho ho.

Look how far we have come. Yet, nothing compared to what's ahead. The sky is the limit, now, my boy. The legislative base is laid to loose the vision of the liberal saints, and outspend Croesus. Are you ready to run your leg of the race?

But Old Redtape gets carried away—back to today. Let the legislative sampler I've given you expand your mind, son. There are hundreds more—that's right, boy, hundreds of laws—backing these up, filling in cracks, picking a cherry or plum here and there, as it were. Learn the game today, son, that you may play it tomorrow, for keeps.

For now, in the Great Hall of dorm-room debate, sell Dan and your pals, first of all, THE SCHOOL TO WORK ACT, the "Certificate of Mastery." This is the cutting edge—the computer network of government-sanctioned resumés replacing the high-school diploma. Job-skill "literacy" and sociability matched to employer needs, creating full employment, bringing on an era of international competitiveness and economic growth, everyone working cooperatively in little groups, happy, busy bees.... Sell, Ticker, sell!

Your impassioned uncle,

RED

Letter the Fifty-seventh

~

Dear Ticker,

Before we leave Education, I want to zoom in on the classroom, give you a slice of student life near the turn of the 21st century. Let's have a look at the firing line.

First, a look at the war of words, and how it is being won. Consider *affective education:* note the *a, affective*, not *e, effective.* Emotions, not results. Many a parent has mistaken this bit of social engineering for "back to [*e*-ffective] basics." Guess what *Outcome Based Education* means, *OBE?* [Affective] outcomes. Ha ha. Remember what I told you about sidestepping parents? We must be, linguistically, a moving target, lest the Adversary home in their artillery.

In the GOALS 2000 ACT, all of the above is referred to as "content-based systemic reform." Reassuring sounds. It would make Humpty Dumpty proud: "When I choose a word," he said, "it means just what I choose it to mean ...." Humpty Dumpty was one of our own.

Now, some classroom examples of affective, outcome-based systemic reform—

A middle school in Kentucky, in order to help children "get in touch with their feelings," gives this sentence-completion test:

I'll never forget the first time I _____

I remember how angry I was when my father _____
I'll never tell anyone about the time I _____

An Ohio school questionnaire helps children clarify their values by answering OK or NOT OK (circle one):

Having sex so I will be popular: OK or NOT OK?
Having sex so I won't be lonely: OK or NOT OK?
Having sex for fun: OK or NOT OK?
Having sex to repay a favor: OK or NOT OK?

In Virginia, on Mother's Day, the children answer questions about Mom:

How much does Mom weigh?
How much does she want to weigh?
Who was your mom's first boyfriend?
What does Mom do that your dad can't stand?

What goes on? Look closely. Situational ethics is encouraged: sex to repay a favor, OK or NOT? Family affairs become the business of Big Lunchbox: *"What does mom do that dad can't stand?"*

Think of the classroom as surrogate family, my boy, and these puzzle pieces will start to fall in place.

Dr. Joycelyn Elders, then Surgeon General of the United States, referring to THE GOALS 2000 ACT, pointed out that the emphasis was on making children *"physically, emotionally, and psychologically fit ...."* Things traditionally associated with the family, the home. No mention of academics.

The following are from a list of subjects Ms

Elders recommended schools teach: "sexuality, contraceptive methods, psychological concerns, pregnancy, welfare benefits, child abuse ....."

What are schools for?

How is "content-based systemic reform" doing? Here are some *outcomes*:

In an international math competition Korean children came in first, American children last—yet American children when questioned, afterward, felt they were *superior* at math. The Korean children thought they were only *adequate.*

Self-esteem! We teach it, and students learn.

In a study comparing Asian and American children in reading and math, American children did significantly worse. On a questionnaire, Asian teachers selected "clarity" in teaching as most important. American teachers rated "clarity" last. American teachers thought "sensitivity" most important. We want *sensitive citizens with high self-esteem!* The 3 C's: *cooperation, compromise, and consensus.* Could we ask for more?

I could go on, pantheism, entitlement, pure democracy, *Scientism* and *secularism* to go with *situational ethics*—sex to repay a favor, OK?—the 3 S's.... But enough, you have the idea.

A *Nation at Risk* is behind us. We are back on track. Congressional, judicial, professorial, and teacher-union leadership is paying off in the classroom where it counts.

Your outcome-based uncle,

RED

Letter the Fifty-eighth

~

Dear Ticker,

Dig in your heels—there is no compromise with "inner voices." Instinctive knowledge is the most dangerous kind. Religion, itself, is rooted in such nonsense. The inner voice today, Sweet Jesus tomorrow. We must turn this around.

The Mastery certificate and *official* resumés remind Dan of the USSR. Pshaw. Russia used brute force, we use infection and allure. Carrot, not stick. Russian secularism and central control wore boots. We wear bedroom slippers—but I digress.

To the real issue: "inner voices." Opposition without an argument, not even a pretense—our boy is at the fork in the road, Ticker. He senses the turn up ahead.

It's not so much the government and mastery certificates he shies from, but liberal glory. We've been building to this. With a lad like Dan, it had to come. THE SCHOOL TO WORK ACT—it might have been a dozen other things—happened to trigger the crisis. The wrong shoe at just the right time, pinching his conservative soul just a little too tightly. Look beneath the issue, son, to the real struggle here.

These "inner voices" are an echo of Dan's early religious training, though it is doubtful this occurs to him. As you say he seems confused, "almost embarrassed."

That, at least, will be helpful.

We move beyond Dan's niggling numbers and fiscal policies to the heart of the matter, Ticker. Religion or Secularism, Right or Left—the fork in the road. Recall Redtape's correction of Paul Elmer More:

> "Politics leads to morals (or amorality),
> which leads to religious faith (or secularism ...)."

Dan takes a critical step, forward or back. There is much ground to be gained or lost on this round.

Rally your Troobs, boy, right down to Mr. Bow Tie. Surround Dan with *outer* voices, friendly and sure. Force a choice. He must listen to reason or the ghosts in his head. Haints, fairies, little green men.... Science versus superstition. There is your line of attack—the more boldly taken, the better, my boy.

"Friend Dan, will you look through the telescope, like Galileo, or retreat into darkness...."

Use your imagination, Ticker—lay it on, son.

Your unblinking uncle,

RED

Letter the Fifty-ninth

~

Dear Ticker,

He doesn't budge. Maybe, Ticker, the problem is you. Your account is all detail, no passion.

You ask, "What went wrong?" You're not dipping deep enough into the liberal well, my boy, not getting down to the living water, as it were.

Perhaps it is time to immerse you more deeply in the art of persuasion, as I promised to do. Yes, I think so.

Liberal rhetoric, my boy, is more than a bag of tricks, more than dexterity. It is a window on the liberal soul.

You know the basics, well enough: half-truths, the Crisis, experts, false definitions and alternatives.... You know the words, Ticker. Now, let's add some *music*.

Two words you must bring to life: "Friend Dan." Relationship! Group! The *circular* genius of Saint Dewey—spell things out for our boy, five to one.

Harmony, son, the 3 C's, *cooperation, compromise, consensus*—a *process*, to be achieved at any cost. As Saint Dewey said, process can become result.

It's like calculus, son—the same old numbers but another world of thought.

Reality, listen closely, must be collectively determined. No private places allowed, no inner sanctums—no holy ghost whispering in someone's ear. The individual outside the collective is not really real. "Nothing *at bottom is real except humanity,"* said Saint Comte.

Stop making points, Ticker. Start selling *principle* with *passion, purpose,* and *pride.* You must go for the heart, as well as the head, with a recovering mystic, like Dan.

Smoke him out of his cave—didn't Saint Nietzsche predict that the shadow of God would haunt us for ages? "Ghosts," "haints," "fairies...." Display Dan's goblins for what they are. Make them stand against Science, my boy, Dr. Postman's *moral imperative.*

But be careful. Recall, you must never force the choice between Science and God. Let the two holy spirits coexist (à la Comte, in their proper order). Many Troobs, as I've said, carry God as baggage indefinitely. The smarter ones wean themselves in time. I'll wager our boy will be one of these.

Go to it. Let the liberal within you loose, son. Persuade, try again, but this time with *feeling.* Try to cultivate a tear in your voice. Learn to cry a little as you speak— study video of the 42nd President. He did this so well.

Give Dan a choice: Science and *progress,* or the little green men in his head? Help Dan take the Left fork.

Here's an incentive for you, Ticker: bring Dan to heel and Phase Three of our project can begin. Win this one and we move out of the dorm-room, beyond causes and issues to *action!*

The real thing, for both you and your boy.

Your managing uncle,

RED

Letter the Sixtieth

~

Dear Ticker,

It sounds like you made the case, this time. Little green men or "enlightenment." Not a tough choice. Give Dan some space—an imperative of persuasion, my boy. Tempt don't taunt. Never hurry.

Ticker, this little development illustrates well the need for the public schools. If our boy had attended, he probably wouldn't be plagued with "inner voices"—religious schools do nothing to cure such things. Public schooling would have put an end to such nonsense years ago. Instead, here we are giving Dan lessons he should have gotten in the first grade.

Dan never learned the real National motto in school: *In Science and State we trust.* Ho ho. But I shouldn't make light. Keeping God out of the classroom is serious business, and a sacred trust as it were—the classroom today, public buildings tomorrow, buildings open to the public the day after that....

Thomas Jefferson showed us the way in a phrase: *separation of church and state.* Don't tell the Troobs that Jefferson never intended the eviction of God from the public square, or that the famous phrase appears nowhere in the Constitution—it calls for Congress to "make no law respecting an establishment of religion, or prohibiting the free exercise thereof" and, regarding religion, not a word more.

No state religion and no state interference with religion—for nearly 150 years of U.S. history that was all there was to it. Hard as it is to believe, today.

Even as late as 1952, Supreme Court justice William O. Douglas in a Court opinion wrote, *"We are a religious people whose institutions presuppose a Supreme Being."* John Adams went so far as to say that the Constitution *"was made only for a moral and religious people...."*

A general reference to God is still made—there is much to do—on the dollar bill, in the Pledge of Allegiance, and there is prayer to open sessions of Congress and the Supreme Court.... But not in the public schools. That turf is totally ours, secure—not even a silent moment allowed to God.

We liberals decided among ourselves what it was Jefferson *really* meant. Never underestimate the power of a bold assertion (and a pocketful of federal judges).

God was erased from blackboards, and, as night follows day, Joseph, Mary, and baby Jesus disappeared from the White House lawn, then the Commandments of Moses from courtroom walls.... The Judeo-Christian heritage, gone from the public schools, will soon disappear from public life entirely.

Note, however, pagan and New Age pantheist icons are allowed. Dagan, the fish-god of the Philistines, sacred whales.... Such things are acceptable—even beneficial. They soften the prohibition. Like a latter-day Disney movie with spiritual overtones, they turn the religious impulse away from more dangerous venues.

Cartoon gods are compliant, never contradictory. They bow down to Big Nanna, or stand respectfully aside, live and let live. Learn from the Soviet and Chinese communists, son, who tried to stamp out the religious impulse entirely and ended up creating a religious underground. Better to replace our religious tradition with ever-milder forms, let the whole thing decay and fall away on its own.

What a coup, Ticker—booting God out of the classroom. It all seems so natural now. Anyone objecting can be labeled a fanatic or kook.

Well, boy, it seems I got carried away, but this is something you *must* understand. Son, the education wars will be yours to fight one day—they will go on for some time. The last sputtering Adversary will have to be put to rest (in jail or the grave, before we finally take over home and religious schools).

It will be awhile before we, as a people, unanimously chorus, "One nation under Big Nanna." Yet, look at the progress we've made, and the recalcitrants are few. The time will surely come.

For the present, our task is to keep public education strictly secular: the Judeo-Christian God *verboten!*

As public education goes, so goes the Nation— imagine if this country were facing not just a handful but a whole army of Dans.

Your stewarding uncle,

RED

ps. Keep the pressure on, slow but steady. Bring Dan around and I'll keep my promise. No more issues, *action.*

Letter the Sixty-first

~

Dear Ticker,

Dan is "analyzing the phenomenon"—a good sign. Discuss the *phenomenon* with him, by all means. Ask if the voices he hears are alto or baritone? When he says it's not like that, refuse to understand.

While we're waiting on Dan to come to his senses, there is a little wrinkle in our Education puzzle we should discuss. The Adversary is pushing something uncharacteristically shrewd, attempting to step past school reform to alternatives. "School choice."

Private education versus the public schools—

The idea is to get some of the money parents now pay in taxes for public education back into their hands to spend, if they choose, on private, at-home, church schools.... Let free-market competition improve education. I'm afraid a few folks are onto our *reforms*.

This takes us all the way back to the first century of this Nation, back into the dark ages of the colonial period. Schools were all private, back then. People chose this school or that—communities subsidized the poor to attend. That was *way back when*, and that is the first argument against school choice.

We need *innovation*, not a retreat into the past. True, the old-time system produced the Founding Fathers and a populace that read and debated the *Federalist*

Papers.... But that was long ago. It couldn't work now. All they focused on *way back then* were academics and civility. Why not go all the way back to living in caves?

What we need now, as Dr. Elders pointed out, are schools that make children *"physically, emotionally, and psychologically fit...."* We need to go forward, not back!

Now, a second argument. School choice would result in the disadvantaged being left behind in a withering public system (never admit that this concedes private schools are better and would win out in competition, at about half the cost). Focus on the *rights* of the less fortunate (humane justice). Things must be, in a word in the liberal vocabulary, *equal-and-fair* (except, of course, for the children of the liberal elite, who attend private schools). Ho ho.

These arguments are working, Ticker. But it is only prudent that we have other defenses. The Public Mind can be fickle, especially about children.

A promising defense is alternative public schools—steal the Adversary's thunder. Alternative schools, by whatever name, Charter, Magnet, Most Excellent and Wonderful, would allow *choice* and yet maintain the public system. Everybody wins! If people want choice, let them have it (within schools run by the government and the N.E.A.). Snicker.

In the end, Ticker, we can always drag out the Trojan Horse and follow redirected tax money into private schools, the same game we played federal-to-state and in the Nation's colleges. This could be our opportunity to take over education completely. We might just hoist the Adversary with his own petard....

We need to keep a careful eye on this initiative son,

but no reason for panic. We have the infrastructure to absorb this thrust: teachers' unions, teachers' colleges, federal funding tied to state educational bureaucracies.... We can fight a thirty-years war. The fire will most likely burn itself out. Time and inertia are on our side.

Back to Dan for a moment. I've thought of a hypothetical for you to pose. Ask, "What if your inner voices, Friend Dan, started advocating murder?"

What would Dan do if a delegation of little green men showed up in his head screaming for blood? Would he listen to reason or go with his Martians? Just how reliable are these little guys?

See if that helps our boy sort things out.

Your helpful uncle,

RED

Letter the Sixty-second
~

Dear Ticker,

Ho ho. The little green men are gone, explained away. Dan sees the light. Brain chemistry and electrons shifting orbit, all triggered by an excess production of endorphins.... Mr. Bow Tie—going to be a psychiatrist, you say—has explained Dan's voices in scientific terms. He, himself, has had similar experiences mixing alcohol and marijuana.... Don't tell me anymore. I don't want to know.

Redtape's hypothetical helped too—the possibility of inner voices waxing suddenly sinister—the little green men disqualified *ex post facto*. Yes, a neat trick. Hypothetical trumps actual, future trumps present and past. *What if* conquers all. One more arrow for your quiver, Ticker.

Plus, Dan and the gang tumbled to protecting the disadvantaged against "school choice." Sounds like you're hot, Ticker. We're off and running again, my boy.

Yes, I promised, and so it shall be: out of the dorm room, into the field. If Dan is not inoculated by now, he'll never be. Time to consolidate and consummate, to take action....

Causes and issues, of course, we do not leave behind. They are the essential first steps, a necessary element, of political action. We take them with us or find them as we go. *All* that you've learned, you must take with you, boy. You have the tools of the liberal trade— now you begin to hammer and saw, to change the world, for real.

Dan comes along, as apprentice, soon to be a journeyman Troob. Our boy has come a long way, but he won't be truly converted until sentimentality and ponderation are put into motion, turned into *deeds*.

As George Herbert put it, "Words are women, deeds are men." Apologies to Ms Jewelry and PJ. Ha ha.

Words can be taken back, thoughts made over. Deeds are permanent. Deeds cannot be undone. They are the steel rods around which the cement of causes and issues harden—the backbone of faith.

Our boy has come along slowly, dug in his heels here and there, but come he has—we now graduate him to the next level. Thank Ned he's in the Ivy League, where our every effort is supported by faculty and friends. Think how difficult this would be at Notre Dame, or, the liberal saints help us, Hillsdale!

Let us be off, Ticker, to taste the world of politics beyond the dorm room. I'll suggest an initial effort in my next letter. Nothing too difficult—we want to start slow.

Make noises to Dan and the others that it's time to stop talking and get into the fray, put liberal deeds in place of words....

Your forward-looking uncle,

RED

PART THREE: HARVEST TIME

"And yet words are no deeds."

—William Shakespeare
Henry VIII

Letter the Sixty-third

~

Dear Ticker,

How is PJ's kangaroo rat?

You know that relatives of that little bugger have shut down farms, halted the making of firebreaks—costing people their homes—and brought on a years-long federal inquisition of an unrepentant Taiwanese emigrant who ran over a rat with his tractor while plowing his fields? I'm sure PJ has regaled you with such stories. "Save the rats, owls, whales ... *at any price.*"

Animal rights, my boy! It's the *Perfectly natural* place to begin the action phase of Dan's conversion. Out of the dorm room and into the *fields*! Ho ho. PJ will lead the way—the piper our Dan is inclined to follow.

We are not talking cruelty to animals here, boy, or poor conservation. We're talking genocide: cuddly creatures being hunted down by an army of drooling conservatives, carrying assault rifles, bent on wrapping their women in furs....

The images of childhood flow freely into this adult fairy tale—saving Bambi and Dumbo and Chip and Dale. Reality need never intrude. Best of all, you and your pals get to be the *action heroes*, the G.I. Joes and Janes, in this righteous war.

But let us not go too quickly: serious politics lie beneath the surface of this crusade. *Animal rights* is only a convenient place to start in a much larger crusade, *the* crusade of the 21st century, my boy.

Study the pyramid below—it is nothing less than the future of liberalism.

earth rights
animal rights
human rights
Perfect democracy

Do I have your attention, son?

We begin at *animal rights,* in the middle, because of PJ's bent and her influence on Dan, and because animals are cuddly. It's the place they start in the public schools. Highly appealing. You, of course, must have the postgraduate seminar—you must do more than pet dolphins and recite the New Age litany.

Let us begin, you and I, with *human rights,* the real center of things. Follow me closely, boy, or I'll lose you on the sharp turns. The future of liberalism—

Nothing is more sacred to Troobs than *human rights*—the lite-Right fairly worship them too. It's a fine confusion, Ticker, this "rights" business, redrawing the very outline of Western Civilization. As with Galileo and Darwin, contradiction, convolution, highly useful.

Human rights, my boy, are hopelessly mixed in the Public Mind with natural law: truths believed to reside in the nature of man. Natural law, in its many forms, proclaims a universal human dignity and defines the individual's responsibilities toward, and just protections from, others. "The Ten Commandments," for instance.

Natural law is ancient, limited, sacred—woven into

the fabric of Western Civilization by Moses, Jesus, and Thomas Aquinas through Christianity, and Aristotle and Cicero through Rome—paralleled in the East in Taoism and Confucianism.

You see the problem: *the transcendental thread.*

The liberal trick is to remove the troublesome transcendence while maintaining the psychic weight of the centuries. Enter our old friend, J. J. Rousseau. Frenchmen! What would we do without them?

Don't be impatient, Ticker. I'll get to *animal rights* and political action in due course. The Frenchman and the future now, Chip and Dale versus the evil giant soon . Pay attention. There are no Cliff Notes for this.

Rousseau proposed a grand theory in place of world history, the "Social Contract." He made of history an elegant hourglass, cleaving time in two, primitive and modern. Before the Social Contract—the top half of the hourglass—JJ said man was primitive and free. At the pinch point in the glass comes JJ's Social Contract: man giving up his freedom, pledging allegiance to Mankind, itself, in exchange for all just benefits from society. Enter the all-powerful state. Into the bottom half of the hourglass falls modern man in his collectivized state....

Man leapt into society, said JJ, no gradual, heavenly revealed, intricately woven binding of men and women into groups with intertwined loyalties and complex commitments among self, family, community, nation, God. The Social Contract was an all-at-once, all-or-nothing deal: allegiance to the state for society's boons. A simple, compelling theory of history, well suited to those who do not wish to spend long hours with dusty old books.

You'll remember, with JJ we are in the heart of the Enlightenment, the French Revolution coming soon....

I know, I know, Ticker—when do we get to the animals and *action*? Soon. But first you must have this background, lest you think *animal rights* is merely a cartoon. Be patient. I'm getting to the present day.

Confused with and colored by natural law, Jean Jacques' Social Contract evolved into the *enlightened* notion of *human rights*—a vague, infinitely expandable collection of things people are owed by society: the human heritage of responsibilities and protections under God, overlaid with a wholly secular Terror of entitlements.

People conveniently forgot what to society they owed and became exclusively focused upon what they were owed, and began lopping the heads off those who hadn't given it to them. We have arrived at the French Revolution, on our way to the Russian and the Chinese....

Now, the idea of entitlements was not, early on, as noted by Tocqueville—a Frenchman, too, but not the *enlightened* sort—well-suited to the American temperament. Notwithstanding this, Thomases Jefferson and Paine— in, respectively, *The Declaration of Independence* and "The Rights of Man"—planted the seeds. They grew.

Rousseau's disciples, Comte, Croly, Father Mann, Dewey, Postman ..., did the watering. You remember these liberal notables, I'm sure.

Presidents Woodrow Wilson, FDR, and LBJ brought in the harvest, each using the term "human rights" to strike the right note in advancing entitlements and the power of the state. Big Nanna, getting bigger and bigger....

The United Nations proclaimed *universal human*

rights, including, along with security of person and equal protection under the law, such things as housing, medical care, unemployment protection, leisure, and holidays with pay: a grand mixture of natural law and entitlement. Confusion, convolution, as I said.

President Jimmy Carter put the idea of *human rights* into U.S. foreign policy, threatening sanctions against those who did not live up to American standards, however ambiguous: things we didn't like, anything undemocratic for instance.

Encouraged by presidents and the press, and pandered to by politicians—here is where the future begins—*the People* began to get the idea that they *deserved* a Perfect, pure, democracy. Wasn't that a *human right* too? Forget representation, parental, fraternal, and religious authority, tradition, and the rule of law.

Wasn't any man or woman as good as any other? That's what democracy is all about, isn't it? One man, one vote. *Public opinion* rules!

Suddenly, it all seemed so obvious. Court cases, for instance, began to be settled with a weather eye to mobs in the street....

A grand idea, Ticker, with a big future: if pure democracy—think about it—is a *human right*, all you need is a vote to spawn more *human rights*.... Demands sanctified by *the People* in a vote (perhaps a poll) become *human rights*, don't they? Or what's a social contract for?

Perfect democracy, theorizing further, *ought* to produce the ultimate *human right*: Perfect liberty and equality for all. Heaven on Earth, Amen! Sound familiar? Yes indeed, but look at the shiny new words and note the new role for democracy. Envy, long the liberal engine of social change, is about to become supercharged.

Look into the future, boy. Who could even pretend to deliver up this expanding world of *human rights*? A bigger and bigger BIG NANNA! "The more things change, the more they stay the same." Step right up, ladies and gentlemen, buy your ticket to ride.

Ha ha. Remember Old Ned's merry-go-round? It spins on, gaining speed. Saddle-up, Ticker. There is going to be a wheel full of bucking broncos in place of those old prancing steeds. Ride-um, Cowboy! Yee-ha.

Human rights and *pure democracy*, son, are the rising stars of latter-day liberalism—rebirth. New possibilities. I did not exaggerate when I said that here lies the future. Let your imagination run, my boy.

I'll connect the dots to *earth* and *animal rights* in my next letter—our furry friends and *their* planet are going to be very important in the new century, son. *Earth* and *animal rights,* taught in the first grade, is the Perfect introduction for the Nation's children into the center of latter-day liberalism, preparing them for *human rights*, for life. I've got to run just now, duty calls. Taxes to raise, property to seize.... We've got to fund this super-behemoth we're birthing (and see to it that it doesn't go nibbling at *our* lunch). I hope you begin to see the future, boy. It can be yours.

Your ringmaster uncle,

RED

Letter the Sixty-fourth

~

Dear Ticker,

PJ continues to work her magic—our boy is nearly ready to march. Chip and Dale should be resting easier, already. Ho ho. Now, it is only left to complete your briefing, son, before we marshal the Troobs.

Direct your attention to the top of the pyramid:

> *earth rights*
> *animal rights*
> *human rights*
> *Perfect democracy*

In a Perfect democracy, *human rights* must be extended to Animals and the Earth: the sovereign People and Animals of the Earth, capitals *P*, *A*, and *E*. Animals should have a vote, too. Flowers and trees, in due course. Rain forests, in particular, should get a vote....

Of course animals and trees can't really vote—we must have some reality. No problem. Everyone knows that Animals would vote liberal if they could, as would the Earth itself. Ask any schoolchild. Big Nanna can simply cast the votes of Chip and Dale in small private elections within the government. Administrative action, regulations, rules.... Millions and millions of votes.

Imagine the howl from the schools, and Hollywood,

echoed in prestigious periodicals and on the evening news, against any who would keep the earth subordinate to man—what an outlandish idea—by challenging the voting rights of ants and flowers and trees. Picture the recalcitrants assaulting Floppsy, Moppsy, and Cottontail with AK-47's, axe-murdering trees, wantonly running over kangaroo rats in their S.U.V.'s....

That's the big picture, boy. Kangaroo rats today, world democracy tomorrow—the New Age Great Pyramid stacking up fast.

No conspiracy, son. The Social Contract is simply being renewed—a liberal face-lift for the 21st century—with a little help from the schools. Take a look at PJ petting Precious, the rat. Whale sounds, on the stereo.... Momentum, son, the world is turning our way.

Your immediate assignment: Heaven on Earth for Animals, Now!

I want *deeds,* Ticker: petitions, letters to editors and Congressmen, marches.... Demand new courses in animal rights, and revisions of history, more animal-sympathetic. We need research to enable us to talk with whales, and sensitivity training for sheep ranchers who have a *thing* against wolves. Use your imagination, boy.

Take to the streets, you and Dan and your little band. Liberty, equality, and fraternity for Bambi and her friends! You're a liberal, boy, born and bred. Think like one, and, now, the time has come, son, *act* like one, too.

Your consummating uncle,

RED

Letter the Sixty-fifth

~

Dear Ticker,

Sorry about Plain Jane's rat—ouch! Yellow-dog sat on it. Tough way to go, and lousy timing. But then I guess rats aren't the thing anymore—and this wasn't really one of *the* kangaroo rats, you say, just *a* kangaroo rat? I wondered about that, having an endangered pet. I'm afraid old Redtape isn't up with the latest fashions on this animal thing. Lucky, we have PJ.

This new crusade of hers sounds better, anyway. Where does she get this stuff—a retirement home for U.S. Air Force monkeys and their offspring in perpetuity! It's such an obvious thing, once you think of it.

These monkeys are explorers who bravely served their country (and not in an unpopular war like the Vietnam vets). They're entitled to the best. Go with it, boy. Petitions, rallies, calls to Congressmen, articles in the school paper.... We're in business, Ticker.

Don't worry about this not being "earth shaking." How many times have I told you, son?: conversion is best achieved on a gentle slope. Steep inclines beget careful forethought. This is just the thing.

But be mindful. Even small crusades are not simple in the field. The liberal vision, easy enough to manage in the dorm room, can be difficult to maintain down on the street. Reality threatens at every turn.

Following are guidelines for maintaining liberalism outside the dorm room—

1. Fraternity first among liberals: liberty and equality
for all later on.

In order to Perfect society, it must be perpetually remade: the existing mold shattered and reshattered, until it is finally gotten right. Prior to the final Perfection, fraternity is all you can expect, and *only* among those doing the shattering. Think about it. Those having their world shattered just aren't going to feel chummy toward the shatterers, however great the new order is going to be some day.

The shatterers, alone, can share the joy of destruction. Barbarians—however elevated and visionary and ultimately benign—must look to each other, not their victims, for love. They, exclusively, are bound in spirit, collectively proud of destroying the city: burning the flag creates a warm glow only the initiated can feel.

This sharing of visceral hate and rarefied love, joyful destruction and righteous rebirth, is the tie that binds liberal reality (and keeps it against all cognition). Shared expressions—continuous declamations—of love for the Perfect future and hatred for the imperfect present and past create a breastwork behind which liberals remain safe in any extreme. Keep your Troobs together, Ticker, singing their song.

2. Keep experience in its place: interpret it Left
and Right.

Modern culture must be viewed dichotomously, style in the Left-hand column, substance in the Right. Place rap music, for instance, in the Left-hand column, "style." Music reduced to grunts and growls, threats and obscenities, is neither dangerous nor degenerate. It is free: uninhibited, spontaneous, *liberal*. Groans and thuds are the equals of soprano and violin. Beauty is relative.

The substantive outcomes of modern culture, on the other hand, totally unrelated to the above, must be placed in the Right-hand column, "substance." Violent crime and illegitimacy ... are the results of clinging to the past and an unwillingness to change. Conservatives are to blame. No relationship to "style," whatever.

Outside the dorm room, son, images and information don't come in neat little packages. You must sort it all out, interpret it Left and Right, lest unfounded connections be made and injurious conclusions drawn. Best to keep the interpretation simple and bold. Two columns: styles Left, substance Right, no connection.

3. Weigh experience carefully: internalize in keeping with liberal values.

A pocket summary:

Value the *ideal*, accept nothing less.

Value *tomorrow*, never yesterday or today.

Value *sentimentality and excitement* not affection and commitment.

Value *fast*, despise slow.

Value *process* over results.

Value *rapid change* versus "old hat."

Much that I have taught you, boy, is summed above. Values are the lens that brings experience into focus. Guard liberal values jealously in the field.

4. Bow down to "the People," thumb your nose at "the Man": copy the ACLU.

The American Civil Liberties Union strikes just the right balance, endorsing Perfect liberty *for* liberal constituents and clients, "the People," while demanding Perfect equality *from* businesses and social institutions, "the Man." On the one hand, they endorse obscenity and verbal violence against police forces, corporations, and universities (expressions of personal liberty). On the other hand, and at the same time, they demand "sensitive" conduct towards blacks, women, and gays from organizations and their representatives (expressions of racial and sexual equality). Perfect!

It's simpler than it sounds, Ticker, once you get the hang of it:

A) Liberals can do as they please, those offended can lump it. *Nude dancing, pornography, prostitution, flag burning, gay teachers, abortion....*

B) But nobody better offend liberals. *Sensitivity, quotas, heavier punishment for hate crimes, no prayer in schools, criminals treated like law-abiding citizens....*

Now, regarding contact with clients and constituents on a more personal level: always confirm their great wisdom and tell them they are in charge.

"That's a *very good* question...."

"*Exactly* right..."

"Enjoy *your* day, weekend, movie...."

"You *deserve*...."

"I work for *you*!"

Study reporters and politicians appearing on call-in shows to get the sycophantic tone just right. "The *People* aren't dumb, they *know*...." Ho ho.

Personal contact with the Adversary, of course, is an entirely different matter.

5. Blast the Adversary: but never with both barrels.

Wounded Adversaries are better than dead ones,

as it were. A dead Adversary may be replaced by another, and what have you gained? Wounded Adversaries can be forever intimidated and manipulated—and you get to watch them bleed.

Except in extreme cases, Ticker, never confront the Adversary with specifics: infringement of rules, regulations, laws.... These can be settled once and for all. Both barrels go off, from both sides. It might even be you who dies.

What, then, should you do? Accuse very broadly, my boy, one barrel of bird- not buckshot. Always generalize: insensitivity, bigotry, greed, lack of understanding.... Demand the accused go to counseling or sensitivity training, not jail.

The troublesome person—"He was sent to counseling, you know"—gains a reputation for insensitivity, bigotry, or whatever, a wound that can be aggravated at will. Politically correct the wounded Adversary will be, or it's back he goes to the interpersonal dynamics guru from Berkeley. Ha ha.

These simple guidelines will keep you out of much trouble, son. Pay them heed. It's trickier on the street than in the dorm room—but I know you'll do well.

Get rolling, you and your Troobs—those monkeys *deserve* a retirement home!

Your streetwise uncle,

RED

Letter the Sixty-sixth

~

Dear Ticker,

I had no idea others were pursuing this. A nation-wide organization, a web site—who would believe it? "Animals First": the name says it all. Sounds like you're in good company, boy. This is going so well, catching fire. Did the Lovelies really livetrap a fly and release it into the wild—and Dan kept a straight face? Oh my! But you're right, boy, this is no time to stand still.

Blue boxes. Yes. A fine next step—and an interesting twist. Let me get this straight: Your little group will weigh the recyclable trash from the blue boxes on each dorm floor. Floors falling below the average will be cited in the school paper, "for shame." Ms Jewelry leads the parade on this one. Good, very good, but be careful.

A certain risk is run with recycling. The environmental costs can outweigh the benefits—extra trucks running about picking up bottles and cans often consume more energy and resources than the recycling saves. Net loss. Just the kind of thing your boy, Dan, is prone to sort out.

If this comes up, claim recycling as a symbol, worth the degradation. It's the spirit that counts, not a nitpicky decimal point here or there. Feeling good about the *correct* things, gaining momentum—that's what's important.

Master stewards of the Earth can't get bogged down in detail. Keep your Troobs focused on slogans and

Earth-saving theories, that's what gets people marching. Leftward. Ho ho.

Remember, environmentalists are *action heroes*. When in doubt, quote the 42nd president's second in command, environmentalist extraordinaire, Al Gore: "[R]esearch in lieu of action is unconscionable." Do *something!*

This can be an important little step, Ticker—more here than blue boxes. Keep the big picture in focus.

Big Nanna spends billions each year saving the Earth. Subsidies, regulations, laws.... Businesses spend billions more applying, complying, appealing, going to court. It's a growth industry, son. Old Ned would love it— advantages for some, obstacles for others, the old merry-go-round.

Corn states, for instance, get subsidies and regulations to encourage the use of clean-burning ethanol over gasoline (agribusiness gets money, politicians get votes, bureaucrats get power). Some move up, others down (everyone switching horses).

Headline: AUTO EMISSIONS REDUCED BY ETHANOL—CANCERS PREVENTED (about one for every billion dollars spent). That's one example, Ticker. There are billions of dollars worth more—some even more cost effective. Ha ha.

On top of all this, environmentalism contributes to the Nation's new spirituality. It is nothing less, my boy, than the capstone of the New Age pyramid:

> *earth rights*
> *animal rights*
> *human rights*
> *Perfect democracy*

Pantheism—holy Mother Earth—rises like the phoenix from a fiberboard pyre, recycled. You don't have to buy all this, boy, or even understand it.When in doubt quote Al Gore: "The lakes and rivers sustain us; they flow through the veins of the earth and into our own...."

What do we gain?

Getting God banned from the schools and the public square was only a start, son. It takes us only so far. This gets God absorbed into the Earth and dissipated into space—better than having Him lurking around outside town somewhere, up to who knows what mischief.

I speak figuratively, of course: there is no God, as we both know, only forms of the Idea more or less harmful, or useful. Pantheism is progress.

"When flies are made in the image of God, religion ceases to threaten the state."—Redtape.

Your uncle the environmentalist,

RED

Letter the Sixty-seventh

~

Dear Ticker,

Dan never got out his calculator—except to figure the *precise* blue-box averages. No eco-productivity calculations, a good sign. See how our boy turns around, facing Left now not Right, but still our Dan?

He endorses the recycling policy in *theory*, insisting selected details be done to Perfection—but he forgets to validate the premise. Hallelujah!

Feast your eyes on conversion, my boy. Next, Dan will be wearing Naugahyde shoes instead of leather, made from "cruelty-free" Naugas. Ho ho. Soon, he will be eating only fruit fallen-not-picked from the tree.... A profusion of symbolic acts of liberal Perfection, a shifting constellation, excruciatingly precise—the pride and pastime of Troobs—will now slowly replace his religion. Keep after him, Ticker. He is all but ours.

You, as well as our Dan, have come a long way. This is, indeed, a good day.

Now to your observation about the press, yes and no. Glad, by the way, you're getting good coverage for your noble project. Thanks for the article—I loved the picture of the chimp in a space suit, really tells the story. But there is more to it than the press being on our side, my boy.

Yes, they are on our side, 89% of the Washington

press core voting for the 42nd President, but no it is not a "fanatic loyalty." The press is not like those in Hollywood or the Nation's universities. There is more here than pseudo-intellectualism and runaway egos.

The press has a natural proclivity for liberalism, and aversion to conservatism, all politics aside. Self-interest, son. Take a good day for conservatives and write the headlines:

EVERYTHING OK, PRETTY MUCH AS IT WAS
MINOR CHANGES CONSIDERED ...

How many papers would you sell, or rating points gain, versus a good day for liberals? Take a good day for us and write the headlines:

DISASTERS EVERYWHERE!
RADICAL CHANGE UNDERWAY ...

Liberalism, by nature, is bold. Conservatism is not. No contest.

We and the press are natural allies. It's as simple as "man bites dog." Or *astronaut* chimps!

So yes and no, Ticker. Yes, the press is on our side, but not really loyal—the first rats off the ship. The only team reporters are really on is their own. The press often act like Troobs, but in the end they are simply whores.

Your perspicacious uncle,

RED

Letter the Sixty-eighth

~

Dear Ticker,

Whoa, boy. Slow down. Recycled pop cans are not sacred objects, a home for your monkeys wouldn't really be theirs.... You're getting carried away, son.

I'm to blame. I've allowed our field trip to eclipse the classroom. Where to begin? Property, I think. Back to school. Animals and Earth: Property 101.

Animals and Earth are property, son. They are owned or *controlled* by someone or something—private or governmental. I'm talking *real* property in this lesson, Ticker: land and what's tied to it, not money and art treasures and such.

So long as there is civilization, however you slice it, *nature is property!* Talk about sovereign Mother Earth, but understand human proprietary control. The question is, and will always be, who owns or controls, who's master? Settling the question is the business of politics, or war.

Think of property, privately owned, as individual sovereignty, the most basic of checks and balances against the state. So long as individuals own and control property, they have weight in the political equation. Do you start to feel the rub?

Private property is also a link among generations, bequeathed from one to the next, a major source of affection for the past and interest in the present, and a check against radical change. Give a man even a postage stamp of land to call his own, and soon he is defending social order, looking to pass his home and ways along to his children in hopes that they might build upon them (not tear things down and revise).

The man with a postage stamp of land, even long-term employment on it, loses interest in Perfecting the world. He gets caught in a web of selfish longing for peace, stability, family, a modicum of comfort, and the romantic notion of continuity.

There is a basic antagonism between private property and liberalism, son. So long as people hold land, they belong to themselves, or to God, not the state.

Property is sovereignty, a measure of freedom. Paul Elmer More declared that the right to property is more important than the right to life.

Never fear, Ticker, liberals who have gone before have not been idle on this important front. Things have been mapped out—the Nation surveyed in ways George Washington would have never imagined. Ho ho.

Let that be our introduction—next time the main body of the course. I am called to the People's business. Continue to save the planet, boy (but don't forget to have the deed signed over to us).

Your proprietary uncle,

RED

Letter the Sixty-ninth

~

Dear Ticker,

"DORM FLOORS SHAMED." Great headline, page one! Dan is the blue-box weighmaster. Sounds like our boy is on the team. Everyone is still "heavy into saving the monkeys." Outstanding, son.

We must, of course, graduate to bigger things soon, put some heavier artillery into the field. But, for now, let's sit back and enjoy the show, let Dan's deeds, baby steps that they are, take their toll. We can use the time to catch up on your education.

Animals and the Earth—

"Property," where were we? The Nation surveyed, I believe—like George Washington never dreamed. But before I spread out the maps, a little recent history.

When I was a young congressman, we liberals faced a difficult task in this Animals and Earth business: to unseat conservatism, the home of *conservation*. It was the Adversary's issue, Ticker. Artful leaps were required to take it away, new thinking, a revolution.

Let us begin with the Adversary's position, so that you, young man, may gain full appreciation of the coup pulled off by Redtape and others before you.

Here is William F. Buckley, Jr., the archetypic Adversary stating their position:

> *"[C]onservatives [support] the natural order of pri-*
> *orities while of course remaining sensible to our ob-*
> *ligation to preserve the vital organs of our planet....*
> *It is essentially conservative to conserve, whether*
> *we speak of energy or timberland, elephants or bald eagles."*

"[N]atural order of priorities." Ha! He means man, made in the image of God, dominion over the earth, and all that. There is the weak link, Ticker: man conserving for himself and future generations. We went them one better. "Environmentalism": conserving for the Animals and the Earth *itself*. Is not that a grander goal? Conservation pales by comparison.

Imagine this: half of North America returned to wilderness, great islands of pristine, primitive Perfection. No humans allowed! Around these wilderness islands, envision buffer zones with Robert Redford views: limited access (to the wise and famous). Ordinary people would live in "zones of cooperation," the outermost circles.

Now, picture wilderness corridors connecting all the wilderness islands, esthetically completing the scheme (joining U.S. states and other countries *together*, into one supreme body). Are you starting to get it?

Guess who would control all the wilderness land all across the U.S., my boy? Guess who would control all the buffer zones crisscrossing the U.S states and other countries? Don't say it out loud: (*bigger and bigger and bigger* BIG NANNA). Shh! Most people are not really ready for this. Let us speak softly, now.

The above vision is quietly being pursued, as it has

been for some time. It has surfaced, of late, as the "Wildlands Project," a plan put forth by a nonprofit organization (with legal foundation and affiliations to a *world* of like-minded groups). But, really, no humans can take credit. The president of Wildlands said so himself:

> *"The oracles are the fishes of the river ... and articulate toads. Our naturalists and conservation biologists can help us translate their utterances...."*

How can anyone argue with fishes and toads? Who but liberal naturalists and conservation biologists could "translate their utterances?" Ha ha.

You're incredulous, Ticker. I don't blame you. "Wildlands" sounds a little too wild. Well, listen up, my boy. We've already come a long way.

The U.S. Senate, in 1973, ratified the United Nations' World Heritage Convention, agreeing to manage places designated as World Heritage Sites (environmentally important, beautiful, historic) in accordance with UN objectives.

It sounds like a pipe dream, I know, World Heritage Sites all over the globe, a vast network. Who could possibly coordinate such a thing, across so many boundaries, against so many laws?

Meet the IUCN, International Union for Conservation of Nature and Natural Resources (an advisory body to the United Nations). Among its purposes: *"promoting alternative models for sustainable communities and lifestyles, based in ecospiritual [fancy word for Pantheism] practice and principles...."* The IUCN, formed

in 1948, has succeeded in knitting together 74 governments, 105 government agencies, and 700 nongovern-
mental organizations. I'm sure you're way ahead of
me, boy.

The IUCN is tireless, behind the scenes, working to
implement not only the UN World Heritage Convention but the UN Man and Biosphere Program and numerous other initiatives. The IUCN, allied with our
own Environmental Protection Agency and private
groups such as the Sierra Club and Earth First, is also
a force behind, you guessed it, the "Wildlands" vision.

In 1996 the IUCN was further empowered to do its
work, by the 42nd president of the United States. He,
by executive order, granted IUCN "privileges and
immunities ... from suit." The President lifted the
IUCN above U.S. law.

What progress? Sixty-seven UN World Heritage
Sites and Biosphere Reserves occupying 50 million
acres have been established in the U.S. It's a start—
every acre owned or controlled by the federal government in accordance with UN objectives. A piece of
the puzzle, son, but only one. UN initiatives are not
the only thrust.

On a single day in 1996, standing alone, invoking
the near hundred-year-old Antiquities Act, the 42nd
President of the U.S., by presidential proclamation,
turned nearly two million acres of U.S. ground into a
National monument, putting it under Big Nanna's
protection and control. "The Grand Staircase-Escalante
National Monument" in Utah: nearly two million acres
under federal control with the stroke of a pen.

That's just one day in the life of this president, son.

He has millions more acres to his credit, obtained for Big Nan in similar ways—and he has birthed bigger plans, by far, reaching beyond his administration into the 21st century.

The 42nd President established, by executive order, the American Heritage Rivers Initiative, modeled on the UN World Heritage Sites: rivers and their basins nominated to receive the special help and protection of a plethora of federal agencies (and of course come under their control). A couple dozen rivers *and their basins*—read carefully—could be half of the United States.

These are only a few highlights, Ticker, but enough for you to see the balance quietly shifting away from state-owned and private property to Big Nanna. Your monkey business and blue boxes are tiny steps, boy, but still part of the big journey. Forest and trees, son. Are you starting to see the forest?

Next time: *personal property,* portable private wealth. Land is not the only thing that can be a nuisance in private hands.

Your acquisitive uncle,

RED

Letter the Seventieth

~

Dear Ticker,

Don't read too much into it. PJ probably saw an ad in the paper and got curious, that's all. I doubt a sermon on *animal rights* is going to do anyone much harm.

This is entertainment not religion, Ticker, perhaps even salutary for Dan just now. You've said our boy stopped going to church. Well, here is something to fill up that space, a fine substitute—I know this church, the big one downtown. Hot topics, a minister who's *with it*. Reverend Pierre. Dan can join, if he likes.

Remember, Ticker, a Troob must keep many balls in the air. If they ever came down all at once—a secular-cum-Pantheist political creed and Judaism or Christianity all hitting the ground—the Troob would have too much dissonance to bear, probably fall into despair. Few would grit their teeth and become consistent, like Sartre or me. How many could stare into the abyss?

So they juggle—but I've spoken to you of all this before. Don't worry. This is a natural part of leaving the dorm room, getting into the field. Go to church with your pals. Take it in stride. Think of it as a lecture with odd special effects, nothing more.

How can I be so confident? As I said, boy, I know this particular church and minister. I've attended myself, near election time, while visiting the college. Not that this church is that unusual. I've seen them all over.

The most staunch of the Adversary agree with me on this: lite-Christianity is not only no threat, it is serving our cause. Listen to Malcolm Muggeridge, defender of Christianity, arch Adversary, a convert from liberalism. What a loss for our side.

Muggeridge, in his own words:

> "It is, indeed, among Christians themselves that the final decisive assault on Christianity has been mounted; led by the Protestant churches, but with Roman Catholics eagerly, if belatedly, joining in the fray. All they had to show was that when Jesus said that his kingdom was not of this world, He meant that it was. Then moving on from there, to stand the other basic Christian propositions similarly on their heads. As, that to be carnally minded is life; that it is essential to lay up treasure on earth...."

Liberalism finds its most unlikely allies in men of the cloth, Ticker. Stand in awe at the plasticity of the human mind, and smile. Perhaps it is the Devil, himself, behind it, boy. Ho ho.

Go to church, by all means—maybe you can figure out what makes these new-wave ministers tick? Keep an eye on our Dan, but I'm sure he'll be fine.

I must delay our lesson on personal property once more. I've given more time to this than it deserves.

Your equanimous uncle,

RED

Letter the Seventy-first

~

Dear Ticker,

Dan got somber during the singing but perked up with the sermon and the animal-sensitivity session after—what did I say? No problem. Dan had to cross this bridge, sooner or later. Better with his pals at his side, Reverend Pierre at the pulpit, than back home in his steel-town church surrounded by family and friends.

This is a milestone, my boy. Dan is integrating his past and present. *Synergising,* as the psychologists say.

Ticker, your thoughts on New Age ministers are interesting. But the problem you uncover—"Redtape's dilemma," as you call it—is an illusion. Let's sort it out.

Your *given* is correct, and useful review. Liberalism, in practice, is indeed a cycle of negation, constant rebellion—the perpetual dismantling of society to be put back together differently. Always tearing down to rebuild, in pursuit of Utopia.

Your *assumptions* are also sound. Rebellion must have something to rebel against, and a base of operations. Liberals must have something against which to swing the wrecking ball, and a place to stand while they swing it. The existing social order is both target and base of operations for the wrecking crew—the existing order becoming evermore liberal as it is continually remade.

Your *conclusion*: In the end, the liberal wrecking ball

has no one left to strike but the rebels themselves and nothing left to destroy but the ground upon which they stand—at this point, of course, in liberal theory Utopia emerges.

Reverend Pierre is, then, you argue, perhaps particularly astute, picking Christianity, an enduring ground in Western civilization, on which to plant his liberal feet. He has a place to stand until the last remnant of the city falls around him, and Utopia rises from the rubble.

A novel thought, Ticker, but, as you say, one raising difficulties—we will skip over that you have probably vastly overestimated Reverend Pierre.

Now, to the chase: Your analysis reveals, you say, a practical dilemma, one that in its insolubility ultimately defeats liberalism itself.

You correctly point out that uncle Red does not subscribe to the Troobic notion of Perfection. Nor do you. What actually comes about through liberal politics is not Perfection but difference, better for some, worse for others (better for *us*, worse for *them*). There is no Utopia. The moon is not made of green cheese.

"*Redtape's dilemma*: absent a Utopian epiphany, a total liberal victory turns liberalism upon itself." If Utopia doesn't emerge, we become toast in our own toaster. Nowhere to stand, burning ourselves.

You cite the French Revolution as a case in point: rebellion proceeding until there is nothing left to attack but your comrades in arms, who have nothing left to attack but you. Chaos emerges triumphant, at least for a while. Napoleon, one way or the other, being the most likely rebirth of order and civilization.

This is first-rate thought. I'm proud of you, boy, even

though your analysis is flawed. You assume that at some point—discounting a conservative triumph—liberalism must prevail. Why? Who says we ever have to be so stupid as to really win? Perhaps the French Revolution failed because it succeeded too well.

Liberalism need not in reality be the straight line that it is in theory. It can be a pragmatic circle that goes on forever, a merry-go-round (everyone down below switching horses, things changing but staying the same). We rediscover the genius of Old Ned. No *enlightened* zealot was he, no Utopian. Nor am I. The trick is *not* to kill the goose that lays the golden eggs, just keep her from getting big enough to keep them herself or give them away to others. Ho ho.

What you have articulated, my boy, is not the fatal flaw in liberalism but the difference between the hardball liberal elite and the Troobs. The Troobs might mindlessly march to the end of liberalism, and scream for Napoleon to restore order when Utopia misses its cue. But not me, my boy, not by a mile.

Let's get back to business, now. I'm overdue on your personal property lesson, and the school year is all but over. How time flies! However, I really must postpone once more. Duty calls. The Adversary is far from leaving us no one to attack but ourselves. Ha ha. Next time, more on property. I promise We must get back to practical politics, son, get our feet back on the present and plentiful Adversarial ground. Puns intended.

Your irrepressible uncle,

RED

Letter the Seventy-second

~

Dear Ticker,

Dan bought PJ a new rat—amazing. She named it Billy, after the 42nd president, her hero. Dan never even snickered. I'm not sure I could have managed that myself. We have turned the corner, my boy. Who could ask for more?

Now, to our long-delayed subject, personal property. Private, portable wealth.

Wealth, of any sort, son, in any considerable amount in private hands weighs against the state. Money, stocks, bonds, art treasures, they all weigh in the checks and balances—they weigh but not so heavily as land and its attachments.

Land engenders responsibility, roots, and reality. Distilled conservatism. Portable wealth does not carry this conservative curse.

Portable wealth engenders none of the deep involvement that comes with the land. A man owning stock in a company is technically an owner, but unlike most landholders he is not a manager. He is unaware of the company's state of repair or of working conditions. He reads reports, window dressing beyond the numbers. Stocks, like bonds and annuities, are a source of income, seldom more. As for money, itself? Well, boy, "a fool and his money are soon parted."

Portable wealth has an insubstantial quality, Ticker, that makes it less troublesome for the state than land. It is less practical, less permanent, less binding. Nonetheless, it reduces dependence on government for protections and services, and it gives a person a certain sense of freedom—the larger danger by far— at odds with the gray compliance required for the smooth running of the social machine.

I exclude here, of course, members of the liberal elite, who run on the inside track—understanding the race and its outcome—not about to get out of line. Remember Old Ned's merry-go-round. I'm speaking here of those on the wheel, not up above.

Big Nanna must protect herself from portable wealth, but not nearly as vigorously as against the possession of land. Exploitation is as important as control, when it comes to portable wealth—and we've got it down to a science, son.

First, striking personal property at its source, are progressive taxes. Nearly 40% of the average worker's income is stripped immediately away. Taxes: federal, state, local, sales.... One hundred dollars earned is nearer fifty (and government grows).

If a worker invests, the remainder is savaged again by taxes on capital gains (defeating the miracle of compound interest, by which many people over a lifetime might become well-off and fail to need government old-age programs).

Inheritance taxes complete the gauntlet that personal—as well as real—property must run, cutting an estate down to size before it is passed on (the game starts over).

Complicated inheritance laws—including those that allow our family to escape inheritance taxes entirely—allow another large bite to be taken by accountants and lawyers (who regularly make donations).

A result of all this is that both parents in most households must work (creating the need for child-care programs, expanded school and social services).

That's a rough sketch, Ticker—you see how it works—and you'd think it would be enough to check the individual, but no. People, in spite of all this, build up small fortunes. They work round the clock, they invent, they save.

Some prosper and begin to do charitable work, endow libraries, put up the money for public parks—trespassing in Big Nanna's backyard.

Some of these *nouveau riche* even get into politics, spending their own money to further conservatism. At least our friends in the press scold them for this. Spending their *own* money in a civic pursuit. Tsk tsk.

So, more taxation is needed, but we must tread lightly now. Elected officials have done, openly, all that can be expected. They, like the IRS, have aroused some ire in even the somnolent masses. There may be a few bites left in the sin-tax apple, down the slippery slope to sport vehicles and high-fat food.... But, beyond that, little more. Time for the shadow government to take over.

Liberal judges and bureaucrats levy taxes—by other names—without the encumbrance of statute or representation: public expenditures ordered for everything from licenses, permits, and fines to required purchases of products and services (our agendas hidden within).

And still, it is not enough. What's left? Personal property is more than money, son. Things! The government can take *things* away too—in ways you wouldn't believe. We're talking lawful seizure, my boy, not "taxes." Ho ho.

You probably have the RICO statute and mobsters in mind. That's just what you're supposed to think, son. It's better than that. Seizure has gotten a life of its own.

There are over 200 federal statutes under which government agents can seize and keep property, some with thresholds as low as *alleged* criminal activity. No due process required. It makes a headline, here and there. But seizures attack no unified group, little chance of organized opposition. People think it won't happen to them.

Concluding Property 101, Ticker, from Earth and Animals to paychecks and Picassos: Put government on one side of the scale, individuals on the other. The liberal imperative, by whatever means—it will be your turn soon to be creative—is to transfer wealth, that's property real and personal, to Big Nanna's side. Absent that, transfer it to state or local governments. As a last resort, simply limit wealth on the individual side, but not too much. Remember, we've got to have someone to tax. Power, son, is what is really being weighed and balanced. Property is simply its repository.

Your bare-knuckled uncle,

RED

Letter the Seventy-third

~

Dear Ticker,

Good question, boy—I see you have taken my advice about diving into books for political pearls. I see no reason we can't spare the time for this. All goes well with Dan. Though we must expand our horizons soon.

Yes, Tocqueville addressed the subject of my last letter—balancing power, individual and state—and proposed a conservative solution. Not to worry, he was wrong. It is actually quite amusing.

Alexis de Tocqueville recognized the political power of private property, wielded by aristocrats in Europe. Aristocrats, he observed, are often powerful individuals, not easily oppressed. "[S]uch persons," he said, "restrain a government within general habits of moderation and reserve." He further observed, way back in the 19th century, Ticker, that America was short on aristocrats, and that by temperament we didn't want any. An imbalance of power favoring government would emerge, he feared.

Tocqueville thought, however, the imbalance would be forestalled by great private corporations rising up to fill the aristocratic gap. Corporations standing up to government would keep it in check. Ho ho. He must have known little of professional managers, their general temperament and fear of risk.

Corporations, happily, did not grow up to be guard dogs. They became cocker spaniels, my boy, not Doberman pinschers. Executives quake at the name of Big Nanna, intimidated by complex taxes, rules, and regulations. A visit from the IRS, FDA, OSHA, or dozens of other federal policing agencies, turns corporate blood cold.

Corporate lobbyists groveling for government crumbs—sweetheart contracts, less regulation, tax breaks, barriers to competition—abound. But nowhere are Tocqueville's Davids willing to face Goliath. Not one in a thousand.

Prescient as Tocqueville was, most of the time, he missed this one by far. Not only did corporations not rise up as a form of American aristocracy, a most unlikely group of others did. Rabid Big Nanna fans, tipping the balance even further her way.

Who could have foreseen the latter-day American aristocracy, a liberal elite: the progeny, got-wise, of titans like Old Ned, Joe Kennedy, John D. Rockerfeller, and Henry Ford, second in social rank only to motion picture and television stars? Beneath this pantheon, an army of knights: preeminent journalists, professors, and ministers.

Not only did Tocqueville's champion, the corporation, not take the field, Big Nanna supporters filled the void. Ha ha. The demon history, son. You can ride it, but you can never predict the buckjumps and rolls.

Your bronc-busting uncle,

RED

Letter the Seventy-fourth

~

Dear Ticker,

Don't get cocky! Yes, we are "running rings" around the Adversary—you ride high with your pals and are winning over our Dan. Even so, you must be vigilant.

Remember the hare and the tortoise. The Adversary—deep within Dan and not him alone—is back there in the dust, plodding along. Look sharp, my boy.

Private property, as you say, is under control. There is not much left to take—unless children, as well as both parents, go to work. Ho ho. But that does not mean we can coast.

The most important property remains outside our control, a *property* of the mind: independence. America still has acres of it, in out-of-the-way places far from the cultural centers most of the time, but there. Sometimes I think it is in the genes brought by the American settlers and by the waves of immigrants ever since.

Independence, son, is a dangerous snake and difficult to kill. Study the state flag of Texas, boy, and be sobered, take warning. "Remember the Alamo!" Do not be so cavalier. So long as a few people think and act autonomously, we are at risk.

Usurpation of physical property encourages but does not ensure docility. The final property, indepen-

232 · LEE WHIPPLE

dence, is the most dangerous of all—and not yet fully in hand.

How do we take a property of the mind? We graduate with this question to the higher math of politics, young man. The answer is artfully, artfully. Taking land and treasure requires only the heart and mind of a thief. Taking a person's autonomy requires the artist's imagination. Listen closely. I'm about to tell you what few people know.

After indoctrination in the public schools, after religion is stripped away, after people have been made totally dependent on government, after private property is all in government hands, after every plank of statism is nailed firmly in place, after the fire of "liberty and justice for all" is put out, *arbitrary power* must still be exercised.

Fire prevention, my boy. Family inspections, obedience drills, smoke detectors that sniff out the unpolitically correct, firebreaks against independence around the town hall, the church, and the home....

Care must be taken, however. In democracies *overt* oppression is a fatal error: velvet along with the iron is required. Object lessons in subservience to the state could be open and brutal in the old Soviet Union, the Third Reich—no imagination at all. But even in these totalitarian states, overt oppression proved in the long run unwise.

The trick is to make people kneel *for their own good*:

Make people wear helmets on motorcycles, then on bicycles and roller skates.... *Force* people to wear safety belts. Their lives, as Saint Dewey taught, belong to the state. How dare they risk what is not their own!

Forbid people from owning and carrying guns, even though research shows that guns in the hands of citizens deter crime. People must never be allowed to protect themselves. That is government's job.

Change the law, arbitrarily making offenses against favored groups more serious than crimes against others: "hate crimes." Dispense justice relatively, *enforcing* preferences.

Insure people's homes in flood planes and hurricane alleys, against all common sense. Teach them to trust Big Nanna—to fear neither God nor nature.

Establish how much people should weigh and what they should eat—asserting the state's will into every corner of private life—and change the standards with regularity. Subtle expressions of state control.

Tell people how to raise their children and how many they should have and what is best for the child's mental health....

Ticker, one day people will walk off cliffs if no guardrail is there, *knowing* that if it were dangerous the government would not have let them do it. Independent thought and action, a thing of the past. Imagine being one of the keepers when such things come to pass, the power and control....

But, once again, I get carried away. Somnambulation is but an ideal, of course. Somnolence, a sleepy state of suggestible subordination, will do: the final property, if not taken away, at least muted and under control.

The progress made by the liberal saints, our dominance today, is only the beginning, son. A brave new world lies ahead for those with the vision, courage, and energy to choose it.

There is work to do, my boy. No sleeping in, not for you: let this letter be your wake-up call. No more premature talk of victory. The complacent, as well as the fainthearted, finish last.

Your rousing uncle,

RED

Letter the Seventy-fifth

~

Dear Ticker,

Yes, time to expand. But I cannot choose the subject for you. You are no longer in the dorm room—you must catch a wave, "go with the flow." Expediency, my boy, is the mother of all liberal action. Whatever moves you Left.

I will, however, offer some guidance, in the form of a poem by Robert Louis Stevenson. His motives were black, to be sure, but his advice is white:

> *Four reformers met under a bramble bush. They were all agreed the world must be changed. "We must abolish property," said one.*
>
> *"We must abolish marriage," said the second.*
>
> *"We must abolish God," said the third.*
>
> *"I wish we could abolish work," said the fourth.*
>
> *"Do not let us get beyond practical politics," said the first. "The first thing is to reduce men to a common level."*
>
> *"The first thing," said the second, "is to give freedom to the sexes."*
>
> *"The first thing," said the third, "is to find out how to do it."*
>
> *"The first step," said the first, "is to abolish the Bible."*

"The first thing," said the second, "is to abolish the laws."

"The first thing," said the third, "is to abolish mankind."

Timeless wisdom, son.

Hillary Rodham, wife of the 42nd President, at the outset of her brilliant career—the man behind the throne, as it were—said it for her generation. Hillary, addressing her graduating class at Wellesly:

"[F]or too long our leaders have used politics as the art of the possible....

We're not interested in social reconstruction; it's human reconstruction."

Abolish God, abolish mankind....

Do whatever is opportune, Ticker, but *know*, as did Hillary and the four reformers and the liberal saints before them, what you are ultimately about.

Your wise uncle,

RED

PART FOUR: SEPARATING THE WHEAT FROM THE TARES

"There exist standards to which we may repair; man is not perfectible, but he may achieve a tolerable degree of order, justice, and freedom...."

—Russell Kirk
The Conservative Mind

Letter the Seventy-sixth

~

Dear Ticker,

Things move too fast. But I don't see how it can be avoided. I'm not blaming you.

Let's sort this out—

A black law student, a conservative, has started a one-man movement against college admission and hiring preferences—shades of the famed California civil rights initiative—speaking to all who will listen, quoting California's Ward Connerly, *the black Judas*: "shall not discriminate against, or grant preferential treatment to, *any* individual...."

The Lovelies, Mr. Bow Tie, and the yellow dog are outraged, of course. But Dan had to go and make friends with this miscreant—Reginald Strong, I believe you said was his name—and has invited him to meet with your group. This is going to be tricky, Ticker.

You can bet this fellow will argue that blacks will never gain true equality until they compete straight up. As long as the game is rigged for them, their achievements will be discounted in others' minds. This Strong wants real equality for himself and his race. He wants respect, not preference.

What we have here, my boy, is a liberal sheep bolting the flock—more dangerous to the liberal cause than a dozen black radicals torching L.A. This fellow doesn't get it. He won't play the game.

Invite other blacks to your meeting with him, to heckle. Choose blacks who oppose Clarence Thomas being on the Supreme Court—there are plenty around. They will know how to shout a black conservative down: "Uncle Tom," "toady," "traitor...." Say nothing yourself. Keep your place. This is about racial equality. Blacks only may speak.

Make doubly sure of your hecklers by selecting bad students. They are dependent on special privileges and inflated grades. Trust me, they will fight fiercely against any suggestion of real equality.

White bigots in the south, not long ago, argued for white preference in the same way. Blacks are just people, Ticker. They'll fight to keep their advantage. We of the liberal elite, black and white, need only encourage them (to remain liberal sheep).

That's right, son. Blacks in the liberal elite stand with us. Many would lose their advantage or their constituencies if equality were ever really achieved. They actually have more of a stake in maintaining black sheep than you or I. Jesse Jackson, for instance, without his sheep, might have to work for a living.

Counsel Dan, in advance. Tell him you think this Strong fellow is an opportunist, trying to curry favor with whites. Disgusting. Ask Dan to reserve judgment until he hears what some *real* blacks have to say.

Your fair-minded uncle,

RED

Letter the Seventy-seventh

~

Dear Ticker,

I really don't understand guys like this Strong. Why does he want to upset the applecart? Why must he earn what someone will *give* him?

We must, of course, face reality, however strange.

It sounds like RS held his own, converted one of the hecklers and hung on to Dan—did far better than I expected. And he comes back next week for round two. This will test your mettle, son.

Let us prepare, Ticker. Mr. Strong could do even better next time *if* we give him the chance. You must be ready for him, boy.

At least the law is with us. *Brown vs. the Board of Education* and the Civil Rights Act have been morphed into lawful preferences. In 1979 the Supreme Court, *United Steelworkers of America vs. Weber*, made it official. Preferences are legal. Judges *evolving* the law— what would we do without them?

The real victory, of course, was in the Public Mind: "nondiscrimination" became "racial balance" became "equal opportunity" became "affirmative action" became "goals," "quotas," "preferences," and, coming soon, "equality of outcomes."

But now, the Adversary has come to life and is trying to turn back the clock to 1964, to the Civil Rights Act and "nondiscrimination," *no* preferences. Leading the charge are some prominent blacks, Thomas Sowell, Clarence Thomas, Ward Connerly—the ingrates— arguing for *actual* equality, giving uppity ideas to others in the younger generation, like Reginald Strong. They call for *evidence* of discrimination, before remedy. I know what you're thinking, Ticker, but it won't work, not with Mr. Strong.

Don't dare argue the underrepresentation of blacks in high places, or low performance in others, as *proof* of discrimination. I know, it's liberal doctrine, but it won't fly here. Guys like RS have thought this through.

The same argument was used in reverse—no black plantation owners—to prove inferiority of blacks in the old south. You see the problem? Our argument is really old Dixie, stood on its head. This won't stand cool analysis. It requires hot blood. You'll end up looking silly if you try this on someone like Strong (you can't cheat an honest man, my boy, one who wants nothing from you but what you owe).

The debate, the one you must avoid, might go something like this—

You charge discrimination in, let's say, lending, citing the fact that blacks are turned down for mortgages more often than whites. There must be a prejudicial hurdle! Has to be....

RS will stop you right there. It follows, he'll say— or I've misread the fellow—that blacks, based on this alleged superior credit required for them to get loans, should default less than whites. But, they don't. The rate is the same. It appears bank standards are sound, and are being applied equally to all—just the sort of numbers game your Dan would relish.

"Aha!" you say, thinking yourself clever. "Blacks *really* aren't as qualified as whites! This is worse yet, a broader, endemic discrimination has caused the poor credit. Now you are trapped, Ticker. You have moved from check into checkmate.

You say blacks in general have weaker credit because of discrimination. How do you know? A moment ago, by the same logic, you were charging a different form of discrimination, but that turned out not to be so. Perhaps you're wrong here *too*. You have blundered into establishing the need for evidence.

Poor performance, or underrepresentation, doesn't *prove* discrimination any more than it *proved* inferiority. Both arguments are unsupported theories, the fallacy of *objectionable cause*. Discrimination turns the wheel one way, preference the other. Either way, it never stops spinning, and no one ever knows.

RS would stop the spin, both ways, insisting on equality *and nothing more*. Those blacks who succeed could look others in the eye, and open the door for more to do so, and for those to help others....

Playing a straight wheel, RS might conclude, may be difficult for blacks, but playing a crooked wheel, for or against them, is impossible: as self-respecting men and women, blacks, barefoot or slipped into wingtips and high heels, on a crooked wheel lose.

Debate will get you nowhere, Ticker. Strong has the high ground, demanding fairness and refusing preference, claiming preference either way in the long term does harm. What are you going to tell him?

"No, blacks are really inferior, after all, and need

special help from whites." I don't think so. You might suggest that Strong, like Clarence Thomas, Thomas Sowell, Michael Jordan, Berry Gordy, Booker T. Washington, Frederick Douglas, George Washington Carver, Scott Joplin ..., is the exception to the rule. Uhn-uh.

Don't dream of debating it, Ticker.

It's a buzz saw—you'll end up as kindling.

Getting discouraged, boy? Well, let me show you what else is in store if Strong gets the offensive—gets to stop fending off hecklers and makes his case. It gets worse.

Something interesting happened around 1960—you remember our discussion of Welfare—about the time government started helping the poor, including large numbers of blacks: illegitimacy, after climbing from 3% in 1920 to about 5% in 1960, shot up to 30% in the 90s, black illegitimacy nearly 70%! A similar story might be told about crime. "Subsidy and preference have not born good fruit," RS might say.

No proof, of course. We could argue that it would have been worse without Big Nanna's efforts—but approaching 70% illegitimacy, it gets difficult.

Finally, Mr. Strong may argue from history. Thomas Sowell has made an international study of government-mandated preference for special groups and discovered patterns difficult to dismiss:

• Preferences, even when explicitly identified as temporary, tend to persist and expand—the U.S., after nearly a half century's experience, is no exception.

• Group polarization tends to increase, non preferred versus preferred, ranging in outcome from hostility to mob violence and civil war.

Ticker, this is just a sample of the debate terrain, the landscape we must avoid. How? When cornered, my boy, get politically correct. Attack! *Pro* minority or *anti* Western civilization and the U.S. Since one of these is the subject, already, and going badly, we must shift to the other. It's time to hate America, son.

The segue couldn't be better: "What about slavery?"

George Washington and Thomas Jefferson owned slaves! The U.S. Constitution allowed slavery, counting blacks as three-fifths of a person! America is the enemy of blacks, a cauldron of hypocrisy, illegitimate power, oppression, and deprivation. "That's the *real* issue, what we *should* be talking about."

Preferences, in a burst of emotion, will be transformed from public policy into penance for the past. Making up for past wrongs will become the focus, not complex questions of legality and effectiveness.

The question is not one of civil rights: the question is whether the white race should be let out of the stocks and allowed not to pay for the sins of the past....

In case you think I am overstating the power of *slavish* emotion to eclipse the discussion of civil rights, listen to this: A Jewish professor at the University of Pennsylvania commented that he, like many blacks, was a descendent of slaves, his race having belonged at one time to Pharaoh. Black students complained, the gall of a white professor assuming ex-slave status!

Under pressure, the professor apologized—not good enough for the students. The Black Student League demanded resignation. A second apology was made and rejected. The professor was suspended for two semesters and required to attend sensitivity training. Believe what Uncle Red tells you. Slavery is dynamite. RS will be blown right off his soapbox, his arguments about current admissions and hiring lost in the noise and smoke.

Get things started, but let some of your new black pals step in and vilify America for slavery. Be careful not to overplay your hand. Keep your place. Wait until the charges have all been made against whites and the United States. That's your cue to step forward: confess, ask forgiveness, be willing to make amends.... Preferences will suddenly make Perfect sense.

Your resourceful uncle,

RED

Letter the Seventy-eighth

~

Dear Ticker,

We got the most votes, but Strong got the vote we wanted most. He was shouted down, but Dan stuck with him. The third and final round, next week. Mr. Strong must move on, spreading his gospel elsewhere.

Good riddance—I hope not too late.

Dan is brooding again, and just when things were going so well. Rats!

Didn't I tell you? The world outside the dorm room can be difficult to manage. *C'est la vie!* We've been here before with our boy. Two steps forward, one back....

Take heart. Redtape's bag of tricks is not empty.

To your general question. Yes, Strong's history is sound. I was betting he, like most young Americans these days, was ignorant of the revolutionary period, but no luck. I underestimated him, son. He ought to go into politics—and let's hope he does not.

The late 17th century frame RS placed around slavery, the nearby Haitian revolution—an estimated 100,000 whites and 60,000 blacks reported dead in a bitter racial struggle—was a fine touch. I have to hand it to him. Puts things in the strange light of the time. Washington, Adams, Jefferson, all feared a black revolt. Tocqueville, in his observations of America, expressed the same fear, a civil war if slavery were suddenly abolished, ending in the "extermination of one or the other of the two races." A point for RS.

It sounds like you hit back hard, son, bloodying Thomas Jefferson. Yet TJ came out surprisingly well. The quote Strong used points up that the Founding Fathers, as well as the blacks, were born into slavery: *"We have the wolf by the ears, and we can neither hold him, nor safely let him go."* The FF's believed instant abolition would lead to vagrancy and poverty, if not war.

Jefferson established a school to ready his slaves for freedom, introduced legislation in Virginia to bring about gradual abolition, and proposed a federal law in Congress—lost by a single vote—banning slavery in the Western territories....

The criticism of Jefferson for owning slaves—perhaps sexual relations with a slave girl—are blunted by the rounded tale. The charges, so robust in isolation, falter somewhat in context. Too complex for good theater.

RS was smart, declining to defend Jefferson. He simply put things in context. It's hard in full light to make TJ out as a monster.

In the end, the slave girl will be remembered and cast her shadow. We come out slightly ahead, tarnishing if not tarring our man (too bad it had to be the Founder who seemed a budding liberal at times).

Others of the Founders, yes it's true, spoke out against slavery. Washington, Adams, Hamilton, Madison, Franklin....

> *"There is not a man living who wishes more sincerely than I do, to see a plan adopted for the abolition of it* [slavery]. *"*—George Washington

"Every measure of prudence, therefore, ought to be assumed for the eventual total extirpation of slavery from the United States...."—John Adams

It's difficult to paint the FF's as weak willed or merely expedient with statements like that.

More important—the strongest point RS scored—the FF's laid the groundwork for the end of the slave trade and for gradual abolition within the states. They were careful in the Constitution never to condone or legitimize slavery—even the "three-fifths compromise" established blacks as human beings. A concession, believe it or not, from the hardline Southerners of the time.

All true, Ticker. The FF's compromised, attempting to form the Union, strangle slavery, and avoid a civil war. A political hat trick.

Indeed, my boy, they almost pulled it off—credit where credit is due, just between you and me. Their strategy worked for awhile. The slave trade was ended, followed by abolition in many states. The battle over the extension of slavery into the territories was joined. Free blacks increased, north and south, after the Revolution. Then the Civil War came, not the war the FF's had feared, it's twin brother.

Frederick Douglas, the great black spokesman of Lincoln's time—RS scores again—argued much as the Founders had: *"My argument against the dissolution of the American Union is this: It would place the slave system more exclusively under the control of the slave holding states, and withdraw it from the power in the Northern states which is opposed to slavery...."*

If the FF's had failed to bring the south into the

Union, in the first place, they would have strengthened slavery. By compromising, they weakened it. The FF's had to be gradualists and compromise with slave holders or recklessly risk missing all three hat-trick wickets: 1) no Union, 2) slavery unbridled in the south, 3) racial war.

There is no point in arguing against this case, Ticker. If we persist, our hecklers might calm down and start listening to RS. Strong has survived, but the hostility toward him is solidly intact. Quite a feat, actually, surviving, the deck stacked as it was. I have a grudging respect for this man. I wish he were on our side.

I love-hated his conclusion best, son, cleverly shifting the ground to the larger question, onto a moral plain. The fellow is good. He ended up talking about slavery in general, moving beyond black and white, robbing emotion. Blacks owned blacks in America, and sold them in the first place. Indians owned other Indians and whites. Whites have owned whites in other places and times....

Slavery, itself, becomes the issue, not black and white. If our hecklers had failed us here, RS might have gotten back to preferences. Finally, he was shouted down.

Count round two a draw: we took every pawn, but RS has our bishop, Dan. Enough of this skirmishing. We must direct our final effort at Strong's underlying principles, his foundation.

We will mount an attack on his king, conservatism itself. Topple the king, my boy, and all the other pieces fall with it. If we take the sovereign—the standard bearer—the game is over and Dan is restored to our side. Redtape has a plan.

Round two has given us the opening: the Founders on two of the three wickets of their hat trick *failed.*

Our rook attacks from the Left—

Assert (RS will agree) that the Founders were Conservatism itself: practical, gradual, steeped in the past, suspicious of centralization, distrusting man's nature, trusting God. True, the FF's founded a democracy, but it was only a decentralized *representative* democracy, neither social nor pure.

Washington and his pals may not have invented conservatism, but they embodied it. Son, that puts them right where we want them, between our rook and a hard place, liberalism on one side, slavery and the Civil War on the other. Now we squeeze. Ho ho.

The Founders' attempt to end slavery and avoid civil war failed, *their conservatism failed*—any praise due the U.S. today goes to the liberal saints coming after the Civil War who fixed things, FDR, LBJ....

The charges:

The FF's accepted the world as it was. They formed their new government not on new ideals but on the model of their defeated enemy and on all of Western Civilization past. They did not know the meaning of the word "revolution." They feared real Change. Tories in rebel dress. Their plan to contain and abolish slavery was doomed by their conservatism from the start. Timidity, boy, the curse of conservatism.

Big Nanna, had she been a Founding Father, as it were, would have torn things up and started over—sweeping evils, such as slavery, away. You see the thrust, Ticker? We attack RS where he lives.

The FF's left the states powerful, and the southern

states, of course, used their power against the state. Big Nanna would have neutered the states at the start—forestalling the Civil War.

The FF's—believing not in the Perfectibility of Man and trusting not in pure democracy—distributed power throughout many levels and placed checks upon it. Big Nanna would have flattened the social landscape and concentrated power in a tiny, enlightened elite. This elite would have done the hat trick, formed the union, freed the slaves, kept the peace.

We will pass, Ticker, on defending our original thrust against the Founders, and move on conservatism itself. Portray the human misery of slavery prolonged, and the carnage of the Civil War—fruits of conservatism—and imagine out loud how much better things would have been if an enlightened liberal few, such as the Lovelies, Mr. Bow Tie, and the rest of your pals, had been in charge instead of the Founders.

Imagine yourselves, in three-cornered hats, quickly bringing about a Perfect U.S. Congratulate each other for what would have happened had you been in charge.

Son, it is time for you to enter the fray. Use all that I have taught you. You might even see this as a final exam, rescuing Dan from Reginald Strong. Yes.

Really, this couldn't be better. Baptism by fire. You will be tempered liberal steel when the smoke clears.

Carry on, my boy.

Your resolute uncle,

RED

Letter the Seventy-ninth
~

Dear Ticker,

You thought you'd won, Dan nodding his head amidst the others' cheers.... I want to picture this, before talking damage control—it sounds most extraordinary.

Son, I can't help but admire this fellow. It's rare you meet a conservative so wily. They usually go by the book—come at you head on, beating the drum.

Well, what's done is done.

We aren't whipped, Ticker. It just turned out your final exam has a second page, the one Reginald Strong left behind for you. The fiend!

I want to picture this—

You finished your speech—like Brutus addressing the Roman throng—using all the tricks I have taught you, an unqualified success. Then, quietly, resigned—I start to see him, the scoundrel—Strong rises to take his turn at speaking, playing Mark Antony to your Brutus.

"Friends, Students of the Ivy League, Classmates...."

Ticker, allow me to hyperbolize, magnify the scene, that I might better see. Let me speak as Reginald Strong.

"Friends, Students of the Ivy League, Classmates:

"I might argue the Founders did all against sla-very they could: choosing compromise to forestall conflagration and create a Union bent on freedom one day for all—but I will not do that. The Founders failed: the Civil War came. Black freedom, delayed, was purchased with blood in the end, nothing saved. That much is clear.

"I might point out that the cloudless alternative, put forth by the noble Ticker, bears striking resemblance to the steerage of the old Soviet Union, Red China, North Korea, Cambodia.... But no, I will not trouble you with this. I will not presume to impose the lessons of history.

"I might argue that much that is good in America be credited to the Founders, but this could not be resolved in a month of debate. I leave this ground unplowed.

"Further, I freely admit the stain upon this Nation. I do not argue the perfection of America, then or now. Each in his own heart must weigh the evidence and judge this Land on balance fair or ill. I will not seek Old Glory's vindication.

"Nor will I plead conservatism's case against Ticker's bold denunciation. I came not to speak of abstract politics but of a practical matter, *equality* in our college: to win your support for a justice blind to color and sex.... But I have failed. I must retrace my steps and consider what best can I do to serve in defeat, victory having alluded me.

"I hearken to the advice of Coleridge: 'To go about doing as much *good* as possible.... [B]ut then,' the poet warned, 'in order that you may not sacrifice the real good and happiness of others to your particular views, which may be quite different from your neighbor's, you must do *that* good to others which the reason, common to all, pronounces to be good for all.' Alas, here is the crux of my failure. I came to you bringing the idea of equality of opportunity for *all*, a common good, I thought. But it was not pleasing to your eye—and from this discussion we somehow strayed, this way and that, perhaps through some fault of mine.

"I will not trouble you more, least I bring to you a *good* that is a good to me but not common to all, and break with the counsel I wish to heed.

"But, still, I think I can leave you one small thing, a suggestion, as you pursue the question, for it does persist: what is, then, *good*, what manner of *equality*? I am defeated—but the question is not resolved. We have looked, as Ticker would have us, through a glass darkly into the past and found no common insight, you and I, to guide us in the present: we did not find the *good* that is common to all. What is, then, *good*, what manner of *equality*? That is the question.

"Perhaps—indulge my humble suggestion—it would be wise to defer the more 'colorful' debate, so inflamed with imperfect history, and choose a more contemporary ground upon which to base your query. In this new light—the subject clear and present—an answer beyond debate may emerge: '*that* good to others which the reason, common to all, pronounces to be good for all.' Two birds taken with one stone:

the one nearer with least plumage, first.

"I speak of course of Abortion, Slavery's twin. Our swirling debate takes root in another form, in our own time.

"Compare the absolute rights of woman over unborn child to those of master over slave. Both powers exercised seeming meet, natural and right, to those who would wield them—then and now—both arguing the *right*. Yes, the slave master held forth eloquently in defense of his right, oft quoting Aristotle. His argument, indeed, quite the same as that of the abortion-minded woman or man of today: two forms of human life, one of less value....

"But, all that is for you to pursue. I only suggest this substitution, one issue for another, in essence the same, as a means of resolving the "question": What is, then, *good*, what manner of *equality*? Are some more equal than others? I confine myself to making this suggestion, and defense of my comparison.

"Compare the antiabortion activist and slavery's abolitionist—each on fire in righteous opposition. Both testing the limits of the law.

"Compare the tangles of the law, itself, the various rulings by states, leading to Supreme Court decisions judging it lawful for a man or woman to have unmitigated power over another life, *Dread Scott versus Sanford, Roe verses Wade.* Was liberty upheld, or equality denied? A towering liberty, the rightful mastery of one life over another, was blessed in each case, and,

necessarily, an inequality condoned, a *preference*.
One human life was judged of less value than
another, to be under the other's complete control, even so far as to put the life less valued to
inhuman servitude, or death.

"I will not trouble you further, my friends. I
take my leave, leaving with you the far-ranging
issue—clearing the mists of time and color, I pray.
The question: Where does liberty end and
equality begin? Who should have *preference*?
Where lies '*that* good to others which the reason,
common to all, pronounces to be good for all'?
Farewell. [Exit Reginald Strong.]"

Ho ho. I've come close, haven't I, Ticker?

I can hear the quiet as RS left the room, leaving us
the issue writ large. Strong lost, but we did not win.
His question persists, a foul mist—Slavery and
Abortion joined together at the hip like Siamese twins.
Preference! Bloody plain and awful. He tossed us a
grenade wrapped in lace on his way out the door.

The *issue* was coming, Abortion, sooner or later, of
course, but I wanted it introduced on our terms and
in our terms and when the timing was right....

We are put to the test, Ticker. I am smarting from this,
I admit. Snookered by a mere student.

Let us not get angry but even, a great man once said.
We will follow his advice. Our revenge will be Dan's
ultimate conversion, sweeter for the adversity. Let us
focus on the problem at hand, and prevail!

Damage control first, then victory.

Point One: At least we are left with an issue, not

action in the field. Imagine if we had an abortion clinic on our hands, or worse, an unwed mother making *the choice*. Be glad we can sort this out in theory. Retreat to the dorm room, boy. Keep this abstract.

Point Two: Establish new terms: "choice," "reproductive rights," "medical procedures...." Insist on an antiseptic discourse, clinical and clean. Accuse of sensationalism any who would speak of flesh and blood, descriptions, details, death. Such things are in bad taste, strictly out of bounds.

Point Three: Draw out Mses Jewelry and PJ—their positions are predictable. Defer to them, always. Establish this implicit ground rule: the women are the only ones who can *authentically* speak on this issue. It is the female body, after all, over which the "right-to-life radicals" wish to seize control. This is a private thing, for women to decide....

Search for compromise, and try to change the subject.

Your unbowed uncle,

RED

Letter the Eightieth

~

Dear Ticker,

Dan remains quiet—there but not there. We've seen this before, how many times? The books, frankly, worry me more than the funk. RS, the devil, *would* give Dan a reading list. Burke, Eliot, Muggeridge, Kirk, Lewis, Sowell, Buckley, Bork.... A dirty dozen, the worst.

Someday soon, Ticker, such rabble rousers need to be purged.... But I digress, and raise my blood pressure for naught. It's a free country, yet.

Let Dan read. He'll find these paper mentors difficult and complex compared with liberal thinkers. Conservatives have never mastered the art of simplifying the world. They are always qualifying and entering into areas that could be easily sidestepped. That's part of what keeps them off television and out of the papers.... But, there I go again. Let us get down to business.

Yellow-dog and PJ are opposing abortion—we don't need this right now. RS got to them: "two forms of human life, one of less value...."

We must put this little uprising down, and get on to subjects more congenial. It doesn't pay to dwell on Abortion, anytime, let alone now with Dan half mesmerized by Strong and reading satanic verses, as it were. What next? Ye Gads!

You say Yellow-dog and PJ balk at the basic premise:

the fetus as part of a woman's body. "DNA configura-
tions *unique* at the moment of conception"—that's
splitting hairs. Stand firm, boy. A woman has as much
right to terminate her pregnancy as Van Gogh had to
cut off his ear. His ear, her fetus. Keep it simple, son.

The slippery slope argument—abortion to infanticide
and on to euthanasia—is false. Those teenagers in the
news dumping newborns in trash bins—slaps on the
wrist from the courts—are irrelevant. *Isolated instances,*
nothing to do with abortion.

Likewise, the parallels between early 20th-century
Germany and present-day America are absurd. Yellow-
dog is majoring in history, I take it. Inform him that
the first euthanasia in Germany was not until 1939,
ordered by Adolf Hitler! An aberration, nothing to do
with those 1930s story problems YD cites from the
German public schools. That was "values clarification"
not "seeds of the Holocaust":

> *"How many new housing units could be built
> and how many marriage-allowance loans could be
> given to newly wedded couples for the amount of
> money it costs the state to care for the crippled...?"*

Modern utilitarian views on abortion are a world
away, my boy. Americans aren't ready for euthanasia
(and won't be for some time). Dismiss the slippery
slope as just another "Right-wing paranoid fantasy."

YD's talk of crushed heads, death throes, and such
is out of bounds. You've let him break the rules. These
are *medical procedures*. Remind YD that he is in the Ivy
League—a certain decorum is required. Rend your

clothes, as it were, at such indelicacy.

Recall for YD and PJ that the 42nd President, our hero, vetoed a bill banning even *partial-birth* abortions. Would he have done this if there were anything amiss? Remind your young friends to look up to our nation's role models, show some respect. Don't movie stars campaign all the time for abortion rights? These people are beautiful! How could they be wrong?

Don't debate these things, Ticker. Declare them! Then, before your pals can regroup, attack their thought process. Suggest they refocus upon *how* one should think about Abortion, not *what*. Remind them of the contemporary wisdom of Neil Postman: "*[T]he theologically related legal concept of abortion is undergoing 'selective forgetting' or unlearning....*"

See if Postman can't bring YD and PJ to their senses. We don't have time for this—we need to concentrate on Dan. We've been put on defense, boy. We need to regain the upper hand. Keep me informed.

Your embattled uncle,

RED

Letter the Eighty-first

~

Dear Ticker,

Yellow-dog thinks abortion is "just wrong." PJ wants to know how she can be against the death penalty and for abortion? Dan has come out of his trance and entered the fray, his old steel-town self, defending them both....

Not one step back but twenty—this is a nightmare.

Dan defends Yellow-dog's "just wrong" position with Newman's "Illative Sense"—his extracurricular reading bearing bitter fruit already. Yes, yes, I'm familiar with Newman's "Illative": a knowledge internally derived, beyond "any technical apparatus of words and propositions." Good *sense,* common *sense, sense* of beauty—"Illative *Sense.*" Man's *sense* of good and evil, a built in gyroscope. Superstition! For the Love of Money, what brings this on? Is there a full moon?

Worst of all is Dan's quote from the mysterious Janius: *"There is a moment of difficulty and danger at which flattery and falsehood can no longer deceive, and simplicity itself can no longer be misled."* Abortion, Dan says, has precipitated this moment. Listen to that, Ticker. Dan declares war!

They have all, the rogue-three, come down with religion in its rawest form. The basic stuff—right and wrong, good and evil. They appeal to a transcendent standard, whether they know it or not. This is the road to absolute morality, son, away from relativity and "situational ethics" and liberalism itself.

We must contain this—cut our losses and move on. *Containment*, boy, like a submarine sealing off a damaged compartment to save the ship.

Yes, I know, an absolute morality, however nascent, in one compartment and moral relativity in another is a contradiction. We have been over all this before. The Troob mind thrives on contradiction, Ticker. It *is* a submarine. Solid internal doors, no windows.

Seal this mummery off—get back to animal rights or the environment, *anything* but this. Agree to disagree, touting tolerance of different points of view as a liberal virtue. Your little group is split on Abortion, three to three. Praise Perfect diversity, and let the Troobs be Troobs. Give in, gloss over, move on.

Great Caesar's Ghost! Who would have thought this little project would turn out to be so difficult? At least, my nephew, you through it have learned and grown—that is the important thing. You are what is important, worth a million others to me.

Your doting uncle,

RED

Letter the Eighty-second

~

Dear Ticker,

Yellow-dog and PJ remain uneasy—that's to be expected. Dan, however, has slipped the leash with this challenge of his. He offers to speak for conservatism against your recent denunciation, "bring conservatism out of the shadows and let it be judged in the light." Your pals are to be the jury, the other four.

The boy has grown bold. I wonder? Could he and Strong be in league, the two plotting this? Or has Dan found himself, the words for what he believes, in those infernal books? No matter, it all plays the same.

I confess, we may not win Dan back this time. But that is really of small consequence this late in the game. Our use for him is nearly at an end. Dan has served his purpose—you have learned much and grown strong.

Dan has been but a sparring partner for you all along, a disposable tool. The others, however, are another story. A complication, obstructing our happy ending.

If you fail to rise to Dan's challenge, let his glove lie, how would you appear—to *yourself* as well as your pals? You must answer this defiance. One last test, Ticker, the third page of your final exam. Redtape promises no more delays, you will graduate after this.

All right. We will hear Dan out, his conservative case. When he is done, all four votes will be counted against him: Ms Jewelry, Mr. Howard Bentley Bow-Tie III, Plain Jane, and Yellow-dog Jake. All four votes will be yours, son. I promise.

Let Dan speak, your answer to come the following week. Claim you wish to be fair, to take time and carefully consider his views. That will give us time to plot our reply. Pointed, my boy, it will be. Deadly pricks in vital places, no beating upon his shield. The Bow Tie and Ms Jewelry will enjoy the show. Yellow-dog and PJ will come around to you, you'll see—Troob minds turn on a phrase.

The stage is well set. Dan turns things to our advantage, stepping forward like this. The boy is incurably conservative, like the heroes of Fenimore Cooper and Sir Walter Scott. He comes out in the open to speak from the heart, while we lie back and plot. High noon, and he walks boldly into the street, the fool.

Poisonous barbs shot from the shadows will be our rebuttal. Ho ho. I trust, by now, you have grown to embrace the full reality of politics, that it is war and in war there are no rules.

Hamlet was wrong. Conscience does not make cowards of us *all*. Wilde was right. "There is no sin except stupidity." Who says we must play by the rules?

Blast Dan's conversion. His humiliation will be a better prize, and he will have served us well. We win from a different perspective, now, that's all. *Finis*. Four votes for you, none for him. A *relative* victory. Ha ha.

Your slick uncle,

REDTAPE

Letter the Eighty-third

~

Dear Ticker,

Dan's conservative thesis is much to the mind of Edmund Burke and in the very words, at times, of Russell Kirk: the Adversary comes into full light. I glean, from your jumbled summary, a baker's dozen tenets. I will sort them out for you, son, that you might better understand my nullification. Think of this as a final review: these black conservative precepts recounting and illumining their liberal counterpoints.

Dan's baker's dozen conservative tenets—

1) There exists a transcendent moral order that properly rules society as well as the individual. This order is made for man, and man for it, and its truths are permanent. Call it religion or natural law—it flows from one God above all.

2) All political, as well as individual, problems are deviations from the above order and are, therefore, at root, religious and moral problems.

3) A profound respect for the limitations of human understanding, and an affection for the proliferating variety and mystery of human existence, should guide all individual and collective action—uniformity, egalitarianism, and utilitarianism are impulses harmful to society and to the human spirit.

4) Man being imperfect, no perfect social order will ever be created by man—those who attempt to create heaven on earth invariably create terrestrial hells.

5) Human society is highly complex—simple solutions to social problems usually do not work and often create great mischief.

6) Practical solutions to social problems are to be preferred over the theoretical and the doctrinaire, the tried and proven over abstract ideas and designs.

7) Society requires prudent restraints upon power and human passions— despotism or anarchy will surely ensue if human nature is left unchecked.

8) Convention, custom, civility, and long-standing traditions are natural checks upon anarchy and political and economic manipulation by tyrants and charlatans. Law may support these natural checks, but it, alone, cannot prevail against despotism and anarchy. Order, justice, and freedom rest on voluntary behaviors.

9) Human talents and motivation being highly variable, society requires a variety of hierarchies to maintain basic order and effectively function.

10) The possession of property protects individual freedom and fixes certain duties and responsibilities upon the possessor, moral and legal, which are accepted cheerfully, as a rule, and confer great benefits upon society.

11) Government should be limited to involvement in those things individuals cannot generally do for themselves, national defense, law enforcement,

and necessary infrastructure such as roads and currency. Voluntary community not involuntary collectivism should be the rule.

12) Society must change to preserve itself and advance, but this must be done prudently with an eye to the past, present, and future. Permanence and change must be reconciled. Nothing should be wholly old or wholly new—this is the means of conservation of society as well as living organisms.

13) *Restrained* by all of the above, the maximum liberty and equality should be afforded to all. Restraint upon liberty and equality distinguishes conservatism from the revolutionary pursuit of both equality and liberty in liberalism and the radical pursuit of liberty in libertarianism. Liberty and equality must be balanced against each other, and against other social and spiritual goods.

There. No one could say I have not summarized Dan's case fairly.

Now, the point of attack. Can you guess? Dan's first tenet, God, of course. Knock this tenet down, and the others fall like dominoes.

Tocqueville—that keen observer of America and human nature—points the way, though that was hardly his intention: *"One of the most ordinary weaknesses of the human intellect is to seek to reconcile contrary principles.... There have ever been and will ever be men who, after having submitted some portion of their religious belief to the principle of authority, will seek to exempt several other parts of their faith from it and to keep their minds floating at random between liberty and obedience."*

You see, Ticker? The Achilles' heel, the sticking point, of conservatism lies not in the admitting of God—have I not always allowed as much for Troobs—but in making Him the *central authority*. Dan's conservatism makes God the iron hub of a wheel, the rest mere wooden spokes. Our thrust, my boy, is not to break the conservative hub but to soften the metal. We will not oppose but instead plant a poison dart, modernity.

God, more progressively viewed, is neither iron nor hub but coloration, blending with other hues, varying in intensity, a tint playing across the many facets of modern life—more for some, less or not at all for others. Your pals will nod, be assured.

Emphasize that Dan is not *wrong*. He has simply "gone too far." He is "too extreme." Phrases, son, that elicit nods from stones.

Your pals are left, now, to shade their liberalism however they like—there is no danger in mere coloration. It is conservatism, not liberalism, that will be changed.

Let each Troob work out his or her own color scheme. A God-colored liberalism for Yellow-dog and PJ—pantheistic, Tocqueville predicted. The Bow Tie and Ms Jewelry may choose an anti-God hue. Merely interior decorating, my boy, a matter of taste. After all, you and your pals are all liberals: tolerant, above all, able to see from all points of view....

Soon enough, even for Troobs who shade deeply toward the conservative, *good* will become confused with caring and concerned....

Didn't LBJ and Jesus both feed the multitudes?

Weren't Mrs. Roosevelt and Mother Teresa both saints?

Jessie Jackson and John the Baptist...

Jane Fonda and Joan of Arc....

Neil Postman and Thomas Aquinas....

Let's have one big happy family (conservatism nullified). "Can't we all just get along?"

Shake your head, when Dan doesn't *get it*.

Say, "Everyone else seems to understand that the world is in living color now, not black and white.

"Really, Dan, this wagon wheel of yours may, once upon a time, have been state of the art, but this is the 21st century! Have you heard of the airplane, or do you still subscribe to the view that man will never fly?"

Dan's way is all or nothing, your way all *for* nothing. He is offering a strenuous swim across a vast ocean, you a dip in a Hollywood pool of unbridled self-esteem and self-gratification. The art of the possible versus *anything* is possible....

Let's vote.

Your merciless uncle,

RED

ps. You and I, of course, know that God is not even the faintest shade of pink but absolutely transparent. Ho ho.

Letter the Eighty-fourth

~

Dear Ticker,

Dan got laughed *Right* out of the room. Ha ha. A rebuff, a repulse, a rout! His archaic, absolutist notions a "hoot," as Mr. Bow Tie put it. PJ, back under Ms Jewelry's wing. Yellow-dog, giving a final horse laugh as Dan made his exit. A fine sound, isn't it boy, an Adversary's derision? Boffo, bravo, well done.

Son, this final victory was more significant than you might guess. Keeping liberals in line, restoring leaners like YD and PJ, is actually more important than gaining converts. We have the Adversary outnumbered already, and the schools increase us every day. Neutralize conservatives, prevent defections—and the future is ours.

Beyond that, turncoats are dangerous. They know where the bodies are buried, as it were, and the tricks of the liberal trade. When they switch sides, it is often with a vengeance and powerful effect: Milton Friedman, Friedrich Hayek, Karl Popper, Irving Kristol, Norman Podhoretz, even Ronald Reagan....

Just listen to Malcolm Muggeridge, after he made his exit from our ranks: *"[L]iberalism. A solvent rather than a precipitate, a sedative rather than a stimulant, a slough rather than a precipice; blurring the edges of truth, the definition of virtue, the shape of beauty; a cracked bell, a mist, a death wish."* Such vehemence comes infrequently from born-and-bred conservatives. This is the stuff of one who has seen liberalism up close, and has been repelled.

Pulling YD and PJ back in line was important work, my boy, fine practice. Always, we must work to prevent the next Popper or Friedman or Reagan from turning on us. Who knows who the next Muggeridge might be?

The last lesson in our course, son: liberals must *never* stray. YD and PJ would have been the loss—Dan was never really ours in the first place.

I will be honest, boy: turning true conservatives around is like making water run uphill, all but a lost cause. I confess, deep-down I was doubtful about converting Dan from the start. My real project was your initiation into grown-up liberalism, all along. You've guessed as much by now, I'm sure. Our boy was a catspaw, no more. I trust you'll forgive me this little deceit, now that you've tasted victory—how I wish I could have witnessed the final drubbing you gave Dan.

Did he really read Eliot to the group, a bittersweet acknowledgment of defeat? How dramatic. It was lost, no doubt, on all but you—I didn't know you were reading Eliot too.

> "Words strain,
> *Crack and sometimes break, under the burden,*
> *Under the tension, slip, slide, perish,*
> *Decay with imprecision, will not stay in place,*
> *Will not stay still. Shrieking voices*
> *Scolding, mocking, or merely chattering,*
> *Always assail them."*

The Parthian shot is straight at you, Ticker. Dan smarting, no doubt, from the lesson in relativism and rhetoric you gave him: *God, the Coloring Book,* as it were.

I might have let Dan just limp away—chewed up enough in our lion's den. But not you. Ho ho. For shame, rebutting his final word in brutal jest:

> "*Words strain,*
> *Crack and sometimes break ....*"
> "But an ancient wheel
> Groans beneath the shriek and chatter,
> True."

Priceless, son—though I admit I was nonplused for a moment, before I saw the mordant wit. Dan's wheel groans *beneath* your "cracked" words....

A fine irony: "So who won anyway," you seem to say.

Am I right, you mock Transcendence as it groans in the dust beneath your words? Ha ha. The sarcasm fairly drips, once you see the cant. You should be in the theater, my boy. Like me, you have the gift.

Thanks, and farewell to Dan—he's served us well—and our little play comes to an end. Son, I've been tough on you from time to time. We've had a few tense moments, but it has all worked out wonderfully.

Si finis bonus est, totum bonum erit.

"All is well that ends well."

Your proud and happy uncle,

RED

Letter the Eighty-fifth

~

Dear Ticker,

You're kidding? Of course, you are: "an ancient wheel, beneath the shriek and chatter, groaning *True*." You meant it literally. Dan spoke *truly*....

Now you play your jest on me, surely.

A joke can be carried too far, my boy.

Talk to me, Ticker. Ticker, Ticker....

AFTERWORD

"Where is the one who is wise? Where is the scribe? Where is the debater of this age? Has not God made foolish the wisdom of the world?"

—*The First Epistle of Paul the Apostle to the Corinthians*

Letter the Eighty-sixth

~

Dear Father ... Ticker,

May I still call you Ticker? How many years has it been? Twenty? It is I who have avoided you, I know—but it is not what you think. It began that way, yes. I was greatly bruised by your defection, or thought it was that bruising me. Where to begin?

I hear of our Dan now and then in the news, a distinguished economist and professor. I have read his *Myths of the Great Depression*. A razor sharp book, no wonder we failed to win him over. What a group you assembled in your dorm room, back then. Who would have guessed? Reginald Strong, a federal judge—I have heard his name whispered for the Big Court one day. And you, a priest. I wonder what became of the others? Yellow-dog, PJ.... So long ago. How to begin?

I took to reading T.S. Eliot after your defection—I still think of it as your "defection," though that is the wrong word. A line from Eliot's *Prufrock* sums me well these days: *"I have seen the moment of my greatness flicker, [a]nd I have seen the eternal Footman hold my coat, and snicker...."* The last laugh is on me.

Like J. Alfred Prufrock: in short, I am afraid. Yes, afraid. You think of me as I was, not as I am. I have changed, these last years in particular. I have not been an idle recluse. I have been thinking. To act is so easy, as Goethe said, to think is so hard.

Let me tell this my way, more slowly than once I might have spoken. I must learn to speak again, for I have known much quiet in these last years. And I must turn you from the boy in my mind into a man, see you in my mind's eye with a few streaks of gray. I wish to speak to you as a man, Ticker, and as a priest....

My first insight—I think that is the right word, though it was only felt, at first, thought following much later—came soon after your defection. Dan stole my pride along with you, and there was *nothing* left. Without my self-importance.... I was Eliot's wasteland. Suddenly nothing but a body, growing old.

Muggeridge put his finger on me—I've been reading him much of late. *"In the beginning was the flesh, and the flesh became Word."* I was the Word, grown hollow, become flesh again—and rotting flesh at that.

Do you remember that devastating Muggeridge quote from one of my last letters? It haunts me. I feel he was describing not liberalism but me: "a cracked bell, a mist, a death wish." I have thought much about death since your defection.

At first, I worried that in death I would leave nothing behind. Your cousins have carried on, of course, but you were always the one. I always knew that. You were my chance to live on.... But then my thinking turned. I *was* leaving something behind, after all: the America I had helped to make. An America with ... my death wish?

In my grief—I do not overstate, for that is the state I have lived in for many years now—I saw America anew, the America I had helped to fashion in my own image. I saw each nail that I had driven as if it were new, being driven again.

I have cried "Wolf" in my lifetime about a coming ice age and global warming, in turns, as it suited my purpose. What will happen, who will listen, if a real crisis comes? I have lured countless people, like sheep, into dependent lives that have ended in illegitimacy, crime, and drugs.... Like Rousseau and all of his disciples, I have labored to set people free from family, church, town, class—and knowingly. Yes, *knowingly.* I was never a Troob. How I wish I had even that to wrap myself in now.

I have built the schools, sleek and well stocked, where no one learns.... No, that is not right. Children learn my creed. I have raised an army of government employees who shoot their superiors over a grievance. I have used democracy to my own ends, flattering and eternally polling the populace, moving us along the road to mob rule.

Ticker, I have used up much of the store of morality and civility bequeathed by Western Civilization, fed off it, eaten the society I inherited—swung my wrecking ball until I have no place to stand. You remember the image? I wish I did not.

I am Liberalism, incarnate. *"In the beginning was the flesh, and the flesh became Word."* And the word in the end was not simply hollow—it was evil. Yes, I believe in evil now. The Devil's greatest trick was convincing me he did not exist, and now that I am old and spent, he has spread my life's work before me.

One day, when I thought I could sink in spirits no lower, the wind turned the pages of a book on my desk to a quote of John Adam's:

> *"The people in America have now the best opportunity and greatest trust in their hands, that Providence ever committed to so small a number, since the transgression of the first pair; if they betray their trust, their guilt will merit even greater punishment than other nations have suffered, and the indignation of Heaven."*

I had thought my spirits could sink no lower—I was wrong. Was it the Devil or God that turned that page?

I dream Yeats' vexed nightmare—and I am the rough beast slouching toward Bethlehem, what irony, to be reborn....

You are a priest—I could not ask this if you were not, for I am beyond the help of any man:

You believe in forgiveness, I know. Is it possible for one such as me? Is the God you worship that large? Did he die on the Cross for us *all*, as they say?

Please write to me, Father ... Ticker. Perhaps we could correspond once again, as we did long ago—perhaps attempt another conversion but of a very different kind?

Your uncle,

RED

Welcome to the *Underbook*

The Redtape Letters, strictly speaking a novel, is actually a hybrid work combining the novel and essay, a technique as old as *The Divine Comedy* and *Pilgrims Progress*, practiced recently to near-perfection by George Orwell and C.S. Lewis.

The essay in *Redtape* calls out for footnotes, sources to confirm the accuracy of statements and statistics, and the inclusion of additional material that would be of interest to only certain readers. However, the novel in Redtape would be disrupted by footnotes, the illusion necessary to the form broken. The "underbook" is a compromise solution. It is here at the end of the book where it will not interfere, containing headings to guide the reader in place of the usual numbers.

The guidelines by which the underbook was developed are as follows—

Quotations from well known people, when the speaker or author is cited within the text, are not cited in the underbook. Quotations from people not well known are cited. Unless it is general knowledge, facts and figures are cited. Remarkable things that might leave the reader wondering whether fiction or fact are addressed and sources given. Finally, the subjective element existing in all footnoting, additional information thought to be relevant and of interest but not fitting well within the main body is included. A suggested reading list is included in the notes on Letter 80, Reginald Strong's reading list for Dan. A brief essay on personal outlook, in the dark face of this latter-day liberal world, is included at Letter 86. This may be of general interest. The intention was to keep the underbook informal and brief.

The term "underbook" is borrowed from William Safire who included something similar to what you are about to read—or scan or leaf through depending on your inclinations—in his Civil War novel *Freedom*. Given that every detail in a work of fiction cannot possibly be covered, he gave his readers a rule of thumb for separating fact from fiction in the Civil War. The rule holds true for latter-day liberalism as well: if it seems absolutely unbelievable, it's probably true.

Lee Whipple
Mark Kundmueller

THE REDTAPE LETTERS UNDERBOOK

Letter 1
admissions people slipping, letting in a conservative
Liberal bias can be found throughout the Ivy League. Robert Bork reports that Yale University, where he was a law professor, has been politically left of center for decades. He was one of only two Republicans on a faculty of 45. At Dartmouth, now retired President James O. Freedman was lauded by the faculty for taking a stand "against *The Dartmouth Review*, a neo-conservative student newspaper." William F. Buckley Jr.'s classic *God and Man at Yale* brims with examples.

Bork, Robert H. Slouching Toward Gomorrah: Modern Liberalism and American Decline. New York: Regan Books, 1996, p. 36.

Rimer, Sara. "Dedicated Intellectual Ends Chapter as Dartmouth President." New York Times 15 June 1998.

Buckley, William F. Jr. God and Man at Yale. Washington D.C.: Regnery Gateway, 1977.

the *"L"* word
A liberal, in current times, is broadly defined as one who "believes in more government action to meet individual needs." This is satisfactory to *start* understanding liberalism.

Safire, William. Safire's Political Dictionary. New York: Ballantine Books, 1978, p. 373.

"Social democrat" has a nice ring
social democracy - "A political theory advocating the use

of democratic means to achieve a gradual transition from capitalism to socialism."

The American Heritage Dictionary. 3rd. ed. 1992.

Letter 2
"sweet mates"
   For those not familiar with the current college scene, females and males sharing a college dorm suite is quite the norm.

Barron's Profiles of American Colleges. 23 edition. Hauppauge, NY: Barrons, 1998.

Perfect, capital *P*
   The belief in man being able to Perfect himself and society versus a fallen man in need of salvation by God is a key tenet of latter-day liberalism. G.K. Chesterton, a believer in the Fall, observed that original sin has been empirically validated by 3500 years of history.

Letter 3
latter-day liberalism
   A dilemma faced in creating *The Redtape Letters* was how to refer to Redtape's political creed. Simply calling it "liberal-ism" would not be true to the word's history. Initially the term liberal meant "one who resisted government encroachment on individual liberties." George Washington used the term to in-dicate "generosity or broad-mindedness." The meaning has definitely changed. In *Slouching Toward Gomorrah*, Robert Bork states the following:

   "Modern liberalism" may not be quite the correct name
   for what I have in mind. I use the phrase merely to mean
   the latest stage of the liberalism that has been growing

in the West for at least two and a half centuries, and probably longer. Nor does this suggest that I think liberalism is always a bad idea. So long as it was tempered by opposing authorities and traditions, it was a splendid idea. It is the collapse of those tempering forces that has brought us to a triumphant modern liberalism with all the cultural and social degradation that follows in its wake. If you do not think 'modern liberalism' an appropriate name, substitute "radical liberalism" or "sentimental liberalism" or even, save us, "post-modern liberalism."

In *Redtape* "latter-day liberalism" refers to the latest evolution of the word, as Robert Bork and to a degree William Safire understand it. It is interesting to note that *The American Heritage Dictionary* still maintains a flavor of the definition Washington held, defining a liberal as "free from bigotry."

As *Redtape* progresses, the "latter-day" is often dropped for convenience. *Latter-day liberalism* is always intended.

Safire, William. Safire's Political Dictionary. New York: Ballantine Books, 1978, p. 373.

Bork, Robert H. Slouching Toward Gomorrah: Modern Liberalism and American Decline. New York: Regan Books, 1996, p. 4.

Letter 4

Redtape's family motto

The phrase "the more things change, the more things stay the same" was coined by the French political commentator Alphonse Karr.

Safire, William. Safire's Political Dictionary. New York: Ballantine Books, 1978, p. 709.

realpolitic

The term *realpolitic* is often used in current times to refer to practical or realistic politics. Redtape employs the earlier meaning of amoral power politics.

Letter 5

Smoot-Hawley Tariff

The Smoot-Hawley Tariff of 1930 was intended to protect American farmers and manufacturers from foreign competition. It resulted instead in other nations raising their tariff rates and diminished the demand for American products.

National Recovery Act

The National Industrial Recovery Act of 1933 was part of FDR's New Deal. It was used to enact codes controlling wages, the length of the workweek, and the price of goods.

Wagner Act

The National Labor Relations Act, introduced by Senator Robert F. Wagner in 1935, gave the federal government the power to compel employers to recognize and bargain with labor unions.

Brinkley, Allen, et al. American History: A Survey. 8th ed. New York: McGraw-Hill, 1991, p. 740, 752, 761.

Letter 11

the growing flock of homeless

Redtape states there are millions of homeless. His numbers come from a Columbia University study which "found that at least 5.7 million American adults were homeless for some period of time between 1985 and 1990." However, Mitch Snyder, the late advocate for the homeless, estimated between 2 and 3 million people were living on the streets nationwide. The National Coalition for the Homeless claims 7 million Americans were homeless at some point between 1985 and 1990. They also state 500,000 to 600,000 persons used soup kitchens or shelters during a single week in 1988. The *USA Today* estimates the total number to be between 300,000 and 600,000. The Department of Housing and Urban Development states 350,000 are homeless. Redtape's guess is as good as any.

Messler, Bill. "The Homeless Learn to Hit Back." Third Force May/June 1995.

www2.ari.net/home/nch/

"Snyder Protests Homeless Census." Washington Post 15 October 1986.

Stone, Andrea. "A Cooling Toward Homeless." USA Today 14 November 1990.

Letter 12
we created the homeless
The connection between the homeless and the mentally ill may seem incredible. The following sources provide evidence and detail of the close connection.

Leepson, Marc. "The Homeless: Growing National Problem." Congressional Quarterly. October 1982, Vol. II, No. 16,

"Outcasts on Main Street: Homelessness and the Mentally Ill." USA Today Magazine March 1994.

Shogren, Elizabeth. "Treatment Against Their Will." Los Angeles Times 18 August 1994.

Torrey, E. Fuller. "Thirty Years of Shame: The Scandalous Neglect of the Mentally Ill Homeless." National Forum Winter 1993.

Letter 13

Spousal abuse

Redtape states that married women are the societal group least likely to be assaulted. This is at odds with the politically correct image of women as victims. Feminist organizations and the media often make wild claims about women being abused by their husbands. One such claim was that because of the extreme violence of professional football, more women were abused on Super Bowl Sunday than any other day. Before being debunked by Ken Ringle of the *Washington Post*, this theory was widely believed. The Associated Press and CBS labeled Super Bowl Sunday a "day of dread" for women and NBC was persuaded to run a public service announcement condemning domestic violence prior to the game in 1993.

The statistics supporting claims of rampant domestic violence are based on incredible definitions of abuse. One Harris poll classified a husband grabbing his wife's arm as "physical abuse" and stomping out of the room as "emotional abuse." Christina Hoff Sommers sites several studies looking at actual assaults that show married women are a great deal safer than we are led to believe, arguably the safest group in our society.

Bork, Robert. Slouching Toward Gomorrah: Modern Liberalism and American Decline. New York: Regan Books, 1996, p. 207.

Hoff Sommers, Christina. Who Stole Feminism: How Women Have Betrayed Women. New York: Simon & Schuster, 1994, p. 189-196.

Ringle, Ken. "Debunking the 'Day of Dread' For Women." <u>Washington Post</u> 31 January, 1993.

Letter 14
the Adversary
Conservatism is defined in ever greater detail as the book progresses, both explicitly and by implication, as latter-day liberalism, is unmasked. For the reader who is reading the underbook along with the main body, an interim commentary is offered here. Kirk commenting on Burke and Adams provides a condensed peek at conservatism. Note the word "prejudice," almost universally employed as a pejorative today, is used in a positive sense, a prejudice against poor manners for instance.

Russell Kirk on Edmund Burke: "A universal constitution of civilized peoples is implied in Burke's writings and speeches, and these are its chief articles: reverence for the divine origin of social disposition; reliance upon tradition and prejudice for public and private guidance; conviction that men are equal in the sight of God, but equal only so; devotion to personal freedom and private property; opposition to doctrinaire alteration."

Russell Kirk on John Adams, from *Discourses on Davila*: "'Is there a possibility that the government of nations may fall into the hands of men who teach the most disconsolate of all creeds, that men are but fireflies, and that this *all* is without a father?' Rather than this, 'Give us again the gods of the Greeks.'"

"Adams ... candor helped to save America from the worst consequences of two radical illusions: the perfectibility of man and the merit of the unitary state."

Kirk, Russell. <u>The Conservative Mind From Burke to Eliot.</u> Washington: Regnery Publishing, 1953, p. 17 and 86-88.

Letter 15

the upper-middle income group pay over 50% of the taxes

According to the Tax Foundation the 24% of the population that earn between $44,147 and $209,105 per year pay 50.1% of federal taxes. This supports Redtape's assertion that 20% of the population, the upper-middle income group, pay over 50% of the taxes.

www.tax foundation.org

Letter 18

ribbons to show one cares

This bit of sarcasm is owed to Rush Limbaugh, from his television program some years back.

Letter 24

man the measure of all things

"Man is the measure of all things" is attributed to the Greek philosopher Protagoras of the fifth century B.C. This statement is considered by William Flemming of Syracuse University to be the "essence" of the Hellenic concept of Humanism. It is central, explicitly or implicitly, to liberal thought today.

Flemming, William. Arts and Ideas. Fort Worth: Holt, Rinehart and Wilson, 1991, p. 49.

Letter 25

the number of defined poor

The economist Thomas Sowell states that social mobility is rarely accounted for in statistics on poverty. Persons included in "the poor" may fall below the defined poverty level in a single year, but be far from poor. Their standard of living may not have changed dramatically. Savings or black-market employment ... may intervene. Voluntary sabbaticals are often counted. Sowell states that "nearly half of the statistically defined 'poor' have air conditioning, more than half own cars, and more than 20,000 'poor' households have their own heated swimming pool or Jacuzzi."

Sowell, Thomas. The Vision of the Anointed. New York: Basic Books, 1995, p. 44.

Letter 28

the telegraph
The history of the telegraph comes from the following sources.

Folsom, Burton. "When the Telegraph Came to Michigan." Mackinac Center for Public Policy: Viewpoint on Public Issues. 8 December 1997.

Coe, Lewis. The Telegraph: A History of Morse's Invention and Its Predecessors in the United States. McFarland, 1983.

Letter 29

poverty in decline when War on Poverty declared
When the Economic Opportunity Act of 1964 was passed into law the number of defined poor had been decreasing for the past four years and was approximately half the 1950 number.

Charles Murray. Losing Ground: American Social Policy 1950-1960. New York: Basic Books, 1984, p. 57.

welfare benefits compete with employment
Redtape claims that welfare has become a more attractive

option than employment. The historian Alanzo L. Hamby
agrees. He claims that the War on Poverty led to diminished
incentives to work and that "among welfare recipients there
suddenly emerged a sense of entitlement at variance with all
past American tradition. Where the New Dealers had stressed
the importance of work in exchange for federal benefits, advocates of 'welfare rights' in the 1960s denounced work requirements. Soon such a position was the new orthodoxy of
American Liberalism."

Hamby, Alanzo L. Liberalism and Its Challengers. New York:
Oxford University Press, 1992, p. 261-262.

welfare budget increased by over 1000%
A thousand percent increase in welfare spending in thirty
years seems unbelievable. However, by 1974 spending had
increased to more than twenty times the amount spent in 1964,
a thousand percent increase in the first decade alone. Redtape
was actually *understating*, choosing a nice round number.

Patterson, James. America's Struggle Against Poverty: 1900-1980.
Cambridge, MA: Harvard University Press, 1981, p. 164-165.

welfare spending as a percentage of GNP
In 1960 the federal government spent approximately 8% of
the Gross National Product on welfare programs; by 1974, 16%.

Patterson, James. America's Struggle Against Poverty: 1900-1980.
Cambridge, MA: Harvard University Press, 1981, p. 164.

clearly stated goals for welfare
President Johnson stated in 1962 that the goal of the War on

Poverty was to prevent dependence on welfare and to "reha-
bilitate" current welfare recipients. He believed that by eliminating the "conditions that breed despair and violence" the
program would put an end to race riots and urban violence.

Sowell, Thomas. The Vision of the Anointed. New York: Basic
Books, 1995, p. 10-11.

welfare, the Social Security Act with racing stripes
The Social Security Act of 1935 was in essence a welfare
law. In addition to the familiar old-age pension and payroll
deductions it included the following programs:
Title III - Grants to States for Unemployment Compensation
Administration.
Title IV - Grants to States for Dependent Children.
Title V - Grants to States for Maternal and Child Welfare.
    Part 1 - Maternal and Child Health Services.
    Part 2 - Services For Crippled Children.
    Part 3 - Child Welfare Services.
    Part 4 - Vocational Rehabilitation.
    Part 5 - Administration.
Title VI - Public Health Work.
Title X - Grants to States For Aid to the Blind.

www.ssa.gov/history/35act.html

Letter 30
never fear or acknowledge failure
Redtape tells Ticker to never fear *or acknowledge* failure.
Many other liberals agree.
John Galbraith, a liberal economist, is described by George
Will as one who never allows "mere facts to inconvenience

the flow of theories." In his 1958 work, *The Affluent Society,* Galbraith calls for increased taxation to correct the "disparities between public services and private comfort." It is now acknowledged by most economists that increased taxes result in economic slowdown, shrinking government revenue, increased debt, and greater disparity between rich and poor. Galbraith, however, sticks to his theories.

Paul Ehrilich is the author of *The Population Bomb* published in 1968. He predicted that major food shortages and widespread starvation would occur by the 1980s. An excellent rebuttal of this sort of alarmist theory concerning population and food supply can be found in Anne Buchanan's essay "Myths About Hunger." Ehrlich's penchant for forecasting the future was not diminished by his lack of accuracy.

Club of Rome was a group of prominent scientists and intellectuals who in the early 1970s predicted that the latter part of the twentieth century would be characterized by major shortages of natural resources and economic collapse. They believed that by the 1990s the earth's supply of petroleum and other fossil fuels would be completely depleted. These *experts* could not have been more wrong. At the end of the 1990s there are large energy reserves, decreasing oil prices, and a sustained economic boom. Prominent scientists and intellectuals have moved on to "global warming."

Will, George F. The Woven Figure: Conservatism and America's Fabric. New York: Scribner, 1997, p. 331.

Rosenberg, Norman L. and Emily S. Rosenberg. In Our Times: America Since World War Two. Engelwood Cliffs, NJ: Prentice Hall, 1991, p. 69.

Buchanan, Anne. "Myths About Hunger." Cooking, Eating, Thinking: Transformative Philosophies of Food. Eds. Deane W. Curtin and Lisa M, Heldke. Indianapolis: Indiana University Press, 1992, p. 329-335.

Meadows, Donella H., et al. The Limits to Growth: A Report for the Club of Rome's Project on the Predicament of Mankind. New York: Universe Books, 1973.

Goldberg vs. Kelly

In this case the Supreme Court ruled that "Procedural due process under the Fourteenth Amendment required that welfare recipients be afforded an evidentiary hearing before termination of benefits." Although there are no official numbers, and cause cannot be perfectly assigned, the number of welfare workers increased dramatically. Some estimates put the number at several thousand in New York City alone to administrate and manage the increased workload.

"*Goldberg vs. Kelly.*" The Oxford Companion to the Supreme Court of the United States. Ed. Kermit L. Hall. New York: Oxford University Press, 1992, p. 341.

pounds added to the tax code

Redtape claims he added pounds to the federal tax code. It is difficult to find consistent figures as to the actual size of the code. *Fortune* magazine states that it began as 14 pages in 1913 and is now 9,451 pages. The Heritage Foundation has the code at only 2,200 pages but requiring an additional 7,600 pages of IRS regulations to be enforced. *The Investor's Business Daily* describes the code as being the size of eight Bibles. Daniel J. Pilla of the Cato Institute states that the tax *system* has 17,000 pages of law and regulations. Regardless, huge!

Birnbaum, Jeffrey H. "Unbelievable! The Mess at the IRS is Worse Than You Think." Fortune 13 April 1998.

Oliver, Charles. "The Morality of Income Taxation." The Investor's Business Daily 4 April 1998.

Pilla, Daniel J. "Why You Can't Trust the IRS." Policy Analysis No. 222 15 April 1995.

Richardson, Craig E. and Geoff C. Ziebart. Strangled By Red Tape. Washington: The Heritage Foundation, 1995, p. 67.

Letter 32
the father-disincentives
   The benefits of fathers in the home has become an established fact. The issue of welfare policies encouraging fatherless homes came to light during the Nixon administration, when republicans *attempted* welfare reform. The debate continues, buried deep in the turf battle between the federal government and the states. Robert Bork states the argument against the father disincentives. "At a time when the institution of marriage is under attack ... it is madness to offer an apartment of her own and a steady income to an unmarried young woman or girl if she will only have a baby while remaining unmarried."

Bork, Robert. Slouching Toward Gomorrah: Modern Liberalism and American Decline. New York: Regan Books, 1996, p. 158.

Letter 33
Secularism

secular - "Worldly rather than spiritual."
secularism - "Religious skepticism or indifference."

The American Heritage Dictionary. 3rd. ed. 1992.

Letter 34
social relativity

The terms secular humanism, situational ethics, and humanitarianism are all closely related.

secular humanism - "An outlook or philosophy that advocates human rather than religious values.

situation ethics - "A system of ethics that evaluates acts in light of their situational context rather than by the application of moral absolutes."

humanitarianism - "The doctrine that Jesus was human only and not divine."

Russell Kirk cites an earlier definition of *humanitarianism* from the *Oxford English Dictionary* which includes the belief that "mankind may become perfect without divine aid."

The American Heritage Dictionary. 3rd. ed. 1992.

Kirk, Russell. Redeeming the Time. Wilmington, DE: Intercollegiate Studies Institute, 1996, p. 193.

Letter 37
Social Security is bust soon enough

Virtually no one disputes that without major overhaul Social Security will soon be out of money. According to Nebraska Senator Bob Kerry, "In 2013, we will be forced to begin dipping into the surplus in the Social Security trust fund to cover benefits payments, an event to be followed by the insolvency of the entire fund in 2029."

Kerry, Bob. "Social Security, Medicare Need Reform Now." Washington Post 5 February 1995.

Social Security withholdings going into general revenues
    Dan and Redtape are correct about Social Security withholdings going into general revenues. According to Senator Ernest Hollings of South Carolina there is no surplus in the Social Security trust fund. Through a practice known as "unified budgeting" this money has been used to hide the true size of the budget deficit since the early 1970s. Already, the government has borrowed $732 billion from the Social Security trust. Whether or not reporting a unified budget is legal has been the subject of much debate. Reorganizing federal funds in this manner appears to be in direct violation of Section 13301 of the Budget Act of 1990 which forbids "the President or Congress from reporting a budget using Social Security trust funds." However, the practice continues.

Hollings, Earnest F. "What Surplus?" Washington Post 5 February 1998.

government not responsible to pay Social Security
    Redtape correctly states that the government cannot be held responsible for making Social Security payments. Contrary to popular belief, the Social Security Act did not create a compulsory insurance program. The Supreme Court has ruled that future Congresses cannot be forced to pay benefits enacted by earlier ones. This means that a person paying into the Social Security system has no contractual right to benefits.

Longman, Phillip J. "Bait and Switch on Social Security." U.S. News 20 April 1998.

Letter 38

"flies of a summer"

Redtape's admission that "we are but flies of a summer" is a deliberate misquote of Edmund Burke. Burke writes that mankind must be mindful of "what they have received from their ancestors" and of what "is due their posterity." If not for this, Burke argues, many (Redtape, The 42nd President...) would act as if they were "the entire masters" and destroy "the entire fabric of their society." Burke argues that without a "contract of eternal society" no one generation could link with another and "men would become little better than the flies of a summer."

Burke, Edmund. "Prejudice, Religion, and the Antagonist World." The Portable Conservative Reader. Ed. Russell Kirk. New York: Penguin Books, 1996, p. 25-35.

Aztec cannibalism

Dr. Tim White, an anthropologist at the University of California, Berkeley, states, "It used to be thought that the Spanish made up all the stories of the Aztecs eating prisoners, as propaganda to justify their own cruelty. But now excavations in Mexico City are finding evidence, such as carefully splintered bones, indicating that the Aztecs really were cannibals."

McKie, Robin. "Cannibalism and Ancient Human Heritage." The Japan Times 18 August 1997.

religiosity of troobs

Redtape's description of the religiosity of the liberal True

Believer is arguably correct. Statistically 90% of Americans claim to believe in God and more than 40% say that they attend church services in any given week. Yet attitudes and behavior, such things as abortion, do not follow in the culture. As Robert Bork states in *Slouching Toward Gomorrah*, "If belief can be said to be present it is a weak and watery belief that is no match for parishioners' personal, secular concerns."

Bork, Robert H. Slouching Toward Gomorrah: Modern Liberalism and American Decline. New York: Regan Books, 1996, p 279-280.

Woodward, Kenneth L. "The Rites of Americans." Newsweek 29 November 1993.

Letter 39
Dan's plan for saving Social Security

Dan's plan for saving and phasing out Social Security is his own. However, there are several plans for Social Security reform currently being proposed in Congress that have similarities. These include S. 1792, the Social Security Solvency Act of 1998 introduced by Senators Moynihan and Kerry as well as H.R. 2768, Social Security Personal Retirement Accounts proposed by Rep. Mark Sanford. The full texts of these plans are available on the Internet.

www.senate.gov/~moynihan

www.house.gov/sanford

Letter 40
Government power grows through saving Social Security

Is increased government power as a byproduct of saving Social Security "conservative paranoia"? Senate Minority Leader Tom Daschle has backed a plan that would allow "the federal government to use the Social Security trust fund to purchase stock in major American companies." According to Michael Tanner, the director of health and welfare studies at the Cato Institute, this plan "would amount to the socialization of a large portion of the U.S. economy. The federal government would become the Nation's largest shareholder, with a controlling interest in nearly every major American company."

Tanner, Michael. "Risky Business." Chicago Tribune 13 December 1996.

Letter 41
education as a separate issue

Redtape would have preferred to discuss education piecemeal, always relative to other issues and agendas. This is indeed how the federal government approaches education. Control of funds and curriculum is divided up among numerous government agencies. The Employment Training and Literacy Enhancement Act of 1997, for instance, gives control of funds reserved for education to the Department of Labor. Thirty-three universities, another example, will receive a total of 900 million dollars from a 1998 highway bill. Other money is given to colleges and universities through the Department of Housing and Urban Development, the Commerce Department, the Defense Department, and the Environmental Protection Agency.... The 105th Congress introduced 1,696 separate bills dealing with education, funneling tax dollars to a multitude of federal and state government departments and agencies and local schools. With this approach, the basic questions about educational purpose and approaches are never asked. Each decision is made in a crossfire of political and financial interests with no guiding priorities. Politics and profit, not principle and policy, drive the federal educational agenda.

"Intellectuals, Your Kids and Your Money." Editorial. The Investor's Business Daily 29 June 1998.

www.congress.gov

Letter 44
gays and Leviticus
The book of Leviticus states "You shall not lie with a male as with a woman; it is an abomination."

The Holy Bible: The New Revised Standard Version Leviticus 18:22. Nashville: Thomas Nelson Publishers, 1990. p. 105.

average life span of homosexual males
The less than 50-year life span for homosexual males cited by Redtape is taken from the work of Paul Cameron. In a study of obituaries from 16 homosexual newspapers over a 12-year period he found that the majority of gay men die young: For those who died of something other than AIDS, the median age of death was 42. If AIDS was the cause of death, the median age was 39.

Cameron, Paul. "Medical Consequences of What Homosexuals Do." The Family Research Institute, Inc. Washington, DC.

gays given Presidential Seal of Approval

As Redtape stated, the 42nd President has had an aggressive policy of supporting homosexuals. The Clinton Administration led the fight to establish the "Don't ask, don't tell" policy in the military, allowing homosexuals to serve as long as they are quiet about their sexual orientation. On November 8, 1998 President Clinton spoke at a seminar for the Human Rights Campaign, a gay rights organization. In his speech he equated the "gay rights movement with the struggle for racial equality." In 1997 President Clinton nominated James C. Hormel, an openly homosexual man, to be the ambassador to Luxembourg, a country that is over 90% Catholic. Mr. Hormel sits on the board of the Human Rights Campaign, a gay rights organization. Hormel's confirmation was blocked by senators who believed he would use his position to advance gay rights.

Baker, Peter. "Clinton Equates Gay Rights, Civil Rights." <u>Washington Post</u> 9 November 1997.

Baker, Peter. "Senators Block Confirmation of Gay Activist." <u>Washington Post</u> 14 November 1997.

Hetter, Katia "The New Civil Rights Battle." <u>U.S. News</u> 3 June 1996.

"Luxembourg" <u>The World Almanac and Book of Facts 1996</u>. Mahwah, NJ: Funk & Wagnalls, 1996, p. 793.

an openly gay congressman
Rep. Barney Frank (Democrat, Massachusetts) is openly gay.

Hetter, Katia "The New Civil Rights Battle." <u>U.S. News</u> 3 June 1996.

the NEA and homosexuality

The NEA has adopted a resolution calling for increased "acceptance of and sensitivity to individuals and groups in a diverse society" including "gays and lesbians." Another NEA resolution states that a teacher's sexual orientation should not be a factor in "personnel policies and practices."

"Racism, Sexism, and Sexual Orientation Discrimination." The 1997 - 1998 Resolutions of the National Education Association. Resolution B-7. 3-6 July 1997 Atlanta, Georgia.

"Protect the Rights of Educational Employees and Advance Their Interests and Welfare." As above. Resolution F-1.

Queer Theory

Unfortunately, Queer Theory is not a fiction. It does exist, as described by Redtape, defined by one of its academic advocates as a "mixture of deconstruction and Marxism ... not primarily an intellectual or theoretical movement, but an effort to make one's private sexual interests the chief focus of one's academic work."

Kimball, Roger. "What Next, A Doctor of Depravity?" The Wall Street Journal. 5 May 1998.

gay Boy Scout leaders

On March 2,1998 the New Jersey Intermediate Appellate Court ruled that the Boy Scouts of America have "no right to expel an openly homosexual man from the position of Scout leader."

Arnn, Larry P. and Glen Ellmers. "Ruling on Gay Scouts is an Assault on Freedoms." Editorial. Bergen Record 5 March 1998.

Letter 45

Erasmus Darwin

Erasmus Darwin foreshadowed the work of his grandson Charles in *Zoonomia* in 1794.

Einstein believed in God

Einstein said, "Anyone who is seriously involved in the pursuit of science becomes convinced that a spirit is manifest in the laws of the universe—a spirit vastly superior to that of man, and one in the face of which we with our modest powers must feel humble." A physicist who worked with Einstein, Professor Henry Margenau of Yale University, described Einstein as "a person of quiet faith...."

Varghese, A., ed. The Intellectuals Speak Out About God. Port Washington, NY: Independent Publishers Group, 1982. p. 43-45.

scientism, scientistic

Scientism -"the application of quasi-scientific techniques or justifications to unsuitable subjects or topics.

Scientistic - "devoted or pretending to the methods of scientists: professedly scientific.

Russell Kirk argues *scientism* is a cause for the loss of religious impulse and conviction in society. He defines it as follows: "the popular notion that revelations of natural science, over the past two centuries and longer, somehow have demonstrated the obsolescence of the church's claims; have informed us that men and women are naked apes merely; have pointed out that the ends of existence are production and consumption merely; that happiness is the gratification of sensual impulses; that notions of the resurrection of the flesh and life everlasting are superstitions of the childhood of the race."

The American Heritage Dictionary. 3rd. ed. 1992.

Webster's Third New International Dictionary. 1981.

Kirk, Russell. The Politics of Prudence. Bryn Mawr, PA: Intercollegiate Studies Institute, 1996, p. 203.

Walt Whitman singing of himself

The Walt Whitman quotation is from the 1855 version of "Song of Myself" from *Leaves of Grass*. The words change somewhat in the many different versions of this work.

Whitman, Walt. Complete Poetry and Collected Prose. New York: Viking Press, 1982, p. 27-89.

President Clinton as cherry on "Enlightenment" cake

Redtape is not alone in this view. The *London Spectator* saw Clinton's election to the presidency in 1992 as a "cultural revolution." They called his election a watershed, concluding that the people of the United States had turned their backs on the old-fashioned values of "private and public Virtue."

"Virtue Unrewarded." The London Spectator 7 November 1992.

Letter 46

A Nation at Risk

A Nation at Risk was published in 1983 by the National Commission on Excellence in Education. It criticized schools for having "a cafeteria style curriculum," as well as low standards and expectations, and called for an improved school curriculum and a tougher criteria for graduation.

Ravitch, Diane. "The Search for Order and the Rejection of Conformity: Standards in American Education." Learning From the Past. Eds. Diane Ravitch and Maris A Vinovskis. Baltimore: Johns Hopkins University Press, 1995, p. 180.

Japanese vs. American schools

The data comparing American schools with those in Japan and China is taken from *The Learning Gap* by Stevenson and Stigler. The book is filled with interesting data but unfortunately draws unwarranted conclusions from it, supporting in the end the educational establishment.

Stevenson, Harold and James Stigler. The Learning Gap: Why Our Schools Are Failing and What We Can Learn From Japanese and Chinese Education. New York: Simon and Schuster, 1992.

other high scoring nations were stingy

The United States spends an average of $5,000 (late 1990s) per student each school year. Redtape points out that most of the nations that outscore the U. S. spend much less. According to Thomas Sowell, "American expenditures on education top those in Japan, whether measured absolutely, per-pupil, or as a percentage of Gross National Product." Russell Kirk, who is not prone to exaggeration, estimates that the U.S. has "spent more money on formal schooling than has all the rest of the world in all ages, combined."

Finn, Chester E. We Must Take Charge: Our Schools and Our Future. New York: The Free Press, 1991, p. 36.

Sowell, Thomas. Inside American Education. New York: The Free Press, 1993, p. 288.

Kirk, Russell. <u>Redeeming the Time</u>. Wilmington, DE: Intercollegiate Studies Institute, 1996, p. 163.

National educational goals

The National Goals were developed by the National Educational Goals Panel in Washington, D.C.

Goal 1: Ready to learn
Goal 2: School Completion
Goal 3: Student Achievement and Citizenship
Goal 4: Teacher Education and Professional Development
Goal 5: Mathematics and Science
Goal 6: Adult Literacy and Lifelong Learning
Goal 7: Safe, Disciplined, & Alcohol- and Drug- Free Schools
Goal 8: Parental Participation

www.negp.gov

are parents necessary?

Redtape's vision of a new family structure based on cloning
is not as far out as it may seem. Radical feminists challenge
what they describe as the "biology is destiny" concept. They
wish to eliminate the terms "sex" and "family." Rather than
the two sexes, they recognize five genders. These include males,
females, lesbians, homosexuals, and bisexuals. Instead of traditional families they advocate "households" that consist of
partners from any combination of the five genders.

Bork, Robert. <u>Slouching Toward Gomorrah: Modern Liberalism
and American Decline</u>. New York: Regan Books, 1996, p. 197.

<u>Letter 47</u>
two professors drawing faulty conclusions

The two professors who did the comparative study between U.S. and Japanese schools were Harold Steverson, a psychology professor at the University of Michigan, and James Stigler, a psychology professor at UCLA. See also Letter 46.

Colorado University: Democratic and politically correct
The Democratic vs. Republican faculty balance and politically correct hiring were reported in *The Wall Street Journal*.

Carroll, Vincent. "Republican Professors? Sure, There's One." The Wall Street Journal 11 May 1998.

Letter 48
the life of Herbert Croly and influence of Comte on his family.

Nuechterlein, James. "Religion and Morality." The New Promise of American Life. Eds. Lamar Alexander and Chester E. Finn. Indianapolis: Hudson Institute, 1995, p. 178-192.

The New Republic **editorialized boldly**

"Father Blakely States the Issue" and "Catholicism Contra Mundum." New Republic 29 July 1916 and 2 September 1916.

William E. Channing writing to Horace Mann

Blumefeld, Samuel L. Is Public Education Necessary? Boise: The Paradigm Company, 1981, p. 188.

students as public property

Rush, Benjamin. "Thoughts Upon the Mode of Education Proper in a Republic." Essays on Education in the Early Republic. Ed.

Frederick Rudolph. Cambridge, MA: Harvard University Press, 1965, p. 14.

Seven Cardinal Principles

Commission on the Reorganization of Secondary Education. Cardinal Principles of Secondary Education. Bulletin 35. Washington: Bureau of Education, Department of the Interior, Government Printing Office. 1918.

"whole-language" method

The controversy over the use of the "look-say" or "whole-language" method of teaching children to read, as opposed to phonics, has been going on for decades. The following sources are recommended for those who wish to learn more.

Flesch, Rudolf. Why Johnny Can't Read and What You Can Do About It. New York: Harper & Row Publishers, 1955.

Blumenfeld, Samuel L. The Whole Language/OBE Fraud. Boise, ID: The Paradigm Company, 1996.

educating "the whole child"

Redtape mentions several *progressive* approaches being used in U.S. schools: "life adjustment education," "affective education," "school counselors...." These are discussed in detail in Thomas Sowell's book *Inside American Education*.

Sowell, Thomas. Inside American Education. New York: The Free Press, 1993.

the shrinking number of school districts

Redtape claims U.S. education has become increasingly centralized. The number of school districts in the U.S. has shrunk from 130,000 in 1960 to approximately 15,000 in the 1990s.

Kirst, Michael W. "Who's in Charge?" Learning From the Past. Eds. Diane Ravitch and Maris Vinovskis. Baltimore: Johns Hopkins University Press, 1995. p. 29.

Letter 49
women in combat

The statistics concerning female anatomy and strength were taken from "Sex and the Soldier" by Stephanie Gutman. She also discusses the high financial costs and the difficulty of maintaining morale in a sexually integrated military.

Gutman, Stephanie. "Sex and the Soldier." New Republic 24 February 1997.

Letter 50
government monopoly on education

Redtape states that the battle for a government monopoly in education is 90% won. He exaggerates slightly. As of 1991 only 13% of American students attended private schools. He should have said the battle is 87% won.

Sowell, Thomas. Inside American Education. New York: The Free Press, 1993, p. 23.

The Committee of 10

A reprint of the Committee of Ten's report can be found in *Secondary Schools at the Turn of the Century.*

Sizer, Theodore. Secondary Schools at the Turn of the Century. New Haven: Yale University Press, 1964.

the proliferating number of subjects being taught
     In 1922 the U.S. Office of Education reported that 175 distinct courses were being taught in American high schools. By 1973 this number had increased to 2,100 different subjects.

Angus, David and Jeffrey Mirel. "Rhetoric and Reality: The High School Curriculum." Learning From the Past. Eds. Diane Ravitch and Maris A Vinovskis. Baltimore: Johns Hopkins University Press, 1995, p. 302.

Herbert Croly on schools

Croly, Herbert. The Promise of American Life. New York: The Macmillan Company, 1909.

Letter 52
do away with the IRS
     There are dozens of proposals for shrinking or doing away with the IRS. They fall into two groups: a "flat" or proportional rate income tax or a national sales tax. The most prominent spokesman for a flat tax has been House Majority Leader Dick Armey. His proposal calls for an extreme simplification of the existing tax code. Everyone would pay 17% of their income, and tax forms would be reduced to the size of a postcard. Representative Armey claims that this would reduce the cost of complying with the tax law, increase compliance rates, and stimulate the economy. Dan's plan for a national sales tax is similar to that of Indiana Senator Richard Lugar. This proposal would completely eliminate the IRS and the national

income tax. Senator Lugar states that this plan would "cause saving and investment to skyrocket" and produce economic opportunity. It would also make it impossible for illegal immigrants, foreign tourists, and the criminal elements of society to evade paying taxes. Details of Armey's flat tax and Lugar's sales tax can be found on their web sites.

www.flattax.house.gov

web.iquest.net/lugar/NSTWORD.html

Supreme Court rules income taxes unconstitutional

The Income Tax Law of 1894 was the first attempt at a peacetime tax on income in the United States. The Supreme Court reviewed this legislation in the 1895 case *Pollock vs. Farmers' Loan and Trust Co.* The Court ruled 5 to 4 that this was a direct tax and thus unconstitutional.

"Pollock vs. Farmers' Loan and Trust Co." The Oxford Companion to the Supreme Court of the United States. Ed. Kermit L. Hall. New York: Oxford University Press, 1992, p. 654.

the first income tax

In 1913 President Wilson helped push the Underwood-Simmons Tariff Bill through Congress. This law greatly reduced tariffs and was intended to bring more competition to American markets. The bill took a turn to the left when Rep. Cordell Hull of Tennessee added an amendment to make up for lost revenue. This amendment called for a graduated income tax. Individuals and corporations earning over $4,000 were taxed starting at 1%. The rate went as high as 6% for those earning over $500,000.

Brinkley, Allen., et al. American History: A Survey. 8th ed. New York: McGraw-Hill, 1991, p. 654.

total taxes being paid

The tax burden on a median one-income family in 1997 was 35.9% of total income. It has been as high as 39% in recent years.

www.taxfoundation.org

the IRS is the hub of an industry

Redtape claims that the IRS is the hub of a major industry. This is backed up by Daniel J. Pilla, a tax litigation consultant with the Cato Institute. He states that in 1993 the IRS had an operating budget of over seven billion dollars and employed more "enforcement agents than the Environmental Protection Agency, the Occupational Safety and Health Administration, and the Drug Enforcement Agency combined." In addition to those who work directly for the IRS there are thousands of tax lawyers and accountants who profit from the system. The number of Americans paying to have their tax returns professionally prepared has increased each year since 1981, the public currently paying $30 billion per year for this service.

Pilla, Daniel J. "Why You Can't Trust the IRS." Policy Analysis No. 222 15 April 1995.

Letter 54

multiculturalism manifesto

The president of the teachers' association putting forth "the manifesto" was William H. Hunter. His organization was the American Association of Colleges for Teacher Education.

Hunter, William H. "Symposium on Multicultural Education." Editorial. Journal of Teacher Education Winter 1973.

Supreme Court champions bilingualism

The Supreme Court case Redtape refers to was *Lau v. Nichols 1974*. A group of non-English-speaking Chinese students sued the San Francisco Unified School District for not providing equal educational opportunities, courses in Chinese. The Supreme Court cited Title VI of the Civil Rights Act of 1964 and ruled that merely treating all students the same did not mean that they were being treated equally.

Crawford, James. Bilingual Education: History, Politics, Theory, and Practice. Los Angeles: Bilingual Educational Services, 1995.

black English

As Redtape stated there have been several attempts to mandate courses in "black English." The Michigan case mentioned occurred in 1976 and was dropped after two years. The "Ebonics" case in Oakland was an attempt by the local school board to "make better use of idiosyncratic speech patterns of many black children to help them improve their reading, writing, and speaking of standard English."

Holmes, Steven A. "Black English Debate: No Standard Assumptions." New York Times 30 December, 1996.

Afrocentric history

Afrocentric history is quite common in colleges and universities in the U. S. Leonard Jeffries, head of the Afro-American program at City College in New York, in conjunction with Asa Hilliard, an educational psychologist, are credited, if that is the word, with creating this new interpretation of history. Mary Lefkowitz, a professor at Wellesley College, states that it is simply myth being passed off as historical fact. Among the beliefs of Afrocentrists is that Aristotle stole his philosophy from the library in Alexandria and therefore blacks, this despite the fact that Aristotle died well before the library was built. Along with rewriting the past, Afrocentrists have much antipathy for the conventional study of history. Jesse Jackson once led a conga line chanting "Hey, hey, ho, ho, Western culture's gotta go" to protest against a required course in Western Civilization at Stanford University. The administration caved in and changed the curriculum to one more politically correct.

Schlesinger, Arthur M. Jr. The Disuniting of America: Reflections on a Multicultural Society. Whittle Direct Books, 1991, p. 32-37.

Lefkowitz, Mary. Not Out of Africa: How Afrocentrism Became an Excuse to Teach Myth as History. New York: Basic Books, 1996, p. 2-4.

Bork, Robert. Slouching Toward Gomorrah: Modern Liberalism and American Decline. New York: Regan Books, 1996, p. 247.

all education should be multicultural education
This quotation is taken directly from the American history syllabus for the New York City public schools.

New York City Public Schools. United States and New York State History: A Multicultural Perspective, grade 7. Vol. 1. New York: New York City Board of Education, 1990.

U.N. Convention of the Rights of the Child

The United Nations General Assembly adopted the Convention on the Rights of the Child on November 20, 1989. It has since been signed by the governments of more than 100 nations. President Clinton pushed for its ratification by the Senate without success. The full text of the Convention is available at the United Nations web site. Those things mentioned by Redtape are in Articles 18 and 19.

www.un.org

NEA lobbying for ratification of Rights of the Child

The NEA has called for its members to lobby Congress on a number of issues, including the ratification of the U.N. Convention on the Rights of the Child.

"Is the NEA 'Molding the Future'?" The Phyllis Schlafly Report August 1997, Vol 31, No. 1.

Letter 55
Neil Postman, in his own words

Postman, Neil. The End of Education: Redefining the Value of School. New York: Random House, 1996.

Postman, Neil, and Charles Weingartner. Teaching as a Subversive Activity. New York: Dell Publishing, 1969.

Letter 56
School to Work Act

Redtape is not alone in seeing major implications for the future of education in the School to Work Act. Rep. Harold Voorhees of Michigan agrees with Redtape's analysis that the

Certificate of Initial Mastery will become a "government-controlled passport to work" and that "with full implementation, a child would not be able to be employed without this Certificate."

Voorhees, Harold J. "Michigan Model of School to Work." <u>Education Reporter</u> July 1997.

tens of billions for education

The federal government does indeed spend *tens of billions* of dollars on education. The federal Department of Education spent over 25 billion dollars every year between fiscal 1991 and 1994. Additional federal dollars are spent on education by numerous other federal agencies. Also see Letter 41.

<u>The World Almanac and Book of Facts 1996</u>. Mahwah, NJ: Funk & Wagnalls, 1996, p.110-111.

double the cost of tuition in high-performing private schools

According to a report produced by the Mackinac Center, the average tuition at private schools is "roughly half of public school per-pupil revenue." Also see Letter 46.

Anderson, Patrick L., et al. "The Universal Tuition Tax Credit: A Proposal to Advance Parental Choice in Education." Mackinac Center for Public Policy. November 1997.

<u>Letter 57</u>
examples of *affective* education

Redtape's first two examples of affective education are in the *Congressional Record*. The third example was reported by Robert Holland in his book *Not With My Child You Don't*.

"Survey, Glasgow Middle School, Glasgow, Kentucky."

Congressional Record, 103 Congress, 4 February 1994. S867.

"Values Questionnaire, Dayton, Ohio." Congressional Record,103 Congress, 4 February 1994. S869.

Holland, Robert. Not With My Child You Don't. Richmond: Chesapeake Capital Services, 1995, p. 2-1.

subjects recommended by Joycelyn Elders

Elders, M. Joycelyn and Jennifer Hui, "Comprehensive School Health Services: Does it Matter and Is It Worth the Fight?" Summer Institute papers and recommendations of the Council of Chief State School Officers, 1992.

Korean vs. American self-esteem in children

An international study of the math skills of thirteen-year-olds ranked Korean children first and American children last. Only 23% of the Korean children believed they were "good in mathematics." However, 68% of the American students tested claimed to be good at math. These results, *after scores and rankings were known.*

"Education Openers," Wall Street Journal, Supplement, 9 February 1990.

clarity versus sensitivity as teacher priority

The survey of Asian and American teacher priorities was conducted by Harold Stevenson and James Stigler. In their study they listed several attributes of a quality teacher and asked teachers from Beijing and Chicago to choose the one that was most important: 50% of the Chinese teachers chose the ability to explain things clearly. Less than 10% of the American instructors believed this was important. The most popular American response, 45%, was sensitivity.

Stevenson, Harold W. and James W. Stigler. The Learning Gap: Why Our Schools Are Failing and What We Can Learn From Japanese and Chinese Education. New York: Simon and Schuster, 1992, p. 167.

Letter 60

separation of church and state

Thomas Jefferson's famous phrase was written as he worked to reform of the laws of Virginia during the Revolutionary War. It was by no means an attempt to remove religion from public life. Rather, he wished to eliminate an official state religion. At the time in Virginia the Anglican Church was subsidized with tax dollars. Jefferson's call for the separation of church and state came in legislative bill No. 82 in which he states "Almighty God hath created the mind free.... To compel a man to furnish contributions of money for the propagation of opinions he disbelieves and abhors, is sinful and tyrannical."

Brodie, Fawn M. Thomas Jefferson: An Intimate History. New York: W W Norton & Company, 1974.

God was erased from blackboards

Redtape's friends on the Supreme Court have made many rulings concerning the presence of religion in public education. In *Illinois ex rel. McCollum vs. the Board of Education 1948* the Court ruled that students could not be released from classes to attend voluntary religious instruction at their schools. Four years later, in *Zorach vs. Clauson 1952*, the Court allowed a similar release program in which students were able to leave campus to receive religious instruction during the school day. Both voluntary school prayer (*Engel vs. Vitale 1962*) and reading from the Bible (*Abington School District vs. Schempp 1963*) were declared to be violations of the First Amendment's "establishment clause." In *Wallace vs. Jaffree 1985* the Court ruled that an Alabama law calling for a moment of silence for "meditation or voluntary prayer" was unconstitutional.

The Oxford Companion to the Supreme Court of the United States. Ed. Kermit L. Hall. New York: Oxford University Press, 1992.

Letter 61
school choice

A good example of the school-choice movement that worries Redtape is the tax credit system currently being proposed in Michigan by the Mackinac Center and others. Under this plan, parents would receive a dollar-for-dollar tax credit up to a certain amount to pay for private school tuition and supplies. This would assist parents in sending their children to private schools while actually increasing the per pupil funding of public education. Parents receiving the tax credit would still be paying some taxes to support the public schools while their children would not be utilizing the resource. A second part of the plan allows unrelated citizens and corporations to give money to private scholarship programs for a specified individual or group. This idea gives a sizable tax break to individuals or companies who help pay for a child's private education and addresses the common objection that school choice destroys the public schools. Similar programs have been initiated in several other states with varying levels of success. In Illinois Governor Jim Edgar vetoed legislation calling for a $500 tax credit for private education. President Clinton has similarly vetoed attempts by Congress to implement school choice at the federal level.

In Wisconsin, Governor Tommy Thompson has proposed tax credits that could be used to defray the expenses of private education, but not for tuition. In Minnesota, a $1,000 per child or $2,000 per family tax credit is currently in place, with a similar program in Wisconsin.... A recent Supreme Court decision holds that such programs are not in violation of the Constitution.

Burr, Richard. "Choice Plan Takes a Surprise Twist." The Detroit News 1 March 1998.

Trowbridge, Ronald L. "School Choice: A Better Way." Wall Street Journal 27 April 1998.

"Yes to Tax Credits For Education." Editorial. Investor's Business Daily 30 March 1998.

The Mackinac Center For Public Policy: www.mackinac.org

education in the colonial period

In colonial times, prior to public education, Americans were one of the most literate peoples on earth. Through private academies, religious schools, and home tutoring there were high levels of educational opportunity and freedom. The education of poor students was paid for through a combination of state funding and private charity. In the state of Pennsylvania, for instance, the State paid the private school tuition of poor students at a fraction of the cost of providing public schools.

Blumenfeld, Samuel L. NEA: Trojan Horse in American Education. Boise, ID: The Paradigm Company, 1984, p 2.

alternative public schools

The proliferation of Magnet and Charter schools in recent

years are examples of the defensive strategy suggested by Redtape. They incorporate teachers' unions and federal controls.... How much different is yet to be seen.

Letter 63
kangaroo rats
   Congressman Richard Pombo recounts many instances of kangaroo rats and other supposedly endangered species being used as an excuse to regulate private property, destroying the livelihood of many property owners.

Pombo, Richard. This Land is Our Land: How to End the War on Private Property. New York: St. Martin's Press, 1996.

natural law
   A summary of the tenets of natural law as evidenced in a wide variety of cultures and belief systems can be found in the Appendix of *The Abolition Of Man* by C.S. Lewis. Its transcendental and absolute nature consistent in its many forms.

Lewis, C. S. The Abolition of Man. 1947. New York: Touchstone, 1996.

Thomases Paine and Jefferson
   Redtape says that both Thomas Jefferson and Thomas Paine leaned at times toward entitlements over personal responsibility. This does not mean that these Founders wished to destroy the existing social order. The signers of the Declaration of Independence promised "unalienable rights" within the context of the moral order they had inherited. An example of this can be seen in the Fifth Amendment to the Constitution. Here, as Robert Bork points out, it clearly indicates "that a criminal

may be punished by depriving him of life or liberty, which certainly interferes with his pursuit of happiness."

Bork, Robert. Slouching Toward Gomorrah: Modern Liberalism and American Decline. New York: Regan Books, 1996, p 57.

Universal Declaration of Human Rights
The General Assembly of the United Nations adopted the Universal Declaration of Human Rights On December 10, 1948. The rights to housing, medical care, leisure time ... cited by Redtape can be found in Articles 24 and 25. The full text of the Declaration is available on the United Nation's web site.

www.un.org

court cases settled with an eye to mobs in the street
One need look no farther than the recent O.J. Simpson trial.

Letter 64
imagine the liberal howl from Hollywood
Several times Redtape has alluded to the left-leanings of Hollywood. A study of the writers and producers of prime time entertainment conducted by Robert and Linda Lichter and Stanley Rothman support the assertion that Hollywood is overwhelmingly sympathetic to liberalism.

Lichter, Robert, et al. Watching America. Englewood Cliffs, NJ: Prentice Hall, 1991.

Letter 65
retirement home for monkeys
The cause that Ticker and his pals fought for really does exist. An animal rights group, People for the Ethical Treatment of Animals,

has begun a campaign to provide a home for the offspring of chimpanzees used in research in the early space program.

www.peta-online.org

violent crime
   Redtape states that increased crime, like illegitimate births, are in part outcomes of government policy. Many statistics support his conclusion. During the 1960s, for instance, the focus in criminal justice turned away from punishment towards criminal rehabilitation. The chances of becoming the victim of a major violent crime tripled between 1960 and 1976. The murder rate more than doubled between 1961 and 1974.

Silberman, Charles H. Criminal Violence, Criminal Justice. New York: Random House, 1978, p.4.

Wilson, James Q. and Richard J. Herrnstein. Crime and Human Nature. New York: Simon and Schuster, 1985, p. 415.

illegitimacy
   See Letter 77.

the ACLU
   Redtape's analysis of the American Civil Liberties Union is owed in large part to the writings of William A. Donohue.

Donohue, William A. Twilight of Liberty: The Legacy of the ACLU. New Brunswick, NJ: Transaction Publishers, 1994.

Letter 66
a certain risk is always run with recycling

Redtape is correct in stating that the environmental costs of recycling often outweigh the benefits. According to Lawrence W. Reed, president of the Mackinac Center for Public Policy, "Simply demanding that something be recycled can be disruptive of markets and is no guarantee that recycling which makes either economic or environmental sense will occur." An example is the controversy over aseptic boxes. These boxes are used as disposable drink containers and are frequently the target of environmentalists who would prefer the use of recyclable glass bottles. However, it requires 50% less energy to fill disposable boxes and 35% less energy to transport the full boxes. Also, Aseptic boxes do not require refrigeration. This lessens the production of CFC gases which many environmentalists claim are destroying the ozone layer.

Reed, Lawrence W. "Recycling Makes Sense--Sometimes." Mackinac Center for Public Policy: Viewpoint on Public Issues 9 November 1992.

when in doubt, quote Al Gore
The Gore quotes are from his book, *Earth in the Balance*.

Gore, Al. Earth in the Balance: Ecology and the Human Spirit. New York: Penguin Books, 1992.

billions on environmentalism and ethanol "pork"
The Brookings Institute reports that hundreds of billions are spent each year to enforce and comply with federal environmental, health, and safety regulations. Pietro S. Nivola, a Senior Fellow in the Brookings Governmental Studies Program, agrees with Redtape's suggestion that these regulations are used as a means of redistributing wealth. He states, "rules

that have encouraged the use of ethanol are a kind of pork for corn farmers" and that billions of dollars are spent on lawyers for every case of cancer that is prevented in the battle to clean up toxic waste.

"Regulation, More or Less." The Wilson Quarterly Spring 1998.

pantheism
> *pantheism* - 1. "A doctrine identifying the Deity with the universe and its phenomena."
> 2. "Belief in and worship of all Gods."

Pantheism is a primary component in most, if not all, New Age religions. Charles Colson in his book *Against the Night* traces New Age religions back to Eastern mysticism and Egyptian, Babylonian, and Caldean religions. He comments, "The New Age belief system, if it can be called that in all its bizarre diversity, is not immoral but amoral. It has no absolute moral standard; instead it exalts the individual and celebrates relativism.... Dostoyevsky wrote that anything is permissible if there is no God. How much more so if everything is God!"

The American Heritage Dictionary. 3rd. ed. 1992.

Colson, Charles. Against the Night: Living in the New Dark Ages. Ann Arbor, MI: Servant Publications, 1989, p. 106.

Letter 67
the picture of the chimp in the spacesuit
Those who wish to see the picture of the chimp in the spacesuit that Redtape so liked can find it at the web site of People for the Ethical Treatment of Animals.

www.peta-online.org

the Washington press and the 42nd President
Redtape claims that 89% of the Washington press corps voted for Bill Clinton. This figure is taken from a Freedom Forum survey that was conducted after the 1992 election.

Parry, Robert. "Media Mythology: Is the Press Liberal?" The Consortium for Independent Journalism Newsletter 17 February 1997.

the press has a natural proclivity for liberalism
Robert and Linda Lichter and Stanley Rothman did an in-depth study of television journalist and news anchors. They discovered that the majority of these media figures labeled themselves politically liberal.

Lichter, Robert, et al. The Media Elite: America's New Power Brokers. Adler & Adler, 1986.

Letter 69
William F. Buckley's conservative rationale for conservation

Buckley, William F., Jr. Happy Days Were Here Again. Holbrook, MA: Adams Publishing, 1993, p. 180-181.

half of North America returned to wilderness
Redtape is not exaggerating the extent of the plans of some environmentalists. The Wildlands Project, developed by the Earth First! organization, was the model for Redtape's scheme. The zones and corridors, and general prohibitions, are not a fiction but a part of the Wildland's plan.

Coffman, Michael S. "Globalized Grizzlies." The New American

18 August 1997.

no humans can take credit for Wildland's vision
The president of the Wildlands Project who gave credit to the fish and the toads is Michael Soule.

Coffman, Michael S. "Globalized Grizzlies." The New American 18 August 1997.

United Nations World Heritage Convention
The Convention Concerning the Protection of the World Cultural and Natural Heritage was initiated by the United Nations Educational, Scientific, and Cultural Organization (UNESCO) in 1972. The United States ratified the treaty in 1973.

McHugh, Lois. "The World Heritage Convention and U.S. National Parks." Congressional Research Service number 96-395f, 19 September 1997.

the IUCN's ecospiritual practices and principles
The International Union for Conservation of Nature and Natural Resources' purpose for existence, as stated by Redtape, was first articulated by its Ethics Working Group in 1996. The IUCN's international influence is evident from information contained on the organization's web site.

Coffman, Michael S. "Globalized Grizzlies." The New American 18 August 1997.

www.iucn.org

IUCN granted immunity
On January 18, 1996 President Clinton issued Executive Order

#12986 which granted the IUCN the "same immunity from suit and judicial process as is enjoyed by foreign governments."

www.whitehouse.gov

what IUCN progress?
There are currently 47 Biosphere Reserves and 20 World Heritage Sites in the United States.

Coffman, Michael S. "Globalized Grizzlies." The New American 18 August 1997.

42nd President invoking the Antiquities Act
On September 18, 1996, in the Grand Canyon National Park in Arizona, President Clinton signed a proclamation invoking the Antiquities Act of 1906 and creating the Grand Staircase-Escalante National Monument. This placed 1.7 million acres of remote canyon lands in southern Utah under federal control and thwarted plans to mine the region's rich coal deposits.

Dolcini, Marie. "Monumental Victory in Utah." The Planet November 1996.

American Heritage Rivers Initiative
The American Heritage Rivers Initiative combines the resources of 13 federal agencies to "protect and restore America's great rivers." Detailed information concerning this program is available from the Environmental Protection Agency and from Representative Helen Chenoweth, who has initiated a bill to terminate implementation.

www.epa.gov/rivers

www.house.gov/chenoweth

Letter 72
nearly 40% of income stripped immediately away
See Letter 52.

inheritance taxes
The federal inheritance tax affects estates of $625,000 or more. The tax rate begins at 37% and gradually rises until estates of $3 million or more are taxed at 55%.

Welch, Mark J. "Estate and Gift Tax Aspects of the 1997 Budget Act." Estate Planning Advisory Newsletter 2 August 1997.

the RICO statute
The RICO statute that Redtape mentions is the Racketeer Influenced and Corrupt Organizations Act of 1970. It was originally intended to help the government recoup the cost of fighting organized crime by seizing property from mobsters. In the 1990s the law has been invoked against a wider variety of supposed "racketeers" including several antiabortion activists.

Leo, John. "Are Protesters Racketeers?" U.S. News 4 May 1998.

federal statutes under which property can be seized
Redtape states that there are over 200 federal statutes under which government agents may seize private property. This figure was provided by the Libertarian Party.

www.lp.org

Letter 74
forbid people from carrying guns
Redtape states that research shows that guns in the hands of

citizens deter crime. A study conducted by John R. Lott and David B. Mustard of the University of Chicago found that "when state concealed handgun laws went into effect in a county, murders fell by 8.5 percent and rapes and aggravated assaults fell by 5 and 7 percent."

Lott, John R. and David B. Mustard. "Crime, Deterrence, and Right-to-Carry Concealed Handguns." University of Chicago, 15 August 1996.

hate crimes
Forty states and the District of Columbia have "hate crime" statutes. Attempts are being made to create federal legislation.

Castaneda, Ruben. "Hate Crime Laws Rely on Motives, Not Targets; Laurel Slaying Illustrates Fine Line." Washington Post 26 October 1998.

insure homes against all common sense
The Federal Emergency Management Agency's National Flood Insurance Program provides affordable insurance to nearly anyone, including those who build in "Special Flood Hazard Areas." Hurricane zones are similarly administered.

www.fema.gov

establish how much people should weigh
In June of 1998 the National Institutes of Health issued new guidelines telling people how much they should weigh based on their height. These new standards increased the number of adults considered to be overweight by 29 million. Among the people who are now too heavy are Baltimore Orioles third baseman Cal Ripken Jr. and gold medal skier Picabo Street.

Squires, Sally. "Pound Foolish?" Washington Post 9 June 1998.

Letter 75
Hillary Rodham
Redtape's quote of Hillary Rodham is taken from the student commencement address she gave at Wellesley in 1969.

Bork, Robert. Slouching Toward Gomorrah: Modern Liberalism and American Decline. New York: Regan Books, 1996, p. 86.

Letter 76
the "black Judas"
In 1996 California voters endorsed Proposition 209, an initiative intended to eliminate affirmative action in their state. The proposition was initiated by Ward Connerly, a black Sacramento businessman. Connerly was seen by many as a traitor to blacks and subjected to lawsuits and death threats.

Fisher, Marc. "Ward Connerly's Campaign to End Affirmative Action in California May Succeed. But In the End He Still Stands to Lose." Washington Post 29 October 1996.

Haverman, Judith. "Limit on Affirmative Action Wins in California." Washington Post 6 November 1996.

Letter 77
United Steel Workers of America vs. Webber
In this case the Supreme Court rejected the argument that Title VII of the 1964 Civil Rights Act prohibited the granting of special privileges to racial minorities. The Court declared that "prohibitions against racial discrimination do not condemn all private, voluntary, race conscious affirmative action plans."

"United Steel Workers of America vs. Webber." The Oxford Companion to the Supreme Court of the United States. Ed. Kermit L. Hall. New York: Oxford University Press, 1992, p. 889.

discrimination in lending
Redtape is accurate. A 1992 study by the Boston Federal Reserve Bank found that 89% of white applicants and 83% of minority applicants were approved for loans. However, the default rate for all racial groups was the same.

Sowell, Thomas. The Vision of the Anointed. New York: Basic Books, 1995, p. 37-42.

Brimelow, Peter and Leslie Spencer. "The Hidden Clue." Forbes 4 January 1993.

the fallacy of objectionable cause
In formal debate the fallacy of objectionable cause occurs when "someone argues for a causal interpretation on the basis of limited evidence and makes no attempt to rule out alternative explanations of the event."

Govier, Trudy. A Practical Study of Argument. 3rd ed. Belmont, CA: Wadsworth Publishing, 1992, p. 345.

illegitimacy rates

Himmelfarb, G. The Demoralization of Society: From Victorian Virtues to Modern Values. New York: Knopf, 1995, p. 222-237.

preferences
The international study cited by Redtape was the basis for Thomas Sowell's book Preferential Policies.

Sowell, Thomas. <u>Preferential Policies: An International Perspective</u>. New York: William Morrow, 1990.

an ex-slave Jewish professor
The story of the professor who made comments that were construed as racially insensitive was recounted by Robert Bork.

Bork, Robert. <u>Slouching Toward Gomorrah: Modern Liberalism and American Decline</u>. New York: Regan Books, 1996, p. 279.

Letter 78
Haitian Revolution
The horrors of the revolution in Haiti and their effects on the Founding Fathers are recounted by the historian Alfred N. Hunt.

Hunt, Alfred N. <u>Haiti's Influence on Antebellum America</u>. Baton Rouge: Louisiana State University Press, 1988, p. 21-22, 39-40.

groundwork for the end of slavery
Thomas G. West makes the case that the Founders intended to slowly weaken and eliminate slavery.

West, Thomas G. <u>Vindicating the Founders: Race, Sex, Class, and Justice in the Origins of America</u>. Lanham, MD: Rowman & Littlefield,1997, p. 10-14.

number of free blacks increasing
There were 59,000 free blacks in the north and south combined at the time of the first census in 1790. By 1810 there were 186,000 free blacks, the majority of whom lived in the south.

West, Thomas G. <u>Vindicating the Founders: Race, Sex, Class, and Justice in the Origins of America</u>. See above, p. 11.

Letter 79
Aristotle on the rights of slave holders
Aristotle saw slavery as a necessary institution. In book one of *The Politics* he states the belief that "from the hour of their birth some are marked out for subjection, others for rule."

Aristotle. The Politics and Constitution of Athens. Ed. Stephen Everson. Cambridge: University Press, 1996.

let's not get angry, let's get even
Redtape's great man who said this is, of course, John F. Kennedy.

Letter 80
Reginald Strong's Conservative Reading List:

Bork, Robert H. Slouching Toward Gomorrah: Modern Liberalism and American Decline. New York: Regan Books, 1996.

Buckley, William F., Jr. "An Agenda for Conservatives." Happy Days Were Here Again. Holbrook, MA: Adams Publishing, 1993.

Burke, Edmund. Reflections on the Revolution in France. 1790. New York: Penguin Books, 1986.

Eliot, T.S. Christianity and Culture: The Idea of a Christian Society & Notes Towards the Definition of Culture. New York: Harcourt, Brace & World, 1940, 1949.

Hawthorne, Nathaniel. "Earth's Holocaust." Mosses from an Old Manse. Columbus: Ohio St. University Press, 1974.

Kirk, Russell. The Conservative Mind From Burke to Eliot. Washington: Regnery Publishing, 1953.

Kirk, Russell. The Politics of Prudence. Bryn Mawr, PA: Intercollegiate Studies Institute, 1996.

Kirk, Russell, ed. The Portable Conservative Reader. New York: Penguin Books, 1996.

Lewis, C. S. The Abolition of Man. 1947. New York: Touchstone, 1996.

Madison, James, et al. The Federalist Papers. Chicago: The Great Books Foundation, 1966.

Muggeridge, Malcolm. "The Great Liberal Death Wish." Things Past. New York: 1979, p. 220-238.

Sowell, Thomas. The Vision of the Anointed. New York: Basic Books, 1995.

Tocqueville, Alexis de. Democracy in America. Ed. Phillips Bradley. New York: Vintage Books, 1945.

Vonnegut, Kurt Jr. "Harrison Bergeron." Welcome to the Monkey House. New York: Delacorte Press, 1961.

Yeats, William Butler. "Second Coming." The Norton Anthology of Modern Poetry. Eds. Richard Ellmann and Robert O'clair. New York: W.W. Norton & Company, 1988, p. 158.

teenage parents in the news
Redtape brings up the topic of teenagers who killed their babies and dumped the bodies into trash bins, but are given minimal punishment by the courts. The *Washington Post* recently reported two such cases. In each instance the convicted teens

received jail terms of three years or less. One young woman, who confessed to smothering her infant daughter, was later granted custody of her two-year-old son.

"Killing Babies." Editorial. Washington Post 11 July 1998.

first official orders for euthanasia in Germany

Redtape is correct in stating that the first official orders for euthanasia in Nazi Germany were issued in 1939 by Adolph Hitler. However, a systematic propaganda campaign favoring this practice was begun much earlier. As early as 1931 German psychiatrists were discussing sterilization and euthanasia as ways of eliminating chronic mental illness. An article in the *New England Journal of Medicine* in 1949 stated that "[b]y 1936 extermination of the physically or socially unfit was so openly accepted that it was mentioned incidentally in a German medical journal."

Alexander, Leo. "Medical Science Under Dictatorship." New England Journal of Medicine 14 July 1949.

1930s math problems

The arithmetic problem that Redtape describes as an early form of "values clarification" was printed in a widely used German high-school textbook, *Mathematics in the Service of National Political Education.*

Alexander, Leo. "Medical Science Under Dictatorship." New England Journal of Medicine 14 July 1949.

Letter 81
the mysterious Janius

Dan "declares war" by quoting Janius, the pseudonym of an Englishman who wrote a series of letters published in the London *Public Advertiser* between 1769 and 1771. The true identity of Janius is unknown.

Bartlett, John. Familiar Quotations. 14th ed. Boston: Little, Brown and Company, 1968, p. 1091.

Letter 83
baker's dozen conservative tenets
Dan's thirteen conservative tenets are heavily influenced by the writings of Russell Kirk, encompassing the wisdom of many generations of conservative thinkers. One can find similar views expressed by Edmund Burke and other authors on the reading list of Reginald Strong. See Letter 80.

call it religion or natural law
The belief in a transcendent order was central to the Founding Fathers. As John Adams stated, the Constitution was intended for a moral people. At the same time the Founders demanded separation between church and state (see Letter 60). The concept of natural law allows a government based upon absolute morality yet free from a state religion, a pluralist yet moral order. See also Letter 63.

Letter 86
pessimism and optimism
Redtape in his despair reveals a deep pessimism about the state of the Nation and implicitly Western Civilization. He is far from alone in his dark view. T.S. Eliot expressed similar sentiments as long ago as the 1940s, when there was less evidence than there is today of the declining state of our culture:

"The Church disowned, the tower overthrown, the
bells upturned, what have we to do
But stand with empty hands and palms upturned
in an age which advances progressively backwards?"

Whittaker Chambers, who like Redtape sinned mightily against God and his fellow man and repented, felt a despair similar to Redtape's. "It is idle," he said, "to talk about preventing the wreck of Western civilization. It is already a wreck from within." The fall of Western Civilization may be well underway. Yet all is not bleak, perhaps even for Redtape.

There is an optimism buried deeply within Redtape's repentance and desire for forgiveness. For others who also see the mounting darkness, the optimism is more evident.

Charles Colson in *Against the Night*—in which he argues we have already entered a new Dark Ages—expresses hope: "Perhaps the great nightfall will soon be upon us.... But one thing we do know: it isn't necessary that such predictions come to pass.... There are no inexorable elements propelling history. God is sovereign over human events.... We never know what minor act of hopeless courage, what word spoken in defense of truth, what unintended consequence might swing the balance and change the world." We never know what *act, word, unintended consequence....*

Redtape has begun the process of repentance and seen the possibility of forgiveness and is contemplating conversion....

Finally, a word of caution and hope from former British Prime Minister Margaret Thatcher. Speaking of turning the world from its present course, she reminds us that salvation comes "[n]ot group by group or party by party or even church by church—but soul by soul. And each one counts." Amen.

ABOUT THE AUTHOR

Lee Whipple is the author of several other books, including college texts, essays, and a true-life novel. His true-life novel, *Whole Again,* won critical acclaim and was the book-of-the-month in the *Reader's Digest.* He has also published in a wide variety of periodicals, including *National Review, The Journal of Rehabilitation Medicine, Home Education, Production Engineering, Disabled USA, Reader's Digest,* and *Galaxy Science Fiction Magazine.* As adjunct faculty, he has taught both undergraduate and graduate courses at several colleges and universities. Mr. Whipple is in strong demand as a speaker, lecturing regularly on college campuses, and to a wide variety of business and civic groups. He lives with his wife and family in St. Augustine, Florida.

ORDER INFORMATION

Obtain *The Redtape Letters* from your favorite bookstore.

If your bookstore does not have it in stock, you can order it directly for $14.95 plus $3.50 for shipping and handling per book. If five or more copies are ordered, send only $2.00 shipping and handling per book. Michigan residents add 6% sales tax.

Call 1-800-706-4636 to order today!
or

Please send_____copies @$14.95   _____

Michigan residents add 6% sales tax   _____

Shipping and handling at $3.50 per book   _____
($2.00 per book for five or more)

TOTAL   _____

PLEASE PRINT

Name _____

Address_____

City _____State_____Zip _____

Phone _____

Credit Card# _____Exp. _____

Name on Card _____

Signature _____

Mail order blank with check or money order payable to Rhodes & Easton

Rhodes & Easton
121 East Front Street Fourth Floor
Traverse City, Michigan 49684
(616) 933-0445